ON THE
Edge
OF
Dangerous
Things

Dear Helen,
Thanks for
your support!
Enjoy!

ISBN-10: 1484015665
ISBN-13: 9781484015667

Dedication

For Nicole, Seena, and especially, Joe T.

Author's Note:

Though some facts about some places in the novel are accurate, Pleasant Palms Trailer Park and Sourland High School are figments of the imagination. Furthermore, resemblances to actual persons living or dead are coincidental.

Acknowledgements

Thank you to my readers, Karen, Mark, Nicole, Seena, Tim, and my parents, Julia and Russell.

Printed by CreateSpace An Amazon.com Company

"Shame, Despair, Solitude! These had been her teachers, - stern and wild ones, - and they had made her strong, but taught her much amiss…"

1850, Nathaniel Hawthorne, The Scarlet Letter,

ON THE
Edge
OF
Dangerous
Things

S. SNYDER-CARROLL

One

Like the fist of an angry god, the hurricane jogged off course and slammed into Pleasant Palms Trailer Park.

Startled by a boom of thunder, Hester Randal Murphy stood stock-still. Lightning crackled. A current of air sucked open the shutters of the pool house, banging them against the outer walls. She hurried from the shower, closed the window, and turned toward the two naked women, who'd been drying off.

"What the hell?" Dee clasped her bra to her bosom.

"It wasn't supposed to hit us!" shrieked Eve.

They looked out at the monstrous black clouds swallowing up what was left of morning, at the mighty palms bent in submission to the howling wind. Rain drummed on the fiberglass roof, the grommets of the marina flags clanged against the poles, dogs barked. They tried to talk, but their words were lost in the deafening clamor, so they gave up.

They were trapped where they were. That much was obvious.

Dee and Eve hurriedly dressed. Hester wrapped herself in her towel as panic rose in her chest, *what about Nina?*

Young, lovely Nina Tattoni, obsessed with finding shells, had gone to the beach at dawn. She'd be looking down, her big, glistening eyes, as captivating as a water creature's, riveted on the flotsam. She wouldn't notice the wind shifting or the clouds hurling themselves into a sinister mountain over the Atlantic. What if a wave swelled and crashed over the sprite of a teenager? How easily she'd be knocked down and dragged out by the fomented sea. One good thing was, Nina didn't scare easily, wouldn't care much about any old storm even if she did see it coming.

After the hell she's been through in her short life, Hester thought, *this sort of wildness would be nothing to her.*

Hester prayed Nina, who was staying temporarily with Hester and her husband Al, had the sense to get out of harm's way. If anything happened to Nina, Hester would never forgive herself, and neither would Al.

Is this how it feels to have a child of your own? Hester's heart turned stone cold in her chest. *Nothing bad can happen to Nina, not now, not ever.* Nina had survived a tragedy that would've ruined a weaker child and had turned out to be a good kid, a really good kid.

Kid? Hester had to stop thinking about Nina like that. She was in college, had, in fact, turned eighteen last week.

"She's legal now," Al reminded Hester, "so for Christ's sake would you stop trying to solve all her problems and let her learn to stand on her own two feet."

Something hit the pool house door hard. Hester flinched. The sound of things being ripped apart and smashing about punctuated the constant, eerie wail of the wind. Their old double-wide was probably a pile of rubble by now. She swallowed hard. If Al hadn't gotten his lazy butt out of bed… She tried to nag him into getting up and doing something. Anything! But he fell back asleep even before she left.

Jesus, please, Hester's mind whirred, *don't let anything…*

Life with Al hadn't always been easy, nevertheless, Hester worshipped the ground he walked on. All he had to do was touch her, kiss her, lead her into the bedroom, and her world of troubles went away. Losing him at this point, after years of holding on, after she agreed to retire early from teaching, and when they seemed, finally, to be starting out on a whole new right foot, would be a damn calamity.

A flash of lightning lit up the room. Hester saw terror in Dee's eyes.

"We'll be all right!" Hester shouted uselessly.

Dee lowered her head.

"Don't cry, don't start crying," Hester screamed.

Eve put her arm around Dee, but Dee didn't look up. The train wreck of a storm screamed on. The cacophony was ear-splitting, and escalating.

"A tornado!" Hester shouted. "It's an effing tornado!"

The window rattled as though it were about to be torn loose from its frame. Hester squatted in the corner by the sink. Dee and Eve crouched next to the wall by the toilet.

Water began spouting up from the drain in the shower, coming in under the door. In no time it was up to their crotches. Hester's head ached. She took a deep breath, slowly released it, and watched a stained tampon float out of the swamped trash basket and blossom into what looked like a translucent jellyfish. Soon it was joined by more bobbing debris.

She had to find Al, and Nina. Good God, she had to find the girl and make sure she was okay.

Hester's drenched swimsuit hung like a thick black noose from a peg on the wall. She thought about putting it on, but her body was wet. It'd be a royal pain getting into it. She stood up and headed toward the door.

A coconut blasted through the window. Glass shards flew everywhere, pinging off the fixtures like flicked crystal. Some just missed Hester's face. Undaunted, she trudged through the water.

Eve saw Hester put her hand on the knob of the door and yelled, but Hester couldn't make out what the woman was trying to say. Hester looked down at Eve, and Eve mouthed, "Where are you going?"

Hester read her lips, but ignored her. She tightened the towel around herself and pushed against the door.

Eve jumped up, tried to pull her back. She shouted in Hester's ear, "You'll get killed!"

Hester shrugged, pushed harder. The wind and the water held the door closed. Hester pounded her thin body against it again and again until it moved enough for her to wedge herself into the gap. The aluminum scraped the skin on her arms; the frame dug into her buttocks.

"You'll get killed!" Eve's voice sounded like a whisper from the other side of the planet. Then Hester was out. The door slammed shut behind her.

The pool, the parking lot, the decks of the marina were under water. Boats, torn loose from their moorings, drifted about ramming into things. Trailers had been blown off their pads and onto their sides, their snapped tie-downs dangling from their rusty bellies like severed umbilical cords. All sorts of junk floated aimlessly on the fickle current.

In a powerful gust Hester, stunned by the spectacle of the damage, almost lost her balance. Her hair lashed her face. The flood was thigh-high. Cold rain pelted her. She pictured Al's yellow slicker hanging in the closet in the trailer. If only she had it now. She tried to make her way along, but it was nearly impossible to move against such a force of nature as this. Cowering against the pool house wall, she dared to look up. Her eyes stung, she saw the clouds roiling above her like heavy smoke about to burst into flame. *The celestial has turned into the demonic.* She closed her eyes, tucked her face down, and gasped for air.

Eve was right. The thought shook her to her core. *I could get killed out here.*

Two

―――――――――――――――――――――――

The mass of clouds, like the lid of a burial vault, slowly slid across the sky leaving Hester bathed in sunlight. Half naked, her towel down around her waist, she opened her eyes.

God has taken pity on me…again.

She'd gotten farther than she thought, halfway around the pool, almost to the laundry room. Pulling the towel up over her breasts, she slogged east to A1A where the flood waters subsided, and headed up Fish Tail Lane in the direction of their trailer. The narrow street was deserted, and up ahead she saw with great relief the double-wide still standing.

A couple of dead lizards and one of the tailless feral cats that populated the park floated in a large puddle next to their patio. Debris was everywhere. Their Odyssey was still in the driveway and seemed undamaged, but behind the trailer Hester noticed half of the old ficus tree was gone. She couldn't determine from where she stood if it had fallen between their unit and the Buchanans' or had crashed into the roof.

"The first thing I'm going to do is trim that old, overgrown tree," Al said as they pulled into the driveway the first day they arrived at Pleasant Palms for the season. That was over two weeks ago. Hester stared at the weepy pulp and felt lousy about it. In China, ficus were called bo trees in honor of Buddha who meditated in the shade of one for six years. Buddhists, considering them to be sacred, planted them outside their temples. Hester liked the connection between her tree and the holy man, and she didn't like it one bit that a raw, fatal-looking wound now ran up its length.

"Damn it, Al," Hester muttered aloud, "if this tree doesn't make it and we get bad karma…"

She angrily tossed some of the garbage away from the sliding door while cursing what a lazy bum her once-ambitious husband had turned into and wondering what she could do to save the ficus. She looked back at the tree. *It's those leaves. The slightest breeze makes them beat like fragile, frantic, green hearts.*

What was left of the leaves were doing it right now, and Hester regretted not trimming the tree her damn self. She slid the door open and stepped over the remaining trash into the living room. As she did, blood dripped onto the carpet from a cut on her calf.

"Son of a…" She took her towel off, blotted her leg, then knelt and swiped uselessly at the spots.

She knew she should be looking for Al and Nina.

"Al? Nina?" she shouted. "Anybody home? I'm cut and bleeding. Al? Where are you?"

She scanned the small interior. There wasn't much space, even in a double-wide. From where she was, she surveyed the living room, dining room, and kitchen. Al's putter and his Prince racket were propped against his recliner. Her half-empty coffee mug, cheaters, and copy of *O* were on the counter. Everything looked fine. Quiet as a morgue, but fine.

She should check the bedrooms. After all, when she left that morning, her husband was curled up in bed snoring like a freaking chain saw. God knows, he might've slept through the whole catastrophe. But Hester couldn't seem to stop rubbing at the blood. She desperately wanted to get the OxiClean, treat the stain right away, save the carpet from being permanently ruined. So there she was, naked as a jaybird, smearing her bodily fluid even more deeply into the fibers and into one hideous purple spot, while a new, larger, beet-colored one formed beneath her still-bleeding calf.

The longer she worked at the mess, the more irked she became with her husband. She warned him they should not to go down to Florida so early in the season, even begged him, "Al, please, I've got a bad feeling. Please, let's wait till December, till hurricane season is completely over."

No, he was adamant. "What the hell do you think I retired for, Hester? To sit in New Jersey and freeze? You can if you want to, but I'm going to the goddamn Sunshine State."

What could she do, but give in.

She shouldn't have, but she was trying to pick her battles, as always. At the moment, though, peeved as she was with Al, she could use his help before their whole carpet turned wine-dark, and before she lost any more blood.

"Al," she hollered, "answer me?"

No answer.

Dust motes floated through the hot sunlight and settled into the hazy surface of the end table in front of her. Hester pulled the cord of the bamboo shade. The light dropped into a thin, white line. The room took on a burnished glow and appeared cooler, but the rising humidity was stifling. Sweat dripped from Hester's body and mingled with the blood she'd rubbed irrevocably into the rug.

She relinquished her battle against the blots and went to flip the switch on the air-conditioner, nothing happened. The power was out. She threw the bloody towel in the hamper behind the sofa and went into the kitchen.

On the counter fruit flies orbited a half-rotten banana. Hester futilely shooed at them. They circled away from her hand, then veered back the minute she stopped. She grabbed the dish towel and mopped her face and armpits and under her breasts. She needed gauze and Band-Aids before she spoiled anything else. She headed down the hallway and checked the guest room.

No Nina.

Maybe she ran to the clubhouse. She wasn't stupid. If she'd come to Hester with anything, it'd been an odd set of survival skills.

Hester turned to her bedroom. If Al was gone too, and if enough hot water was left in the heater, she'd take a shower, fix herself up, and then go find those two. They couldn't be far away. Though the hurricane had caused tons of damage, it didn't seem so bad now that Hester was back in her own little place.

The bedroom door was closed. She turned the knob and tried to push it open, but it went only an inch or two. She peeked in. Nothing but leaves.

"What the...?" She pushed again with her shoulder. It widened a bit more. *Wow, the effing bo tree...* Half of the bo tree was in their bedroom.

"Jesus Christ, Al, are you in there?"

Petrified he might be trapped, all Hester's annoyances with Al vanished. She threw her body hard into the door. It hurt, but she didn't give up until it budged enough for her to squeeze into the room.

It was a jungle of leaves and branches. The trunk jutted up into the air like a giant spear. Broken ceiling tile, plywood, Styrofoam, aluminum, some stuff she couldn't identify, and the bed were under it all.

Hester pushed her way through the branches. She was getting pretty scratched up when she felt something touch her thigh. It was Al's foot. She looked down and saw his hairy lump of an ankle and the high arch of his instep. He was trapped!

"Al, answer me, you son of a…God, just answer me!" She grabbed his foot and shook it.

No response. She broke off enough branches to open the door all of the way and began flinging more of them behind her into the hallway. She worked feverishly, moving what was loose till she could squat beneath the trunk, lift it on her shoulder, and slide it off Al.

A large piece of the roof was still on top of him. She gripped the end of it and yanked with all her strength. Her breasts swung uncomfortably. She tried again, but it slipped out of her grip. *No time to go get a pair of gloves. No time to go for help.* She wiped her hands on the saturated carpet and took hold again of a corner and pulled with all her might. This time it moved, so she kept pulling. As she did, she worried it might be scraping off some of Al's skin. She almost had it, but the room was small, and it got jammed against the wall.

Hester hurried to the kitchen and grabbed a hammer. Panting heavily, she ran back to the bedroom and began hacking at the piece of roof with the claw end. She was careful not to land any blows near

Al. She persevered, made a hole, and pounded and pounded until she broke a big chunk off. Finally she was able to tilt it on one end, push it upright against the wall.

Al was under a soaking wet comforter. Hester, exhausted, couldn't lift it, so she knelt and gathered it to her like a fisherman would his net. She heard her own breathing, uneven and labored in the quiet. The soft hair on her arms bristled. She stood up slowly. The trauma of the hurricane, the weight of her worry over Nina, the fear that gripped her at the thought of losing her husband, all hurtled in on her.

Al Murphy was not alone.

Three

Lying there, next to an average-sized man, the young woman looked pathetically small. Arms flung out in abandon, legs spread-eagle, she seemed to have landed where she was after falling from a great height.

She had on a thong.

A frilly, pink thong.

Where the hell are the rest of her clothes? Hester stared in disbelief at her husband and the girl positioned on the bed like a pair of bronzed bookends. Despite the way their skin glistened in the heat, Hester was sure they must both be dead. Shocked, she shrunk from touching either of them. She had to do something, yet she was unable to think of what that something was.

God, she didn't want to keep looking at them, but she couldn't turn away. And what conclusions might she draw? What were they doing here? Together?

A cloud began passing in front of the sun, and since the roof was gone, she watched its shadow advance across them until they were in the shade. The room turned cooler and Hester shivered. If they were dead, it was for the best, because then she wouldn't have to kill them herself.

The cloud moved on, and the sun forced Hester to shield her eyes. *Walk away, go in the kitchen, find the cell phone, call the goddamn police.*

Instead, she fixated on the tendrils of wet pubic hair that had escaped from Nina's pink thong.

Shells? Where were the shells she'd gone to find?

Nina must've listened to Hester warning to keep an eye to the sky, that computer models weren't perfect. "You never know with Mother Nature, Nina."

Hester had offered to make the girl breakfast, but Nina hadn't wanted any. Every day since she got here last week, she seemed to be eating less and less, and she didn't seem to have a whole lot to say to Hester. When Hester confided that Nina might be having some kind of problem, Al said, "For God's sake, Hester, she's fine. It's all in your imagination."

My imagination? Hester could see Nina was too thin, and Hester worried she was starving herself or depressed or something mental like that. Hester worried about her like a mother would her own child. From the first time Nina walked into Hester's English classroom three years ago, Hester had been...well, drawn to her, inexplicably drawn to her.

Al, who was the school's vice principal, warned Hester, as he always did, not to get too attached to any of her students. "When they graduate, they'll forget all about you, and then I'll have to listen to how miserable that makes you so, please, for Christ's sakes, save me the trouble."

Hester, uncharacteristically, ignored Al. Nina was her favorite. Nina was special. Nina and she were close and would remain close. So when the girl called crying because she was having terrible problems at the community college and needed to talk to Hester, Hester sent her money for a flight down to Pleasant Palms. She didn't tell Al about it until after the fact, until it was too late for him to stop her, until she could gloat, "See, Mr. Know-It-All, Nina hasn't forgotten me. She needs me. She needs us both."

Al, true to form, was completely against what Hester did. He tried several arguments on his wife, the main one being that Nina Tattoni was plenty old enough to take care of herself. Hester didn't often cross Al, but in this case whatever he said didn't matter. What mattered was, Nina was coming to Florida.

"Thou doth protest too much, husband," Hester joked. "Besides, it's a done deal. I already sent her the money."

As soon as Nina got off the plane, though, Al seemed to change his mind. He paraded her around the trailer park, introducing her to everyone as though she were an exotic pet who said nothing much but was so unusual and cute it didn't matter. He sat next to her on the beach, pretending to read the latest from Corbin or Patterson, while Nina slathered her bikini-clad body with lotion and stretched out on her towel like a well-oiled princess.

Hester watched them and stifled any nasty thought that tried to surface. Al's interest was fatherly. They never had any children, so why wouldn't he enjoy pretending Nina was his? And all along hadn't she wanted them to be close?

This fascination of Al's would wane. Hester would help it along. She'd have sex with her husband, lots of sex, and maybe even do to him what she seldom did anymore, but what she knew he liked best. It would reignite things between them, take his mind off Nina, and all would be as it should.

That had been her plan, but now the sight of Nina lying next to Al sickened her. What glaring proof that everything had backfired. Sweat was blinding Hester. She wanted to curl up somewhere, fall asleep, and wake up in the recent past, before this. She closed her eyes; fireworks exploded inside her head. She squeezed her eyes tight. The vision of Nina's naked body emerged through the blackness. And— she had to admit it—she was momentarily satisfied by how, despite the sweltering heat, frozen-in-place the girl seemed. *Maybe she really is dead.*

Hester opened her eyes and forced herself to look at Al. He was on his back, mouth agape, limp penis resting on his thigh like a half-stuffed sausage. His feet flopped out sideways. His arms were over his head, the hair in his pits as black, wet, and curly as his pubic hair. The salt and pepper hair on his head thick and stubborn. Sunspots dotted his tan face. His neck sunburnt. His Roman nose as aesthetically sculpted as ever. His brown nipples hard and nubby like pinched dry clay. His appendectomy scar, a pale, lipless, closed mouth.

Yes, she recognized each separate part of this man; but right at the moment she couldn't reckon the sum of those parts—the whole person, Alexander Bruno Murphy, whom she had loved long and intensely. If the man in front of her opened his eyes, she would have nothing to say to him, except maybe, who the fuck are you, really?

She wasn't one to curse, but that expletive came to mind easily. Why should she feel like the intruder in her own home? Why should she feel like she opened the wrong door? Like she interrupted them in the middle of…something secret?

Hester rolled her aching shoulders up and back. She was burning hot. She spread her feet a bit to steady herself. Another cloud came. A slight breeze lifted the ends of the sheers on the window and jiggled the heart-shaped leaves that were still all over the room. They twinkled like flashing bits of green neon. Then the cloud was gone, and the air in the room collapsed in on her.

Shame on you, Al, shame on you, she thought, as something on the periphery of the moment jogged her memory.

"Two shall be as one."

Isn't that what Father Ferrara said when he married us? Two are one. We are one and the same in marriage. His sin, mine. His humiliation, his guilt, his shame, all mine.

Hester blinked the sweat from her eyes and caught a glimpse of herself in the mirror on the opposite wall. She ran her fingers through her tangled long hair, trying to get it off her face. It fell into a natural center part, and her silver roots looked like a bald streak down the middle of her head. Already she needed to get another dye job. What a project it was keeping up with what used to be her honey-colored tresses. She didn't want highlights. She didn't want to be a bleached blonde. She just wanted to look like she used to.

But she didn't, and wouldn't ever again. The round apples of her cheeks had thinned. Her eyelids were puffy. Her mouth was a sad little hill. Her breasts looked like two barely inflated *U*'s, her nipples putty-colored asterisks in their valleys. One was streaked with blood.

She was covered with cuts and scratches from her valiant effort to clear the mess away to save her, son-of-a…, philandering husband. She looked more like a boy than a middle-aged woman. She looked like that boy, Ralph. Was Ralph his name? She was trying to remember. It had been a while since she'd taught British lit, *Lord of the Flies,* but wasn't Ralph the name of the one who ran from the others, the one they tried to hunt down?

Hester's body looked thin and powerless. How had she had the strength to do what she just did?

"I can't recall ever looking like this," she said to the mirror as her knees stared back at her like the faces of two upside-down babies. She hardly recognized herself, and that was distressing to her, but now was not the time for self-pity. She turned away, remembering how Al always used to say she "cleaned up well." There was never anything wrong with her that something from the makeup counter couldn't fix. She had to tell herself that. She had to believe it. She'd constructed her life on a fault line. A tremor of doubt, the whole foundation might crack. A quake of significant magnitude might make her whole damn world crumble.

Bad enough I found them together, the two…? What were they? She hesitated to form the word in her mind. *Lovers?*

You think you know your man, and then, even after decades together, he arches an eyebrow or laughs a certain way or does something you've never seen him do before, and suddenly you are struck with the most frightening feeling of all: ignorance.

Hester struggled to reconcile the lingering "before" with the clamoring "now." And she couldn't, because they were galaxies apart. It was beginning to make her go mad trying to put two and two together. Before she retired at the end of last year, when she was still teaching

English, she asked one of her students why she hadn't turned in her research paper.

"Shit happens," was what the brazen teenager said to Hester.

Shit happens? That was it, and Hester was supposed to know what that meant, to accept that kind of an answer, that kind of disrespect.

Hester decided to let the fact that the girl had used foul language go in order to get to the facts. "Exactly what kind of s-h-i-t happened, Angela?"

Angela let her jaw drop. Her mouth fell open like a puppet's before she smirked and answered, "Shit, all kinds of shit. It happens all the time. You know what I mean, Mrs. Murphy."

And that was supposed to get her off the hook. The big, old, screwed-up universe was to blame, not anyone as powerless as poor little Angela.

Hester might not have agreed with Angela's philosophy then, but she did now because here she was knee-deep in s-h-i-t, and she certainly had done nothing to cause it.

Al still hadn't moved, so Hester stepped closer to the bed, rallied what courage she had, and put two fingers on his carotid artery. He looked older in the unforgiving light, but not old enough to be dead. She wasn't sure if there was a slight pulse or not. Touching him felt weird, and she removed her fingers quickly.

She was still holding the hammer as she shuffled through the loose leaves and broken branches and trailer parts to the other side of the bed. Against the pattern of white shells on her favorite sheets, Nina's long curly brown hair spread out around her face like damp seaweed on a beach. Her wet, matted bangs covered her eyes and nose. Her mouth was open, the inside like the pearly inside of a conch. Her small chin was tilted as though she were trying to balance something on the tip of it. Hester, standing there with sweat running down the small of her back, had the chilling sensation there was no hope for Nina.

What to do?

Hester felt the weight of the hammer and squeezed the handle. Gently she bumped it against her thigh.

Again and again.

There! There. She thought, *I don't know what to do.*

She felt stuck between them now, just as she probably had been for a while without ever knowing it. Or had she? Had she known deep inside and done nothing to stop it? Had she, perhaps, wanted it to happen?

No, never.

She heard…no, she saw something. At least she thought for a second she had. She stopped swinging the hammer and held her breath. She stared around the bedroom, remembering all that happened in it since Al and she first bought the place several years ago. They'd fly down from New Jersey for long weekends. She'd bring a stack of essays to grade. Al would take them away as soon as they got on the plane. He wouldn't let her look at them until the flight home. The rest of the weekend they lounged on the beach, ate, drank, and made love. *Love, love, love, all I ever needed was love.*

Hester looked down at her husband, at her former student. Something inside her snapped. *Throw yourself on the bed between them, be with Al one last time before the truth has to be faced, before the police come, before everyone finds out what a sham our marriage is?*

She imagined Nina waking up, watching her and Al, wanting Al. It was absurd, yet the black feeling welled up. She hated Nina. No, she hated Al.

Let it go back to before. Nina on the beach, Al taking a shower, me sipping coffee, paging through a magazine.

But her life would never be the way it was, because of them.

It was quiet, so unearthly quiet, like the split second when the tide pulls a wave out and the next one hasn't broken. That split second of absolute silence.

They deserve to die for what they did to me.

Hester fought against this hateful conclusion, against the wave of anger breaking over it.

It passed, but something worse came into her head.

Nina's nipples, large and dark, glistened like eyes watching Hester, the only thing watching her. They made her look back at them. She couldn't help it.

Swing the hammer high. Bring it down into the smooth, flat skin between those breasts. Swing the claw end into the pink thong, the pubic hair, and finally into that face, that beautiful angel face.

Hester had loved Nina, had believed, until now, Nina loved her too. Hester must have been wrong. The hammer burned in Hester's hand; she wanted to hurt her, again, and again, and again.

Four

Hester must've blacked out for a second. Then she heard Al groan. His eyes opened. He stared at the girl.

"Nina, are you alright?" His voice was weak.

For a split second, Hester was relieved to hear him say something, but in the next instant, she was overcome by the impulse to smash his head in. She could've gotten away with it, made it look like a concrete lawn ornament had flown through the air and landed on his skull, maybe one of the silly miniature leprechauns that populated the O'Neals' patio or Gerri Trainer's oversized smiling duck. It could've happened.

"No, she's not, you fool." Hester was looking at Nina, at her thin neck arched like a swan's. Her hands were upturned; her fingers curled inward, their long, narrow nails like white-tipped claws. Hester started crying.

Al winced with pain and tried to turn toward Nina. He couldn't, so he stopped. His eyes met Hester's before he glanced down at her breasts and saw the one caked with dried blood and stared at it.

"How dare you?" Hester bent over to lock eyes with him.

He rolled his head to turn away. "What are we going to do?" He whined like a baby.

"There is no 'we' anymore."

"Hester, please? I'm hurt."

"Too bad." Hester smeared her tears from her eyes with the backs of her hands.

Al grimaced, rolled his head back to look at her, and begged, "I can't move. Please? Hester? Goddamn it, call an ambulance."

"I think she's dead, Alexander," Hester said distinctly. It didn't matter. Her words had fallen on deaf ears, Al was unconscious again.

Hester pressed the palm of her hand against her hot forehead. Al's slack face had a frown on it. Lately he always seemed to be frowning.

Was it displeasure? With her? She tried to get what was wrong out of him, but he insisted nothing was wrong, barking at her, "It's all in your head, Hester, so quit bugging me about it, will you?"

Hester leaned close to the frowning face and whispered, "Do you hear me, Al, you son-of-a-bitch? I think she's dead!" She threw the hammer on the floor. Roused by the thud, Al moaned, "Did you call the ambulance?"

"No, so shut up." Hester turned and walked to the dresser. She took a towel out a drawer and began wiping herself off.

Al watched her. "What in the hell are you doing?"

"What I have to."

"Hester, listen to me…"

"No, you listen to me," she spat out. She never spoke to him like this, in this harsh tone of voice. She turned her back to him and reached down to wipe the insects and dirt off her legs, and realized he had a full view of her buttocks and between her slightly spread legs, he would see her breasts hanging like small white eggplants. Quickly, she spun around to face him.

"Do you think I want everyone to find out about you and her? Do you think I want this all over the park? You've spoiled everything. I don't care about you. I'm looking out for myself now." Even as she said it, she knew she was lying, knew what she was about to do would be for Al too. If no one found out about what happened, they could go on as before, and at the moment that seemed to be the only thing Hester could bear.

She grabbed a clean bathing suit from another drawer and stepped into it. She struggled to pull it up.

"But, Hester…" Al was watching her while she reached in and settled each breast in its foam cup.

"But, Hester, nothing. I'm not talking to you anymore. Just lay there and suffer."

As if on cue, he was unconscious again and that was for the best. The less Al knew, the easier it would be for her.

She had to think of something to do with Nina's body.

Beyond the partially collapsed wall, the top of the long gash on the bo tree was visible. It gave Hester an idea. She hurried outside to examine the damage. The weight of the top-heavy branches had severed the trunk down to the roots, pulled them out of the ground, and left a shallow four by five-foot hole—big enough for a body.

Hester checked to make sure no one was around. It was early in the season, and the few people who were in the park were probably in the community center trying to organize the cleanup. Still, she decided to wait until dark to bury Nina.

Hester had never touched a dead body before, except at a wake, when sometimes she felt obliged to kiss a stone-cold forehead. And now she would have to touch Nina's dead body. She looked down at her former student, her skin had lost all color and looked like white jade streaked with sap. Hester's rage subsided. Minutes ago she wanted so badly to hurt Nina, but now she felt sick at losing her. Whatever happened wasn't this child's fault, because that's what she still was, a mere child. Hester could see that now, and she would bury her as decently as she could.

She went into the bathroom, got the bucket from under the sink, filled it with hot soapy water, and grabbed a washcloth and towel. She came out of the bathroom and bent over Nina. The musky odor of her body mixed with a putrid smell coming from her open mouth. Hester pushed her chin up and closed it. Then she dipped the cloth in the sudsy water and wrung it out. She smoothed Nina's hair back off her forehead. It shocked Hester that Nina's eyes were open. She didn't shut them. That would seem too final. Gently, she washed the girl's face, neck, and shoulders. Nina's breasts jiggled when Hester cleaned around them and ran the cloth over her nipples. With her other hand, Hester pressed down where Nina's heart was. Could her touch spark a pulse? Bring Nina back to life? No, the girl's body was slowly turning colder.

Hester wiped Nina's flat stomach and her legs. A pool of urine and stool spread out beneath the body so Hester rolled it on its side. The stench made her gag, but she pulled off the pink thong and threw it on the floor. Nina's rear end curved out from her spine into two firm mounds. Hester washed the filth off her, then rolled her back onto a clean spot and washed between her thighs, the back of her calves, her feet, between each toe.

Hester worked methodically. After she rinsed Nina with clean, hot water, Hester got her best lotion from under the sink and rubbed it into Nina's skin hoping the scent of verbena would overpowered the smell of death. It didn't. She brushed the knots out of Nina's thick mane of hair. Hester was getting tired so she sat on the bed next to Nina and reached out to pat her calf. She felt the soft stubble. She reached up and touched one of Nina's stubborn curls and twisted it around her finger. A sob caught in Hester's throat.

Don't cry, she told herself. She'd lose it if she started to cry again. Hester slipped from the bed, knelt down, bowed her head, and whisper a Hail Mary. When she finished and looked up, she saw Al's profile beyond Nina's and…

Hester begged the Blessed Virgin to intercede, to stop her from doing something horrible to Al. Then a strange thought came into Hester's head, and she couldn't seem to stop herself from getting up, from sitting beside Nina again, taking her in her arms, and doing something she never should have done. It was as though it were all a dream. Hester felt she was floating somewhere above watching some-one else do such an unthinkable thing.

After a while Hester left Nina on the bed next to Al, who was still unconscious. She went and got two jumbo plastic trash bags. She straddled Nina's body to lift her legs into one bag. She pulled it up to the girl's chest. Then before she put the other bag over Nina's head, she tried to smooth Nina's hair away from her face, but it wouldn't stay. Hester was losing her nerve. Quickly, she pulled the bag down. It was done.

She rolled Al on his side, pulled the sheets out from under his dead weight, and shoved them into the top bag over Nina's breasts and face. She got Al's duct tape and wrapped it a dozen times around where the bags overlapped.

Out of the corner of her eye, Hester saw Al squirm. The sudden motion scared her, but when he didn't open his eyes, she ignored him. She was on automatic pilot and started humming while she rolled Nina's body off the bed and dragged it by the feet into the spare bedroom. She rolled it under the guest bed and pushed it as far back as she could.

"Alexander," she shouted into the next room, "I'm going to call the ambulance now."

He didn't answer. She went in and shook him.

"What?" His voice was weak.

"I'm going to call the ambulance."

He turned his head to look at the empty spot where Nina had been. "Where is she?"

"She's fine." The lie rolled off Hester's tongue. Keeping the truth from Al made her feel like she had some control over him, and right now, as on several occasions in the past, she knew her whole future depended on that.

"Good." He struggled to open his eyes. He was squinting in the sunlight. He lifted his head as high as he could to face Hester. "Hester, look, I…"

"Don't waste your breath, Al." She stood at the foot of the bed with her arms folded across her chest and her feet spread apart, a pathetic Colossus.

"It's not what you think." Al was so weak, he dropped his head back onto the mattress and closed his eyes. When he rallied, he enunciated each syllable of what he had to say. "I was not having sex with Nina. My God, Hester, I would nev—"

"Shut up, Al! Just shut the hell up!" Hester took a step toward him and dropped her hands into tight fists.

"Hester, I did not do anything wrong! For God's sake, ask Nina, she'll tell you the truth."

Now what? Hester hadn't figured out what she would say about where Nina was or what had happened to her. She turned away from Al, walked toward the foot of the bed, and said sarcastically, "Go ask Nina? Right, like she wouldn't lie to me too."

"She doesn't have to lie. I tell you, nothing happened between us." Saying it took the last of his strength. Al shut his eyes and grimaced.

Hester was on the verge of screaming, but she didn't. She wanted to hit Al, hurt him, but his mouth dropped open. He was out of it. She collapsed onto the floor, hugged her knees to her chest, and lowered her head.

Five

A long while passed before Hester pulled herself together and got on her feet again. She noticed the pink thong. Picked it up and, dirty as it was, shoved it in the back of her underwear drawer. She had to tend to Al. He was completely unconscious, like a rag doll. Putting his swim trunks on him made her sick to her stomach. She resisted the temptation to get a knife and cut his balls off. She called the ambulance.

Hester didn't know Dee all that well yet, but she was exhausted, needed some help to face the EMT's so Hester called her on her cell. It was getting dark and the electricity was still out. Dee came over, lit all the candles Hester had in the house, set them on the coffee table, and insisted on clearing the debris in the hallway. The ambulance didn't arrive for an hour—there were worse cases inland, and the bridge over the Intracoastal was closed. The squad leader questioned her about Al, and why she'd taken so long to call them. The storm swept through the park over eight hours ago. Hester lied, said her husband was wide awake the whole time and refused to let her call. She left him for a minute to go to the bathroom and was shocked when she came back and found him unconscious. She tried, honestly she did, but she couldn't get him to wake up.

It was after eight by the time they were ready to transport Al to the hospital for a severe concussion, some broken ribs, maybe a slight heart attack. They'd know more once they examined him at the hospital.

Hester watched them strap him onto the gurney. She shoved his health insurance cards into her old passport holder, looped it over his head, and stepped back. No way was she going to the hospital with him. The men who were ready to hoist the stretcher into the rear of the ambulance hesitated, and one of them looked at her oddly. She forced herself to go to Al, lean over, and kiss him on the forehead.

"You'll be alright, honey. I'll see you later." The words caught in her throat. She had no intention of going anywhere to see him. Not now, maybe never again; but despite her anger and disgust, she hadn't wanted to raise suspicion. She was angry with Al, but her life, the one she wanted, depended on him. If anyone else had found Nina and Al like that…

Hester should've never invited Nina to Florida. She should've seen the whole thing coming, knowing how weak her husband was. But Hester believed she was like a mother to Nina, helping her was the right thing to do. So how did it turn into such a nightmare? Nina dead, Al to blame. *Thank God I got here first, the park's half empty, no one gives a damn what's going on at 23 Fish Tail Lane.*

After the ambulance drove away, Hester almost said something to Dee about all that had gone wrong, but she didn't. Instead she asked Dee to leave.

"I'm so sorry, honey." Dee hugged her. Hester was touched by this gesture from someone she only recently met, and Dee had said the one thing Alexander Bruno Murphy, in his moments of lucidity, hadn't.

Sorry…I'm so sorry.

Yes, the whole day and the whole night would go down now and forever for Hester as sorry. Everything Hester had counted on her entire adult life had almost been wiped out. Before, whenever Hester learned of one of Al's mistakes, she forced herself to bury the knowledge of it in a dark corner of her brain. This worked for a while, but eventually each memory sought light and air, and popped up into her consciousness again like a real living thing. The memory of what Al had done had to be constantly weeded out before it could grow and choke her heart to death. Hester had to live in strict denial of many occurrences if she wanted to remain married to Al, and being married to Al Murphy was, since the first day she met him, all she ever wanted.

As much as it would give Hester some relief to unburden herself to someone like Dee, she knew she couldn't. She could trust no one with this latest knowledge.

It was past nine o'clock when Dee went back to her trailer. The candles had burned so low, they sat in their pools of wax, watching her like a field of winking yellow eyes. Hester blew them out and decided to wait in the darkness to finish what was left to do. She sat on the sofa facing in the direction of the ocean. If she were to sit there during the day, through the slider beyond old Chet's trailer, she could see one small square of the Atlantic. The sound of the pounding waves reached her. The sea was in a fury that had not yet subsided.

Not since her freshman year in college had she felt this low or this scared. It was the only other time her life intersected so intimately with death. Dredging up that old nightmare now might paralyze her, and she couldn't stop now. The worst was left to do.

She thought instead of Edna Pontellier, the heroine of Kate Chopin's *The Awakening*. She's on the beach alone in the moonlight. She takes off her "unpleasant" and "pricking" garments, throws them down, and walks out into the waves. The water feels colder on her naked body then she expected, colder still the farther out she goes. Though she's so cold, she doesn't stop. She keeps struggling until she knows she's in too deep to turn back. She should try to save herself, but she doesn't. She gives into the sea and lets it take her under, swallow her up.

Edna tried to make her marriage work, played the happy house-wife, and it'd gotten her nowhere. Death was better than waiting for the love that would forever be denied her. Death was better than living a lie for one moment longer. The hopelessness, the character's utter despair tied Hester's stomach in knots the first time she read the novel, and now again as she recollected it.

Hester was so god-awful sick of lies, believing them, telling them. It didn't matter which. She was sick of going along to get along. She didn't know anymore what exactly would make her happy, what she wanted from life, why she was even on this earth.

The night before, Hester had gone into the guest room after Nina was asleep. The air was cool, and she wanted to make sure Nina was warm enough. She pulled the blanket up over the girl's bare shoulder. Nina stirred and turned her head enough for Hester to notice the gentle curves in the topography of her perfectly shaped ear. Hester thought, *delicate, like a child's, like my child's would've been.*

What made sense a few hours ago to Hester, now seemed insane. But it was already too late to do what she should've done, call for help, turn everything over to the authorities. What would she say now? "Oh, by the way, I forgot to report that there is a young dead woman in my trailer, I found her naked in my bed next to my naked husband, I think her neck was broken, and I stuffed her in plastic bags and hid her body."

If she did call them now, with their advanced technology it would be no problem for the police to figure out exactly what happened. Hester had watched enough *CSI* shows to know they would find Al's DNA, and her DNA, all over Nina. They'd probably find his sperm too.

Sperm? Hester couldn't bear the thought of anyone finding out Al had sex with Nina. She wouldn't be able to bear the humiliation if anyone ever knew. Damn it, she should not have stuffed the filthy sheets in the bag with Nina's body. She should've waited and, when they'd dried, burned them. That would've been the only way to get rid of all of the evidence, for good. Too late now. She couldn't fathom opening up those bags, reaching in, pulling them out. Maybe seeing Nina's dead face again. No, it wasn't a good idea, but the lapse in her thinking gave her a sharp stab of doubt and made her more anxious than she already was. And then there was that pink thong...*they'd put us both in jail.* She shivered at the possibility, but try as she did, she couldn't remember what she'd done with the pink thong?

Then she thought, *what if Al wasn't lying? What if he didn't do anything to Nina? What if nothing was his fault?*

Hester sat up straight. There was a thread of hope, and that made her feel slightly better, slightly less hateful toward Al.

Better I act like nothing happened, she told herself, *because I may never know what really happened.*

Hester got up from the sofa, walked to the hall closet, grabbed Al's shovel, and slouched toward the spare bedroom.

Six

Hester had done all she could do to put an end to the "accident," as she was now trying to think of the tragedy that had occurred at 23 Fish Tail Lane. She stood on the patio and watched as the full moon rose up behind the palms transforming their tops into giant black spiders. She listened to the rush of the surf and the distant hum of traffic on Route 95. Her sweaty body, covered in a scrim of dirt and bugs, ached. She leaned the shovel against the side of the trailer and went in.

After showering in the tepid water that was left in the tank, she put on a thin nightgown, lay on the couch, and prayed for sleep. It didn't come. Sick of struggling to reach the oblivion she so desperately needed and without bothering to get dressed, she headed to the beach. No one was around, and if they were, she didn't care if they thought she was crazy. She was, wasn't she?

From their trailer all the way to the beach, the street was littered with trash. Garbage-cans, clothing, flowerpots, broken gutters, beach umbrellas were a few of the things strewn about that Hester could identify in the gloom. She saw a cat tearing into what looked like a package of hot dogs, and there were other small creatures like lizards and rats scurrying about. Hester passed the clubhouse and cut through a patch of sea oats.

The beach too had been ravaged by the hurricane. Hester had to navigate piles of seaweed matted with trash and large pieces of timber. There was a deep drop-off where the pounding surf had eroded the shoreline. Hester jumped down it to get to the water. She walked for what seemed an hour along the edge watching the luminous foam of the waves until she was about to collapse. She climbed back up the ridge and found a spot above what she thought was the high tide line and lay on her back. The moon was far to the west, and the stars looked so close she reached her hand up and pretended to touch them. She wished she could fly up in the sky and be one of them, be light years away from the fact that Nina was dead, that Al might have had sex with her, might have choked her until her neck broke, might have had rough sex with her and accidentally broke her neck. He might have…

Would she ever sleep again with these thoughts looping through her mind?

And then there were the damn bloodstains on the carpet, her trail of blood leading to the bedroom. In the morning she'd phone Stanley Steemers, get them over early, and get rid of at least one mess.

But the bigger mess? The one in the bedroom.

She closed her eyes. The stars she'd been staring at zoomed around inside her head like bullets ricocheting off metal.

There was no cleaning that up. Ever.

She was damned for good now, and she knew it. That stupid hurricane had blasted through Pleasant Palms, destroying many things, including—she had to accept it—the life she formerly lived, the one she'd worked long and hard to have.

Why me? Why now? Why...

The next thing Hester knew she opened her eyes and saw a thin line of light on the horizon. She sat up and looked behind her at the part of the sky that was still dark in time to see the last star disappear.

She had a long walk back to the park. When she arrived at the trailer, it was sunny and bright. The brilliant clouds had grown into a chorus line of giant round-shouldered trolls. The power was still out so Hester filled a pot with water and headed out to the gas grill. She watched a tongue of fire leap from the burner when she turned it on. She boiled the water, stirred in instant coffee, and added powdered creamer. It made her think of Carly Simon singing about clouds in her coffee. The words came back to her: "You're so vain, you probably think this song is about you...don't you?"

It reminded her of Al, of how everything always had to be about him.

Seven

Years and years ago, during her interview at Sourland High School, Hester wanted to be the shining star, but it was Vice Principal Alexander Bruno Murphy in his navy suit, crisp white shirt, and thin red tie who stole her thunder. He was gorgeous, and the cock-sure smile on his face made Hester think he knew it.

When he stood to introduce himself, Hester blushed. Her hand turned sweaty. She wiped it on her skirt before she shook his. "So plea-sed to m-meet you," she stammered. What kind of temporary insanity was gripping her? She needed this teaching position. She was broke and owed a fortune in college loans. She took a breath and focused on Mr. Heck, the principal, instead of on the handsome, young VP. But his eyes seemed riveted on her breasts, and shockingly she was enjoying the attention. It had been a long time since she wanted a man to look at her, desire her…since she was seventeen years old, her freshman year in college, when her heart was broken, and her spirit crushed.

In order to survive, Hester adopted a strict routine—Sundays go to Mass, weekdays work the cafeteria line, go to class, go to the library, Saturdays volunteer work with the amputees at Walter Reed Hospital, call home twice a week, even though no one answers. No time to get in trouble, no time to make another mistake. And she stayed away from her friends too. They were burning their bras, fighting for equal rights, fighting for birth control. Birth control? The only real birth control was to not want a man. Love was a hot stove that burnt you when you touched it. She swore that she'd never go near it again, not with a ten foot pole. From that time on, Hester stifled all romantic notions and lived a life of strict chastity.

Now, at age twenty-two, she was stunned, and, yes, petrified, by the way she was reacting to Vice Principal Murphy.

She was so distracted by his strong profile when he turned to look at Mr. Heck that Hester almost missed hearing the principal say, "Miss Randal, I think we can conclude this interview by offering you a position in the English department."

Mr. Murphy stood up and extended his hand and said, "Congratulations, Miss Randal, glad to have you on the team." Hester was faint with gratitude. She put her hand in Al's, and it fit like a glove. He squeezed it gently, and her body hummed with longing.

As time passed, Hester's yearning only grew more intense. Many times she tried to talk herself out of falling for Alexander Murphy, but he had so much going for him: beauty, brains, a strong work ethic. Hester liked that he took his position seriously. And he had a sense of humor. He made her laugh, and he flirted with her. She began to let her guard down.

By Christmas, she found herself completely under his spell. Her life consisted of two main components, working like hell at teaching and dreaming of nothing but Al. She was convinced he was a good man, not at all like the young man she'd thought she loved in college. No, here was a man she could trust, so she was willing—more than willing—to do just about anything to get Al Murphy. She had done a complete about-face. She was ready now for love.

Right before the winter break he dropped into Hester's classroom for a surprise observation. As he was leaving, he turned and said, "In my office after the bell?" It was a question, but his clipped pronunciation made it sound like a command.

"Yes, Mr. Murphy."

There were still ten minutes left in the class.

What had Hester been saying about Daisy Buchanan anyway? She was so flustered she couldn't remember. All she could think about was what might happen—what she wanted to happen—when she went to Al's office.

Her students looked at her curiously like another head had sprouted out of the one she already had. When she said nothing, they looked away and started talking and laughing, and soon the room was full of noise. Still in the afterglow of Al's visit, Hester stared blankly at them. *God, how unkempt,* she thought, *those boys with greasy hair, wrinkled shirts. The girls, their ratty hair clumped with spray, those tight, slutty-looking tops.*

They were a noisy, motley bunch, and not easily contented. How dissatisfied they seemed with their teacher for not being more…more entertaining. Hester knew they'd probably rather watch her immolate before their very eyes, than to have to sit there and listen to her talk about *The Great Gatsby.*

Hester wasn't a very entertaining teacher, but she tried to lead them to the nuggets of insight she found so fascinating in most of what she read. They, however, even if they understood her point, never seemed to care about it. Her first year of teaching was falling far short of the high expectations she'd had for it. In retrospect, even her near-disastrous student-teaching experience seemed a success, compared to the circus her classroom was turning into.

"So, class." She started talking over the jabbering. "Even though Daisy seems so perfect on the outside…how does Fitzgerald put it?"

Here she paused to give them "think time," but no one was listening.

"Come on, have a little respect." She hated saying stuff like this because it never worked.

"Okay, so no one remembers?" She felt she had to keep going. The clock was ticking, and she wanted to get past this whole part of the novel today. She didn't want to stop and discipline Ashley or Pete or anyone. She just wanted to move on, and the class to end.

"Open your books. Go to chapter two. Find the description of Daisy," she said, sounding like a platoon sergeant. A few actually followed directions. It struck her that they liked being told exactly what to do.

"What in the description would make a reader think Daisy Buchanan is attractive?"

Beth Humbolt's hand shot up. "Hester, I mean, Miss Randal." Snickering.

Beth quickly looked back over her shoulder. Hester had the feeling she must have made some kind of funny face to the kids behind her, because several of them burst into laughter.

Beth paused before she continued, "We already discussed Daisy, Miss Randal."

Another pause, then, "Remember?"

She dragged out the middle syllable of "remember" and rolled her eyes toward Amy Watson who chuckled.

"Daisy has a 'low thrilling voice,'" Beth said, making her voice low and husky. Her fans guffawed. She waited till the noise died down. "It was 'a promise that she had done gay, exciting things.'" Beth strung out the words "gay" and "exciting" in such a way that the whole class erupted in laughter.

Hester, despite being annoyed by Beth's sarcastic tone, had to admit the girl could quote directly from the text.

In a mocking sing-song voice Beth continued, "I think anyone who does 'gay, exciting things' is probably attractive to a lot of people. Don't you, Hester, I mean, Miss Randal?" She didn't pause for an answer. "Anyway, we're supposed to be discussing Tom, Daisy's husband. You re*mem*ber who Tom is don't you, Miss Randal?"

"What?" Hester was again at a loss for words. *The little brat thinks I don't know who Tom is? Is she kidding?*

Hester opened her mouth to say something, but as soon as Beth saw Hester's jaw drop, she kept going. "You asked about how Mr. Frederick Scott Fitzgerald described Tom Buchanan; and while you were flirting, I mean chatting, with Vice Principal Murphy, we were supposed to be looking it up. Remeeeeeember?"

The whole class was in stitches, and Hester felt like Miss Carolyn, that teacher in *To Kill a Mockingbird* who didn't know what to say; and when she did, it was the wrong thing. Hester surveyed the room: big gangly teenage bodies stuffed into seats too small for them, heads thrown back, mouths opened, ha, ha, ha. They couldn't stop laughing.

"Hey, settle down. Settle down. Please, come on now. Settle down." Hester knew her words were falling on deaf ears. It was useless. They laughed and laughed and laughed.

At her wit's end, Hester put her book on the chalk tray, walked to the side of the room, picked up the trash can, and slammed it down on the floor again and again and again. The laughter stopped. She raised the can up and slammed it one more time. Silence.

"There," she said, struggling to control the frustration in her voice. "There."

All eyes were on Hester. She held her breath as she stared Beth Humbolt down. Then in the calmest voice she could muster, "Thank you so much, Beth, for getting us back on track."

Hester walked in a dignified manner back to the center of the room thinking, *calm down, don't drop to their level, don't do what you feel like doing, don't slap little Miss Know-It-All in the face, don't let them make you lose your job…better to act like nothing happened.*

"So, Beth, how does Mr. Francis Scott Fitzgerald…" Hester emphasized "Francis" just so the one or two kids who were on the ball, including Beth Almighty herself, would know Beth had made a mistake and that their teacher wasn't a total idiot after all, "describe Mr. Tom Buchanan and explain what that description implies about his personality?"

"Well, Mr. Frederick, I mean, Francis…who cares? Really, Miss Randal, who really cares?"

Boy, thought Hester, *what a little pain in the ass. She can dish it out, but she can't take it.*

"Anyway, in chapter two on page nineteen," Beth continued, "it says he had, and I quote, 'a rather hard mouth,' 'shining arrogant eyes,' and 'a cruel body.'"

"Sound familiar, Miss Randal?" It was Robby Pherson from the corner of the room. Now most of the students were chuckling and back to having a good old time as Hester wondered what Robby was referring to.

"God, give me the strength," Hester mumbled half to herself. "Continue, Beth."

"Well, men with hard mouths, arrogant eyes, and cruel bodies, although no doubt attractive, are dangerous and just plain not trustworthy. It's easy to see that Tom can do more damage than just giving poor old Daisy a bruised—"

The bell rang. Beth stood up, turned from her front row seat to face the class, and announced, "I'll finish tomorrow, class." She glanced at her teacher, "Bye, Hester, I mean, Miss Randal."

Hester flushed, her eyes widened with disbelief, and she clenched her teeth so tight her jaws ached. Beth sashayed her way to the door. Hester watched her and couldn't help staring at the girl's bulky behind. *God, what a mess, her own mother probably has a hard time loving her.* And just as Hester thought this, Beth whipped her head around and caught Hester.

"You are so sick."

Thankfully, no one but Hester heard what Beth said. Still Hester wanted to stop the girl and say, you're wrong. It's not what you think. But Hester knew if she said one thing to Beth, it would set her off, and she'd yell something outrageous back like, you were staring at my ass! Weren't you? Yes, you were and don't try to deny it.

Beth would make sure her friends thought Hester was a pervert. Even now she was probably telling them that. Hester had no choice. She had to let the incident go, or she'd be the one in trouble. Discouraged and anxious, Hester grabbed her keys, followed the last student out, and locked the door.

In the main office, Gladys was slumped over her new electric typewriter. Her dirty blonde hair teased on the top resembled a bird's nest from the back.

"Hi, Gladys, is Mr. Murphy available? He asked me to meet him here after class."

Gladys didn't look up, but Hester saw her hands hesitate above the keyboard before she grumbled, "Check the gym."

"Thanks, Gladys. See you later."

"Yeah, later." Gladys still didn't look up at Hester, who stood there for a second and wondered why Gladys didn't like her. It bothered Hester because she knew everybody loved Gladys, and Gladys seemed to love them all back, except for her, whom she seemed quite content to ignore. It made Hester feel like such an outsider. She longed for some degree of closeness with her coworkers, but she wasn't mixing in the way she'd hoped.

It's me. Something's wrong with me, she told herself. *It's January. I've been here since September. I have to try harder.*

Hester blamed herself for being somewhat of an outcast, but she couldn't help thinking that the staff of Sourland High were all a bit stuck-up. They took pride in the fact that their school wasn't an educational badland. Students passed the county, state, and college admission tests with no trouble, and that was something to brag about in the seventies in a state like New Jersey. Okay, so it was a great high school. Did that mean that a new teacher couldn't break into their tightknit circle?

Hester forced herself to stop thinking about the sad state of her social affairs. Who cares? She had plenty of work to keep her busy. She listened to the noisy clip of her heels on the linoleum as she hurried down the hall toward the gym. She had seventy-six more essays to read, two parent phone calls to make, and Supervisor Zeigler was observing her tomorrow. She should've asked Mr. Murphy if she could meet with him tomorrow after Zeigler's visit. She could turn back now and leave a message for him with Gladys. She was sure he would understand. But she didn't. Instead she walked faster until she was in front of the closed door to Coach Stalmeyer's office.

She knocked. "Mr. Murphy? It's me, Miss Randal…"

"It's open."

Al Murphy was alone in the small room, sitting behind an old desk. He had taken off his suit jacket, and the muscles of his chest strained against the fabric of his striped shirt. His tie was loose. He was leaning back in the office chair, and the tips of his fingers were wedged into the top of his pants. His wavy black hair was combed back neatly and carefully trimmed around his ears. His skin shone a deep honey-color even though it was the dead of winter.

The wall behind him was lined with shelves stacked with disheveled piles of paperwork and some binders labeled Phys Ed 469 through Phys Ed 488. A dusty plastic fern in a red pot was on one side of the desk and a folding chair on the other. There were no windows. A small white poster was taped on the wall above the fern. It read, "Be a force of Nature instead of a feverish selfish little clod of ailments and grievances complaining that the world will not devote itself to making you happy. Shaw, 1903."

Hester read the sign before she looked down at Al and smiled.

Al smiled up at her, cleared his throat and said, "Well, Miss Randal, something will have to be done about your inability to control your class."

Hester's smile quickly disappeared. "Excuse me, Mr. Murphy?"

"You heard me, Hester." He frowned, but his dark, deep-set eyes were warm and friendly.

Flustered, Hester felt weak. Her voice trembled as she made an attempt to defend herself. "Well, Mr. Murphy, it is true that…"

"Call me Al."

"Okay, well, Al, it is true that some of the students in some of my classes misbehave some of the time, but I believe I am progressing in the area of discipline. As a matter of fact, today I was planning on speaking to several parents concerning just this sort of thing. I really am trying to get a handle on each one of…" Hester couldn't stand the way Mr. Murphy was staring at her "…them. It's just that there are certain students like Beth Humbolt, Amy Watson, and Robby Pherson, who just seem to be able to…"

"The three musketeers of Sourland High? You think they're the worst?"

"Well, yes, I do think they talk too much and that…"

"Tape their mouths shut."

"What?"

"Lock them up in the janitor's closest."

"Mr. Murphy, you must be…"

"I said, call me Al."

"Al, you must be kidding."

"I am." As he said this, he got up, went to the door, and locked it.

"What are you doing?"

He didn't answer, but walked up to Hester and took her hand in his. "I don't want us to be disturbed; and yes, I was kidding around with you."

"Thank God, I really don't want to lose this job." Hester's hand felt warm in Al's, so she tried to pull it away, but he squeezed it and put his other hand on her wrist.

"You're not going to lose your job, not if I can help it. Besides, it's good to know you can take a joke. I love a girl with a sense of humor."

He led her around the desk and tried to kiss her. She pulled away.

"Come on now, Hester. I won't hurt you." He leaned in slowly. His breath was hot on her face. It smelled minty. His lips touched hers. They were soft and full and made hers tingle. He pulled away and looked in her eyes and she noticed his were the color of hot fudge. He kissed her again, this time longer and harder, and she found it difficult not to kiss him back, not to open her mouth, not to let him in.

Al backed off, sat in the chair, and pulled Hester sideways onto his lap. The quickness of this maneuver surprised her. She stiffened and whispered, "No."

But Al had one arm firmly around her, his hand on her waist. "It will be alright. No one will know."

His face was full of concentration. His features took on a look that could be described as disdain, though it wasn't. Hester knew he was aroused, seriously aroused.

"Hester Randal, do you know how hot you are?" His eyes met hers.

"Mr. Murphy, please, we're bound to get…"

"Stop calling me Mr. Murphy, for God's sake, and lighten up."

Before she could decide if what he had said was out of line, he kissed her again, and she sank deeper into his lap, where it became easier for him to reach under her blouse and massage her back and press her closer to him. He kept that hand there, and with the other, pulled the front of her blouse up, reached into her bra, and cupped her breast. He massaged it, then rolled her nipple between his thumb and forefinger until it hardened. He pushed her blouse up under her chin and pulled her bra down until her breast was out. He sucked on her nipple, then he sucked her whole breast into his mouth.

Hester looked down, saw her blouse bunched up, saw Al Murphy's lips stretched out around her; and despite her shock at what she was letting this man, her boss, do to her, she was on the verge of an orgasm.

He touched the zipper on her slacks. Hester froze. She could not let him inside her like that, even though she was so close to coming, even though she wanted so badly to come with him inside her. But she had learned her lesson, and she would never be careless about getting pregnant again. She took a deep breath and put her hand on his. "Stop. Please. Stop."

He did. He leaned back and looked at her. The pupils of his eyes were black pinpoints, the irises the color of wet bark. His gaze was unflinching. His mouth was slightly open and he was breathing heavily. Hester longed for him, longed to satisfy this handsome, beautiful man. Her hand was on his forearm and she could feel how strong he was. He took his hand from her zipper and pulled his down instead. She slid off his lap, knelt between his legs, and tried to stay lost in the heat of the moment. But she couldn't stop the image of Tom Buchanan and his "cruel body" from popping into her mind.

Eight

A t noon the power in Pleasant Palms was still out. Hester was on her patio, lying on the chaise lounge, staring at the scarred bo tree. Two board members came by with clipboards and made notes about the damage to the tree and her trailer. She told them about Al being in the hospital, and they said how sorry they were and moved on. When they left, the quiet grew so intense Hester fell into a trance and no longer even heard the ocean. When a sea gull squawked, she almost jumped out of her skin.

She got up and went for a walk north on Old Ocean Road, which bordered the beach and led out of the trailer park. On the west side, through lush landscaping Hester could peek at the mansions. She spied a Burberry plaid beach blanket hanging over one of the balconies. A recycling bin full of empty Johnny Walker Black Label bottles had been left outside one of the gates. There was not much else to look at. No one seemed to be around.

Other than palm fronds, coconuts, and sea grape leaves scattered along the roadside, little here seemed to have been disturbed by the storm. Hester picked up her pace, and soon she was sweating. It felt good to put one foot in front of the other and leave Pleasant Palms and all that happened there behind.

She made it all the way to the Boyton Inlet, three miles from her trailer. No boats were going out, and the pelicans sat on the concrete pilings looking bored and hungry. Hester stopped by the marina restroom, but it was locked. The sun was high in the cloudless sky. She sat on a bench near the pelicans and watched them watch her. It had a calming effect on her, being so near the birds. When they flew away after an incoming fishing boat, she headed back past the "mausoleums of the living rich," as Al called them.

Hester really liked one particular residence. The facade was Tuscan Revival, and the color of the stone made her think of mango honey. Through the black wrought-iron gate, she could see a giant bronze sculpture of a woman in a toga wearing sandals and holding a sword. One of her breasts was exposed, and the broken shaft of a javelin stuck out of it. The position of her body and the way the long braid of her hair flowed out behind her made her appear to be running. Hester knew she was a goddess and at first thought it was Diana, but after she wracked her brain, she remembered. Because of the wounded breast, it had to be Camilla from the *Aeneid*.

As Hester passed by the replica of the fleet-footed Amazon, she wished she lived in the giant house behind it. She thought if she could just push a button and open the gate and walk past Camilla into the cool glass foyer and stand beneath the glinting crystal of the chandelier (the size of a shed), she just might be able to forget burying

Nina's body by moonlight, scrubbing every inch of the trailer in the dark, hiding Nina's belongings in her cheap suitcase, and shoving it under the bed.

When Hester got back to their trailer, she found two messages from the hospital on her cell phone. Her husband was asking to see her and could she come as soon as possible. No, she couldn't. She didn't call back.

Hester made herself a Captain Morgan and Coke—heavy on the rum, light on the Coke. She drank it down quickly, then switched to wine. She lit one of the candles that were still on the coffee table, and stared at it. She polished off half a bottle of Bogle Pinot Noir before she began to feel dizzy.

She stretched out on the couch and closed her eyes. She knew she drank too much, knew it would sit in her stomach and make her queasy, and give her one hell of a hangover tomorrow. She got up from the couch, went into the bathroom, and stuck her fingers down her throat.

Her vomit reeked. Undigested Coke and red wine splattered the sides of the toilet bowl. It wouldn't easily flush, so she pushed the handle down several times in rapid succession until toilet water spilled over the top. It was a mess, and it stunk. It wasn't that she was too drunk to clean it up. She wasn't now. In fact she felt better, sleepy, even a little peaceful inside. She didn't give a damn about the mess.

She went back to the couch and curled up on her side. Before she drifted off to sleep, she realized that for tonight, anyway, she didn't miss Al at all.

Nine

The minute Hester left Al in the Phys Ed office, she began thinking two things. One, she could really love Alexander Bruno Murphy for the rest of her life; and two, she shouldn't have done what she did. Not since Arthur Kendall and her freshman year in college, had she been at once so afraid, and so alive. It was like leaping off a cliff and thankfully discovering she could still fly.

Al didn't call her that evening as she'd hoped, but he did come by her classroom at the end of the next day to ask her out.

Friday night the temperature dropped into the twenties. With the wind chill it felt like the teens. Al picked Hester up at her apartment in Trenton, and they drove north on River Road along the Delaware River to Lambertville. He was taking her to a place he claimed had the best food in town, Bell's on Union Street. Al parked in the empty lot of Niece's Lumber. When they got out of the car, the cold made Hester gasp.

"It's freezing," Hester shouted.

"It's not that bad." Al hunched his shoulders and started walking toward the restaurant.

"Yes, it is," Hester insisted. She was a few steps behind him.

"Don't be such a baby, Miss Randal."

"I'm not, I'm just really freezing, Al."

Al stopped and turned to look at Hester, who was wiping her dripping nose on the back of her gloved hand.

"Alright, get in the car. I'll see if I can park closer." He didn't sound happy. He sounded like getting in the car and finding somewhere else to park might be a problem, but he hurried back and held the door open for Hester. He got in the other side and started the car. Before he put it into gear, he looked at Hester hesitantly.

"Thanks." She ventured a quick glance.

Al turned the heat up full blast. "Hot enough yet?"

"Yes, it's perfect now." Hester wanted to start a conversation, but she could think of nothing clever to say.

"Here, move closer to me if you're still cold." His voice was softer. She slid over. He put his arm around her. She put her head against his shoulder and watched the lights on the dashboard. Their breathing condensed and steamed up the inside of the windshield. It was like they were inside a silk cocoon. Hester sat there silently berating herself for not knowing what subject might interest Al, so they sat in silence until he kissed her. She kissed him back.

Too fast, she told herself. She swore she was going to slow things down, hold back, make him wonder whether she wanted to do anything with him at all, despite how far she'd gone the other day, and in school at that. *Temporary insanity.*

But his lips were on hers again. His warm, demanding tongue in her mouth.

It was over before Hester could resist.

She pulled her panty hose up from around her one ankle, hooked her bra, and buttoned up the top of her shirtwaist dress. She was breathless, and fretful. What in the hell had she done! Al, though, quick, had excited her intensely, touching, massaging, sucking her body to its breaking point. All thought ceased, all common sense went out the window. He knew what to do to her and did it passionately. As if he'd known her body for a long time, how it worked, what it wanted. As if he'd been down this road before and knew all the bumps and curves. How easily he'd driven her mad with desire.

Al zipped his pants up, put the car in drive, and rode around the small town looking for a parking space. He put the radio on. Wolfman Jack was reviewing the top twenty hits. Al turned the volume up. He couldn't find anywhere to park. After circling the block two times and over Cher belting out "Dark Lady," he said loudly, "Guess we'll have to call it a night."

They drove back to Trenton listening to the Wolfman, and not talking, except for Al lowering the volume on the radio once and saying, "You are on birth control, aren't you?"

Hester's first impulse was to lie. Al would think she was an idiot to have sex with him and not to be on the pill. But she wasn't about to go to a gynecologist to get a prescription. She had her reasons.

"No," she admitted with some trepidation. She knew what it felt like to be lied to, and she didn't want to start out lying to Al.

"Well, maybe you should get some," he replied flatly.

"Okay, I will." Hester was relieved. Al was planning on seeing her again. Maybe she could figure out a way to get something on a black market, not that she knew anything about that sort of commerce, but she'd sure as hell try.

Despite the even colder temperature now that it was later, Al walked Hester to the door of her apartment.

"Why don't you come in? We could talk." The night had gone by, and she didn't know one new thing about this man she'd just had torrid front-seat sex with.

"I'm beat. Maybe some other time." And he turned and left.

Later, starving hungry and rummaging through the refrigerator, disappointment descended on Hester. *Not even a goodnight kiss.* She'd wanted to impress Al, to dazzle him with her wit and vivaciousness, but she'd failed miserably.

Well, not at everything. So they hadn't talked much. So what? They hadn't needed to.

When she closed her eyes, she could still hear the sound of his voice saying her name, "Hester, Hester." She was on top of him. He was squeezing her breasts. She put all her weight into each thrust.

Ten

The kitchen light shone into the living room, startling Hester, who had finally fallen asleep. She checked her cell phone. 3:12 a.m. The power was back. She found the remote and clicked on the television. The ShamWow infomercial guy was fast-talking about their super-absorbency. Hester clicked it off. Her head buzzed. She stood up slowly and went into the bathroom. When she flipped the switch, she was stunned. She'd forgotten about throwing up, clogging the toilet, and it spilling all over the place. The rug was soaked, the linoleum slimy. She gagged on the foul odor. Jesus, the thought of cleaning it up made her sick.

"Mrs. Murphy, you in there?"

Hester recognized Chet Blount's nasally voice. She wished her nosey neighbor would go away. She didn't answer.

"Just want to know if you're alright. Got in from Ohio around midnight and couldn't unpack without electricity, so sat in my lounger till the lights came on. Saw yours were on too. Figured I better check on you." He was hollering through the kitchen window. "Maybe I'll see you in the morning."

Hester said nothing and held her breath until she heard the sound of his footsteps scraping through the gravel as he shuffled back to his trailer. Hester thought Chet asked too many questions, but Al said she shouldn't let that bother her. Still, she didn't like the way his beady eyes darted around when he was talking to her, and he was always talking. If she tried to get a word in edgewise, he stared at her blankly which gave her the impression he was skeptical of the veracity of what she was saying. He reminded her of her father who used to look at her the same way after she came home from a date. He'd ask her where she'd gone and what she'd done, then wait to catch her in a lie. Hester could barely remember what her father looked like, it had been that long since she'd seen him. He could be dead for all she knew.

The next morning before Hester had a chance to figure out what she was going to do about the damaged roof and ruined bedroom and stinky bathroom, she saw old Chet coming around the side of his trailer, holding his mug of coffee in one hand and scratching his scruffy beard with the other. She hurried out of the sliding door and met him on the patio before he could get any closer, or God forbid, inside her trailer. It'd be impossible to get rid of him then.

That's how lots of people at Pleasant Palms were, and it was one of the few drawbacks—she was discovering—the place had. Most residents were retired with nothing to do, so they spent eons of time talking, mostly about themselves; and when that topic was exhausted, they seemed to be on a pointless, yet thorough, fact-finding mission.

"Well, Mrs. Murphy, aren't I glad I didn't come down any earlier. My niece-in-law insisted I stay and have Thanksgiving with them.

'It wouldn't be the same without you, Uncle Chet,' she said. So, you know, how could I refuse? My nephew would have been stuck with all those women from Beverly Ann's side, that's my niece-in-law's name, Beverly Ann. Her mother, her three sisters—they're all single—and her girlfriend Nancy Lynne all pile in on poor Matthew. He's really always so out…"

Hester's head was spinning. *I've got to get rid of him,* was all she could think.

"And he doesn't enjoy his football game if I'm not sitting right there next to him."

Hester shifted her weight, ran her fingers through her hair, and sighed audibly.

"Not quite awake, are you, Mrs. Murphy?" He took a sip of his coffee, and Hester thought, *thank you, God, he's going to stop,* but he quickly continued, "I'm so glad you and Mr. Murphy will finally get a chance to spend the whole winter down here. It's just a shame that storm hit. Who would've thought we'd get something like that so late in the season? The weather people had it passing south of Key West. It was just a freak of nature. Wasn't it now? And where is Mr. Murphy anyway?"

Chet looked over Hester's head at the sliding door. "Thought I'd like to say a welcome to him too. See if he needs any help with fixing that mess you've got in the back there."

Now what am I going to say, thought Hester. She didn't want to have to explain things. She appreciated his offer, but as she looked at how his eighty-five-year-old head hung down like a turtle's and how the mug in his hand jiggled so much that coffee splashed out of it when he tried to drink from it, she knew he had no intention of making good on it.

Hester crossed her arms in front of her chest and sighed again. "Al was injured when the roof collapsed. It was minor, but they admitted him to the hospital anyway, just to be sure."

"Oh my, well, that is a shame. When will he be home?"

"I'm not sure."

"Well, if it isn't serious, then it should be soon. Right?"

"Yes."

"Well, it's already been almost forty-eight hours since the storm hit, so did the folks at the hospital say if it would be today or not? If it's not serious, as you say, then he should be home today."

Who cares when they send the bastard home! Hester wanted to yell at the old man. Instead, she heard herself saying in a pathetically small voice, "I hope you're right. It's so lonely here without him."

"I'm right next door, Mrs. Murphy. You don't have to worry about being lonely. Why don't I come over tonight? We'll play some Yahtzee. I could bring some cheese and crackers. I love Yahtzee. Counting up all those black dots on the die has a way of taking your mind off your troubles. Games are good for you, Mrs. Murphy."

"Oh, thanks, Mr. Blount, but I don't feel up to playing."

"Please, call me Chet, and we don't have to play anything. Talking is just fine with me."

"After I get back from the hospital…" Hester lied—she had no intention of going anywhere near the hospital, "…I'll most likely be exhausted, so maybe some other time, Chet."

Hester thought that would settle it.

"Well, when I see you're back, I'll just come over to make sure you're alright."

"Please, I don't want to bother you."

"No bother, it's the Pleasant Palms way. You'll see. We are like one big family here. We look out for one another."

Great, thought Hester, *that's just great*. She shifted her weight from one foot to the other again to buy some time to concoct another excuse while the old man wiped some coffee from his chin and said, "Oh, I almost forgot, where's your young friend?"

Hester drew in her breath and held it.

"I spoke on the phone with Marvin Bridgeford, his wife is Eve— nice-looking woman with short auburn hair."

"Yes, I've met Eve."

"Well, the night before the storm, I talked to him, and he said you had a young visitor staying with you, a former student. Let's see, her name was…" He held onto his chin as he tilted his head. "Now don't tell me. I like to try to remember things on my own."

Hester's mind raced.

"Nina!" he shouted with delight. "Yes, Marvin said she was a nice-looking girl. So how could you be lonely with such a young treasure around?"

Hester wanted to rip the mug out of his feeble grip and dump the rest of the coffee over his head. She hated being cornered like this, and it felt like the old hoot was drilling her on purpose, almost taking delight in making her scramble for answers she hadn't yet concocted.

"The hurricane scared poor Nina near to death. As soon as it was over, she made me take her to the station and put her on the next train back to New Jersey. I'll miss her, I mean, we'll miss her, but the good part is, she decided to give the community college up north another try." Hester was satisfied with her spur-of-the-moment fabrication.

"Why didn't she fly home?"

That was it. What difference did it make to this old guy if Nina took a plane or a train or a hot air balloon? He didn't even know her.

"She had, I mean, has…" Hester caught herself, "…a tremendous fear of flying. Well, nice chatting with you, but I have a million things to do. Thanks for offering to help, Mr. Blount, I mean, Chet."

Before he could say another word, Hester pulled open the slider, stepped inside, and dropped the shade. She peeked through a gap and saw he was still standing there like a pale specter from the underworld. Hester felt bad. In truth Chet Blount seemed to be a perfectly good-hearted man, a congenial, kind man; but Hester's nerves were so frayed she wasn't seeing things clearly, and she knew it. At the moment she didn't have the luxury of getting too friendly with someone who lived only ten feet away and, obviously, watched her like a hawk. Besides he seemed to be a bit of a gossip, who wouldn't hesitate to tell everyone he met everything he knew or thought he knew about her. She had to set boundaries. She had no choice.

"Okay, Mrs. Murphy," he shouted through the door, through the shade. "See you tonight."

Hester couldn't believe it. She heard the satisfaction in his voice, triumph even. He paid not one bit of attention to what she said, to what she wanted. Instead he sounded like he was coming over for a goddamn date whether she liked it or not. It made Hester go cold inside to have her wishes so blatantly disregarded.

Okay, so maybe he's not all that kind, maybe he's stubborn and narcissistic, concluded Hester. *That the man is ancient doesn't make the fact that he's getting his way come hell or high water any easier for me to take.*

She went into the kitchen and once again got out the bucket and some clean rags. Boundaries? Maybe it was already too late.

Eleven

In March, not quite three months after her first date with Al, Hester was driving home from work when she saw a robin by the side of the road trying to yank an earthworm out of the dirt. Ordinarily such a harbinger of spring would've put a smile on her face. But today, she didn't give a shit about spring. She gripped the wheel and prayed, *Please, God, help me, help me, help me.*

If she didn't get her period tonight, then she had to be pregnant, and it would've happened that night in Lambertville in the parking lot of Niece's Lumber because Hester had not done "it" with Al since then. They'd dated and done other things, but since she couldn't figure out how to get the pill without going to a doctor, she'd been firm with him about not going all the way. And now she'd held him off for nothing. Who said lightning didn't strike twice?

At home she dug her sneaks out of the closet, put on her only workout outfit, and jogged from her apartment on Concord Avenue to Cadwalder Park. As soon as she got through the gates, she began to run at full speed. She passed the deer pen, the empty subterranean bear cages, the rickety old monkey house. Her chest tightened. Her heart pounded. She was sweating, and her breasts ached from bouncing up and down, but she forced herself to finish out the loop only slowing to a walk out on Stuyvesant Avenue. Her pelvic area throbbed with what she was sure were cramps, and she hugged herself in gratitude for the pain. She'd get her period for sure now. She thought of the robin and smiled to herself as she crossed the railroad tracks and turned up Concord. But by the time she got home, the glorious cramping had stopped.

In the bathroom she took off her pants and top, and studied the curve of her abdomen in the mirror. It was flat and tight; but when she turned sideways, there was the slightest bulge below her navel. Had it always been there? She wasn't sure. She ran her hand from her rib cage to her pelvic region. It felt puffy. She took off her bra. Her nipples were dark red and covered with bumps. She cupped them and sighed. They looked and felt exactly the same as the last time she was pregnant.

How had she let this happen, again? She put on her pajamas, sat at the kitchen table to grade some papers, and burst into tears. The awful memory was back.

How cold she'd been, sitting alone in that dilapidated waiting room in Philadelphia, staring at the filthy, crooked blind, the chipped paint on the frame of the half-opened window, the darkness beyond. She prayed with all her might for God to give her the strength to get up and leave, but she didn't. Her boyfriend would never talk to her again if she didn't go through with it. She watched the snow pile up on the sill and blow into the room. It hit the grimy linoleum and melted. The word "forlorn"—a vocabulary word Hester encountered often in literature—popped into her head. It was exactly how she felt.

Her boyfriend, Arty, couldn't come with her. At the last minute, he had something, as he put it, "important to take care of." They were walking past Holly Bush toward Main Street to catch the 4:30 bus from Glassboro to downtown Philly when he told her.

A lump rose in Hester's throat. She thought from the beginning (he'd told her from the beginning) that he'd be with her the whole time.

"I can't do this by myself, Arty," Hester explained.

"You'll be fine. You don't need me there. Lots of girls go through this all by themselves."

"I'm not 'lots of girls.'" She'd fallen a few steps behind him and hurried to catch up. "Arty, please, I don't really want to do this at all, let alone by myself."

They were standing side by side now, looking down the deserted street. Arty was frowning.

Hester gathered her nerve and blurted out, "You're the one who wants me to do it." Her voice was strident, and immediately she regretted how she sounded. After all, Arty, who was a senior, did have a lot on his mind. Tomorrow was the lottery for the draft. All the guys on campus were upset. So she moved closer and whispered, "Please, please, come with me?" She turned and kissed his cheek just as the bus pulled up.

"I can't. I just fucking can't." Arty rubbed his face where her lips had touched it. "You don't understand. Look, don't be such a god-damn big…" He stopped himself and stepped back.

The doors of the bus opened. Hester stepped up and looked back at him, hoping he'd follow, but he didn't, and she noticed a hardness in his eyes she hadn't seen there before.

Hester wanted to scream at him and call him a bastard or something as she watched his back hunch up in the cold and his head disappear between his raised shoulders as he lowered it against the wind and walked quickly away.

Every time the bus made a stop, Hester thought about getting off; but she knew Arty would be furious if she didn't get rid of this baby.

Sitting in that disgusting waiting room was like being in limbo. The sound of the traffic six stories below coupled with the hissing and banging of the radiator were driving her nuts. She kept one hand in the pocket of her pea coat clenched around a thick wad of small bills that added up to exactly six hundred dollars. She'd never had that much money in her life. Nobody she'd met at Glassboro State College, bordered by cornfields and woebegone trailer parks, had that much money. She knew it was tough for her friends to help her out the way they did. She'd felt guilty even asking, but she was desperate. Arty had only been able to come up with forty dollars so she had to go around begging for the rest. It was humiliating, but she'd done it, and here she was, sitting here hating herself.

The older man who finally came into the waiting room had a body that filled the door frame. His head grew out of his short, thick neck like an oversized upside-down apple. He was bald. His thin, dark eyebrows had a feminine arch to them, as though they had been plucked and penciled in. His nose, which looked ridiculously small on his full face, was ruddy; his bottom lip hung down, revealing a set of pointy lower teeth and whitish gums. He smiled weakly, so Hester smiled back.

"Randal? Hester Randal? Come into my office and let's get this over with." The sound of his voice was so sullen, it wiped the smile off her face.

"Okay, I mean, yes, sir." Hester didn't know what to say. She lowered her head and followed him. Her clogs clomped loudly on the bare floors. Why had she worn the stupid things? She stood behind the man as he took a wrinkled jacket, which looked exactly like a chef's jacket, from a coat rack and put it on. The office, as he called it, Hester could see was just his rundown bedroom that doubled as a place where he could conduct his nasty "business." It smelled faintly of urine and something tangy, like an Italian hoagie. There was a double bed with a rumpled coverlet along one wall, and at the foot of it a low dresser with a large console television on top of it. The T.V. was on. The screen was full of nothing but static, but the man stopped to stare at it anyway.

On the other side of the room near the bathroom door was a narrow table covered with a white sheet, and on top of that a pink towel. The table was outfitted with stirrups fashioned from two-by-fours and what looked like bicycle pedals. Hester had never been to a gynecologist, so she had only a vague sense about how to mount such a contraption. The thought of lying up there at such a vulnerable angle made her sick to her stomach. At the foot of the table was a garbage can.

The bathroom door was open. A bulb hung from the ceiling. The mirror on the medicine cabinet was webbed with cracks. The sink was coated with soap residue.

"I'll take the money now. You do have the money?" The man was still staring at the grainy image on the television. Hester handed him the roll of bills. He counted them carefully, then stuck the wad in his pocket.

"Take off your coat, pants, and panties. Give them to me. Get up on the table. Lay on your back." The man's voice was matter-of-fact. Hester did as she was told. She sat on the table and pulled her T-shirt down and watched as the peace sign on the front elongated into an oval. She covered her naked pubic area with the pink towel. The man watched her and then went into the bathroom. She lay down. The bathroom door was still open and the light bothered her eyes. She shut them.

She fought with herself not to cry. What good would it do? There was no one there to comfort her. The man didn't seem to care about much of anything, and if she cried, it might annoy him, and everything might be worse. Hester took a deep breath and exhaled and tried to think only of Arty. Already she'd forgiven him for not being there.

"It's our only way out," Arty decided quickly on the abortion when Hester told him she missed her period. He was upset and seemed angry with her. It was as though she was confessing a grave sin to someone who had no part in it. She was the one, the only one, responsible for the transgression. She waited for her penance, and he pronounced it. The sinner would have to have the sin ripped out of her.

"But, Arty, the thought of it makes me sick. Can't we…" She hoped they could…what? Get married? She knew it was too soon to say that to him. Something like that had to come from him.

Hester couldn't go to her parents. Since she left home for college in late August, her parents called on the pay phone in the dorm hall every Saturday night at eleven o'clock. Had she made curfew? Did she remember about Mass tomorrow?

"I know you're a good girl, Hester," her mother would say, then she'd hand the phone to Hester's father.

"Remember, we trust you. You have a big responsibility to set a good example for your sister." He'd clear his throat and continue, "Say your prayers and stay away from the young men down there. I'm your father and I'm telling you, they are only after one thing. And we didn't raise you like that." Hester knew the translation: make sure you don't lose your virginity.

God, she hated the sound of her father's voice. She'd lost her virginity before she'd even figured out the layout of the campus, so it was difficult for her to hear him hammering home this dictum about saving herself for marriage and all that. Her father couldn't begin to understand how deeply in love she was, how it was only human nature to want to give yourself completely to the person you truly loved.

She'd hang up the receiver seething with anger, then slowly it would subside, and she'd start thinking maybe she should tell her parents about Arty, maybe they would understand. And guilt would begin slithering around inside her. She shouldn't be doing what she was doing with Arty, and she knew it. And when she was on the brink of resolving to never let Arty touch her again, her heart would start racing, *but one day he will be my husband, one day we will be together forever.*

The man coughed and Hester opened her eyes. He came out of the bathroom with two pills in one hand and some sort of tool in the other. Hester started sobbing. The contraption looked like a big claw. In a flash she knew she should've gone home to her parents—they'd been right all along. Boys were nothing but trouble. Dear God, she was sorry she'd ever met Arthur Kendall.

"What is that? What are you going to do with it?"

The man cleared his throat, but said nothing. He moved closer until he stood next to her.

"No! No! No!"

"Calm down. Take these." He sounded impatient.

Hester was shaking and crying.

"Lean up and take the pills." He dropped the pills into her palm. She swallowed them down dry.

The man lifted the towel off of Hester and moved to the foot of the table. He told her to put her feet in the stirrups and slide toward him. She tried to adjust her legs and feet and wiggle her bottom down toward him, but she wasn't doing it fast enough so he reached up, grabbed her by her hips, and pulled her buttocks to the end of the table. Hester gagged at his touch. She was weak with dread. He was impatient now. She could sense it. She watched him as he adjusted the claw. He started talking. Or was it singing? Everything began to sound like it was coming from far away. He put his forearms between her knees and tried to force them apart. Hester tried to keep her legs together, tried to say something, tried to keep her eyes open, but they kept closing. She felt awful, then limp, then like dust, and finally like she was being blown away.

When she awoke, she was in the middle of a dream. A team of surgeons was trying to remove a tumor from inside her head. She had floated out of her body and was up on the ceiling looking down at it. They were leaning over her, and the backs of their white coats and their heads looked like a tightly closed chrysanthemum. She tried to get a glimpse of the tumor, but couldn't. The doctors began talking, and she drifted back into her body. They congratulated her because they had never seen anything like the strange growth they had just removed. They brought it over to show her. It was a lump of slimy flesh that looked like a fat chicken wing with two small feet, one perfectly shaped, the other so deformed it looked like a hand with two fingers.

"Why, at first, we thought it was a baby coming out of your skull!" One doctor was smiling at her, and her inclination was to thank him, but before she could, she woke up.

She was not on the table, but in the bed still naked from the waist down. Something was wedged up into her vagina. Dizzy and sweating, Hester threw off the thin blanket and put both hands between her legs. The bulge of cloth was soaking wet. She pressed on it and the pain was excruciating.

The man was asleep in a threadbare chair. His head was back, his mouth open. He was snoring loudly. His puffy chins jiggled when he exhaled.

After several minutes Hester stood up slowly, walked to where her coat hung, got the belt and sanitary napkin she'd wrapped in toilet paper out of the pocket, and went into the bathroom. She closed the door and struggled to put the pad on over the bloody wad of whatever it was that the man had shoved up her. She was in agony as she tried to pull on her panties and jeans. In the mirror the image of her pale face was fragmented by the cracks in the mirror. Her hair was oily-looking and damp. She stared at herself. Her eyes in the glaring light looked like black ticks frozen in amber. Hester went back into the bedroom, grabbed her coat, and left.

The snow had stopped, but the wind was wicked cold. She stood at the bus stop hugging herself and waiting, for what seemed like forever, for the bus back to campus.

S. SNYDER-CARROLL

Finally it came. It was practically empty. She took a window seat near the front. On the Walt Whitman Bridge there was a backup. The bus stopped, moved forward, stopped. Hester grew impatient. She felt horrible, and she wanted to get back before curfew to see Arty. Seeing Arty would make her feel better. It always did.

Arthur Kendall was one of the first people Hester met when she arrived on campus for orientation. He saw her sitting alone in the lounge, introduced himself, and invited her to the Trailer, an old Airstream, he explained, parked behind the place he rented in town. Hester liked his long sandy-colored hair, bell bottoms, the fact that he was older. She felt flattered, and curious.

The Trailer was pretty dirty, but it had a groovy atmosphere. Arty and guys he lived with ran an extension cord to it from the house, screwed a black light into the ceiling, taped day glow posters over the windows, and threw an old mattress on the floor. It was a hang-out, a place to smoke weed. Arty turned Hester on, and it wasn't long before she was a regular at the Trailer. But there were always so many people around, so getting high was about all they ever did for the first few weeks.

On his birthday, though, they were alone. That night the black light made everything magical for Hester. The whites of her boy-friend's eyes, his teeth shone like milk glass. As soon as they were high, Arty leaned over and kissed Hester. He pulled her hair back and licked her neck and kissed it. Hester, not being experienced, did the same to him. Their hair, the color of the top side of a deer's tail, was so identical they looked like twins kissing.

She felt his long fingers first. He slipped one hand down the back of her jeans and touched her between her cheeks. This made

80

her squirm away from him so he stopped and began massaging her breasts through her blouse. He kept his mouth on her neck until he moved his hands down to her jeans and unbuttoned them. He maneuvered Hester onto her back, pulled her pants off. Before she had time to say a word, he was on top of her, then in her, and all she could feel at first was pain, unbearable, then bearable, then something that wasn't pain but was nearly impossible for her to describe.

When it was over, Arty told Hester he was shocked by all the blood and a little worried that the guys would be pissed about the old mattress being ruined. Why hadn't she told him she was a virgin? But she had, he probably hadn't heard her.

The worst of the damage was already done, according to Arty, so he lit a joint, and they smoked it, and then they had sex until he came two more times. Hester wasn't sure she came at all. But when Arty asked, she said she did because she thought that was what he wanted to hear. He told her she was the best birthday gift he ever got. That was September 14. Now it was November 29, so—Hester counted out the time on her fingers—it was less than ten weeks and that made her feel only slightly better. The baby would've been very small. How small? She wasn't sure, but she was hoping it was small enough not to have felt anything.

Two weeks ago her belly seemed to swell up overnight and none of her pants fit. Arty gave her a pair of his to wear while he was figuring out where she could go, to take care of the problem. She had them on now and rubbed her hands on the soft, worn denim. She tried to think about Arty but was having difficulty picturing him. His face, his hands, even his penis were nothing but a blur. She couldn't picture what he looked like up close while they were making out, how his tongue tasted, how his lips felt on her neck, how he sounded when he laughed. Hester pressed the side of her head against the bus window and tried like hell to visualize the object of her undying love and affection, but all she conjured up was a clear image of that garbage can in that dirty room and, lying cold and dead in the bottom of it, her tiny naked baby.

One time when Hester was around eight years old, right after her sister was born, she was watching her mother nurse the infant—her mother was big on breast-feeding. She even started a club for it. There were more than a few people, though, who thought Mrs. Randal was disgusting. Hester overheard them say bad things about her mother and wished she would just stop doing it. But she didn't. So this one day, when Hester was staring at her, her mother reached around Hester's waist and pulled her close. Hester saw how tightly the infant's lips latched onto her mother's breast. The sound of the sucking was loud, the smell of the milk sweet and overwhelming. Hester felt the urge to suck on her mother's breast too and almost asked if she could, but instead reached down and touched her sister's hand. The tiny, almost translucent fingers wrapped around Hester's pinky more firmly than seemed possible.

The bus was still stuck in the traffic on the Walt Whitman Bridge, and Hester was floating in and out of the past. She saw her baby sister's fingers in her mind's eye, remembered the warmth and strength of that touch.

I shouldn't have left my baby there, I should've taken it with me, Arty and I should've buried it.

Her heart was in her throat. Some girls, who claimed to know about these things, told her it would be about the size of a pearl.

She'd believed them then, and thought it would be an easy thing, but not now. She was in so much pain, her baby had to have been bigger than a stupid little pearl!

Maybe it had come out alive, and she could've baptized it— splashed a little water on its forehead and made the sign of the cross. It would've been better than nothing. Maybe it had cried. Maybe the man had pounded her poor baby to death with that claw thing.

Hester started to weep. It came on her hard. *I'm only seventeen and going to hell…for Arty.*

Snot ran with her tears into her mouth, and the sourness of it all, of everything that happened, of everything she'd done, made her want to kill herself. She thought about getting off the bus and jumping off the bridge into the river.

She was crying so much, she bit down on her fist to shut herself up. She didn't want the other people on the bus to hear her sobbing. She didn't want anyone to ask what was wrong.

It was almost eleven o'clock when Hester walked into her dorm. The drugs were completely worn off. Her pelvis and groin throbbed. She had to see Arty. If he held her in his arms and told her he loved her, then she would know she'd done the right thing. She would heal, and they would go on loving each other. But it was late, too late to go to the trailer and look for him. She couldn't afford to miss curfew and have a letter sent to her parents. After all, they were paying for everything. If they found out about tonight, they'd never, ever forgive her. They'd make her come home, and then she would never see Arty again.

When she got to her floor, Hester went straight to the pay phone. Hearing his voice would be enough until tomorrow. Gene, a guy who lived with Arty, picked up on the second ring.

"Hester?" His voice sounded like it always did, like he'd just inhaled nitrous oxide. "What the hell are you calling here for?"

"Look, Gene, I don't feel all that great. Please, just let me talk to Arty."

"Hester, shit, I don't know what to tell you. Look, I didn't think you'd be feeling too great tonight." He made a noise that sounded like a chuckle.

Did he know what she'd done? How in the hell...?

"Just get him, Gene. Come on." She was almost out of strength and completely out of patience. Then for a split second, it hit her that maybe something bad had happened to Arty, and Gene was just trying to break it to her gently.

"Gene, tell me the truth," Hester pleaded. "Is Arty alright?"

"Well, he's not hurt or arrested or anything, if that's what you mean. I just don't know what to tell you."

"How about the truth?" *Asshole*, Hester almost said it. She knew Gene was just trying to keep her on the phone. He was always trying to outdo Arty like he was jealous of him or something.

"You asked for it, Hester, and remember, I didn't want to be the one to tell you. Personally, I think you're a groovy chick and that Arty is a real asshole for..."

"Please, Gene, I'm really sick here. Please, don't tease me."

"Well, he's not here for a couple of reasons. He got loaded, he went to see Trish. The girl from his home town he's been in love with for four fucking years. The girl he's engaged..."

Hester didn't think she heard him correctly.

"Hey, look, Hester…," he continued, "want me to come over and sneak you out? We can go somewhere and get stoned. You know, help me celebrate, help you get over that asshole."

"You're an effing liar, Gene!"

"No, but for your sake I wish I was. It's the fucking truth, and it's about time you knew it."

Hester slammed the receiver on its hook and held onto wall phone as though she were tethered to it. If she let go, unseen forces might pull her away bit by bit, cell by cell, till even her bones might disappear. All that would remain would be her broken spirit. She leaned her head against the cold wall. The peace sign on her T-shirt stretched across her breasts. She saw it, but it didn't register. She looked down beyond it. How far away her feet looked—those stupid clogs, like two small wooden boats sinking in a puddle of scarlet blood the saturated napkin could no longer contain.

Twelve

Hester wasted half the morning sitting in Al's La-Z-boy feeling nauseous and ruminating about the past. She'd barely slept. During the night she was awakened by the goofy hip-hop ringtone Al had downloaded on her cell. After she saw that it was him, she turned it off.

She stood up. Stretched, and looked out through the sliding door. Old Chet was shuffling his way over to the shuffleboard courts with Ernie Stamford. Thank God. She could go out now and not have to worry about being forced to listen to more of Chet's commentary. The patio and small yard were a mess. Hester got to work picking up garbage, hosing the asphalt down, scrubbing what was left of the outdoor furniture, raking over the fresh mound of dirt beneath the bo tree. Gratefully, she lost track of time and only stopped when she heard the mockingbird. It was sitting atop the Buchanans' flagpole. She closed her eyes and tried to follow the pattern of the whistles, the tweets, the long shrill slides from one octave to another. The wild abandon of the bird's warbling made her ache inside. If only she could be free as a bird. The creature flew into the bo tree. She thought of Atticus Finch.

"It's a sin to kill a mockingbird," she whispered. "All they do is sing and make the world a better place."

That's what I wanted to do, make the world a better place.

How short she'd fallen of her high aspirations. Her time of giving, of mattering, over. Her life narrowed down to Al, dominated by Al. She never should've retired so young. How much more alive she'd felt in her classroom, the endless stream of teenagers with their angst, their neediness, their natural inclination for melodrama. She loved helping them to sort it all out, to stay on track, to make something out of what they thought was their nothingness. Look at Nina. Look at what Hester had done for her.

Nina Tattoni walked into Hester's English class for the first time a few months after 9/11. She looked like a mix between Tinker Bell and someone from the chorus of *Grease*. She was cute and petite, but she had on too much make-up and wore outdated clothes. Hester liked her immediately, though. She had good posture, a long neck, and curly light brown hair pulled up into a really high ponytail. Hester shook her hand. How small and fragile it felt in hers. There was something about Nina that was familiar to Hester, very familiar. *Maybe,* Hester thought, *I've taught relatives of hers.*

Nina was a sophomore and woefully behind in her studies, according to the guidance brief, which had no other helpful information in it. An aunt was identified as her legal guardian. She'd moved from Queens into her aunt's house in Moretown. Her last report card was abysmal. Well, this wasn't the first time Hester had to deal with an almost blank slate.

Hester tried to get more information out of Nina, but the girl was good at not answering questions, good at examining her raggedy fingernails or staring into space. Despite the fact that her new student wasn't more forthcoming, Hester volunteered to tutor Nina during Hester's lunch periods. The rest of the class had just finished *To Kill a Mockingbird,* and Hester wanted Nina to catch up, but Nina was looking for the easy way out.

"Just tell me what I need to know. You think I'm stupid, I ain't. I can remember something if you tell it to me." Nina looked down at the thick book, then back up at Hester and tilted her head to one side just like a little bird. "Pleeeaaaseee, Mrs. Murphy, jus' tell me. I ain't got time to read it now. Please, please, please?"

Hester stared into Nina's big, brown eyes, and almost laughed. Did this little freshman think for one minute that she, the teacher, would actually summarize the novel for her, the student, so she wouldn't have to read it?

"Please, please, please, nothing. Miss Nina Tattoni, you read this book starting right now, because I will never, ever tell you what it's about. And while we're on the subject of what you are, or are not, going to do when you are with me, you are not ever going to say "ain't" again. Got it?" Hester said this half-jokingly. She smiled at Nina. Nina pursed her lips and wiggled her head on her long neck.

After a rather long and ominous silence, Nina said, "I can't read to silently to myself, I'll lose my place."

"Then you can read it aloud, to me," Hester couldn't believe she was offering to listen to the whole novel as read by this stubborn, and most likely lazy, creature. She had tons of other things more important to do on her lunch break. But the offer had come out of Hester's mouth for whatever reason, and Nina whispered, "Alright, Mrs. Murphy, if that's what you want."

The girl's voice was hesitant at first, like a stream drying up on its way to the river; but as she read along, she found her confidence and somewhat of a pace and the words began to flow. She got into the character parts, especially Mayella's. She added lots of expression.

Hester began to genuinely look forward to her time with Nina. True, Hester had read the novel dozens of times, but she'd never had the pleasure of listening to it; and Nina's voice, full of delight, reading the words of Harper Lee, was haunting. When Nina came to the end, she ceremoniously closed the book.

"And that is the end of the greatest American novel ever written. Goddamn, Mrs. Murphy, this is the best book I've ever read," was all Nina could say. Hester's eyes glistened with tears.

Much later Hester would find out that Nina neglected to tell her that it was also the first book she'd ever read.

Now, standing in the middle of her patio in the bright Florida sunlight, staring dumbly at the wounded bo tree, and fighting off yet another wave of hangover nausea, Hester marveled at how the memory of Nina's triumph, only three short years ago, seemed a lifetime away.

When their tutoring sessions ended, Hester found she missed being alone with Nina. Hester forced herself to go back into the English department office and eat her lunch with her colleagues. She had to stop thinking about Nina, but try as she did to distract herself, she knew something—what, she couldn't say exactly—had begun between them.

Thirteen

In her apartment in Trenton, Hester sat at the table until dark, trying to see some way out of her dilemma. If she was pregnant again, she was screwed. She had no answers, no game plan, no one to talk to about the mess she'd gotten herself into for the second time in her life. Her mother wasn't there to say, like she used to, "Hester, honey, you'll get through this." But that was before the abortion, before that night the infirmary nurse called her parents to inform them their daughter was bleeding badly and was being rushed to a hospital. The nurse gave them no further details, so they sped down the turnpike and were at Hester's bedside in an hour. When she finally recovered enough to talk, she confessed to her father she had an abortion. The word dumbfounded him. He stood before her, mute with anger, his penetrating eyes boring through her. Finally, he said coldly, "What you did is unforgivable. You murdered your own baby; you killed our grandchild. I cannot forgive you."

Hester couldn't look at him, so she looked to her mother, who kept her eyes on Hester's father. He turned away from Hester and faced his wife and whispered harshly, "I told you naming her Hester was a bad idea. She's turned out to be a worse sinner than the Hester in that stupid novel you always loved so much. I can't for the life of me see why you insisted on naming our daughter after a character like that."

"Honey, I didn't," Hester's mother pleaded. "Hester means star, it's a good…" But her father wasn't listening to her mother; he was walking out of the room. Her mother touched Hester's shoulder, but quickly withdrew her hand when her daughter burst into tears and cried, "Mom, what am I going to do?"

"I don't know, Hester." Her mother lowered her head, turned and left. Not one word of solace for her desperate, sorry child.

Her father's rejection, her mother's silence, it was more than Hester could bear. The bond between them broken, Hester's shame took on a frightful shape. She wanted to run away and hide from them and never see them again. Never. But she'd lost so much blood she was near death. Her parents took her home and cared for her. Her mother cried in front of Hester at the drop of a hat without explanation, and her father avoided being in the same room with her. Then when her father knew she wouldn't die, he asked her to leave. If she went back to college, it would be without any help from them. They weren't going to pay for their daughter to go somewhere and fornicate and then murder the innocent child she'd conceived. They were good Catholics, they had raised her better than that and didn't like what their eldest daughter had done, not one bit.

Eventually her parents moved to California to be away from her and near her sister, the good daughter, the one who hadn't aborted their first grandchild.

There was no one from work she could call either, because if anyone at Sourland High found out she was pregnant out of wedlock, she'd lose her job. So she sat there on the verge of crying, staring at the light coming from the street lamp. It almost seemed saner to her to go into the bathroom and get a razor and slit her wrists than to sit there alone in the dark and sob. How she'd struggled all these years to accept her solitude, to hold back her desolation! And here she was on the verge of giving into it, of hurting herself. She whispered a Hail Mary and somehow found the nerve to call Al.

"Hey, Al, it's me."

"Hester, what do you want? It's the middle of the night."

"It's around midnight."

"Well, it's late." She could tell by the sound of his voice he wasn't thrilled she'd called.

"I had to talk to you."

"I just saw you eight hours ago at school. Can't it wait till tomorrow?"

"No."

"Why?" Now he sounded completely annoyed.

"Because it's important."

"What could be so important that you didn't tell me about it today and now you can't wait till tomorrow to tell me? Huh, Hester, what could be that important?"

Al's angry tone of voice bristled in Hester's ear. She had been down this road before with Arty wanting her and then not wanting her. But she was older and she thought wiser now. And she was sure Al was the right man for her, and for this child. She had to make this work, but the anger rising up in her scared the hell out of her. She took a deep breath and tried to stay calm.

"What could be so important, Al, is that I missed my period."

"You what?" His voice cracked.

"I missed my period is what." She fought the impulse to be sarcastic, but she hated the way he sounded so…shocked. What did he have to be shocked about? Wasn't he the one who put his penis into her vagina before he said one word about birth control? Oh, this was all going down the tubes. He was her vice principal, her boss, and knew as well as she did, it was unacceptable for teachers to have babies out of wedlock. It was board policy. There was no way out, Hester had to get him to marry her and deal with the fact that she really didn't know him all that well. What she did know was that he was very into her physically, but not into talking to her and confiding in her. This hurt her, but she couldn't let him know that. Everything had to go right this time; she would never have another abortion. Never.

"Al, I'm scared," she said, and that was the truth.

He didn't say anything.

"Did you hear me?" She knew it was a stupid question.

Again, silence. Now what? Hester was close to breaking down, and she didn't want to in front of Al. She hung up.

For two weeks they didn't speak, not even at work. Hester sat through a half a dozen stupid meetings with Al in charge, talking about plan books, final evaluations, graduation duties, parent conferences, the poor condition of the faculty lounge, the new procedures for fire drills next fall. It was torture. Then school was over and Hester was more of mess than she'd ever been. She couldn't sleep, couldn't eat. She unplugged her phone and locked it in the trunk of her car to stop herself from calling Al. One minute she thought, *he can go to hell. I can take care of myself, the baby too. I'll go off somewhere where nobody knows me, start over, just the baby and me.*

The next minute, though, Hester was mired in grief. How lonely she'd be for Al. How their baby would grow up like a weed without a good father. Her heart rapped wildly on the inside wall of her chest, *don't give up, don't give up.*

When she didn't think she could make it through another night or day, Hester woke up with cramps and her sheets were wet with blood.

She was elated. She cleaned everything up, went to her car, and got the phone out of the trunk. She was about to call Al and tell him, everything's okay, honey, I got my period, when her thinking began to go along a different line.

How long would he have gone without finding out how I was doing? Without trying to help me? If I really was pregnant, and he'd totally neglected me, I could've gotten him fired.

She hung the phone back on the kitchen wall and didn't call Al. Each day that passed and the phone didn't ring made Hester more resolute in her silence and madder at herself for falling for another loser, another man who knew how to chew women up and spit them out.

Then on the last day of June, Hester heard a knock on her door. She opened it. Al, who was entirely too dressed up for the hot summer morning, didn't smile.

"I've been trying to call you."

Hester thought, *what an effing lie*, but for some insane reason said, "Oh really, well, my phone must be broken."

"There's something I want to ask you. May I come in?"

She stepped back and let him pass. He smelled of lime scented aftershave and perspiration.

"Hester, how are you feeling? How's everything going?"

She knew what he meant by "everything." It ticked her off, him being all ambiguous, not having the balls to utter the word, pregnancy. He might as well have said, how's the weather? She looked him in the eye and said, "Great. Everything is just great."

She sounded annoyed on purpose. She wanted him to squirm, to be ashamed of himself for neglecting her. She looked at him long and hard, and started to go soft inside. His skin was golden and moist, like he'd just come off the beach. His dark brown eyes peered directly into hers. The slight cleft in his chin looked deeper, his lips fuller, more inviting than ever. She watched them move and listened in disbelief to the words they formed.

"Hester, things could work out between us. We have an attraction to each other, and I'm sure we can build on that."

"Al, what exactly are you saying?"

He glanced down at the floor then back up into her eyes. "I'll be a good father to our baby. I want our baby to be legitimate."

Legitimate…the word made Hester want to keel over with joy.

Al took a breath and continued, "This summer. As soon as possible. Will you marry me?"

Alexander Murphy wanted to be a good father to their baby, to make everything legitimate, to marry her! She turned away. Wringing her hands, she prayed for guidance. She wanted to marry Al more than anything. She didn't know what to say since there really wasn't a baby anymore. If she told him that, he'd leave, and she'd never have this chance again. Nasty thoughts popped into her head. *He didn't say he loves me. Didn't say a goddamn thing about how he feels. It's damage control. He's only looking out for himself.*

But that was as far as Hester's negative thinking went. She turned and faced him. She'd tell him the truth. She'd gotten her period.

But he was staring at her intently. His face was flushed. She was so attracted to him, to his beautiful face, his strong, beautiful body. In his eyes she could see how vulnerable he was. At this moment he was more like her than any man she'd ever met.

The word leapt from her heart to her lips. She spat the single syllable out more forcefully than she intended, "Yes." It hung in the silent air between them before fluttering away like a wounded moth.

Nothing happened for several minutes. Then Al stepped forward and kissed her. His lips softly touched hers. How sweet they tasted. She wanted this man. She did not want to be alone, and lonely, again.

Al made short order of getting Hester's clothes off. When she was naked, he held her by the waist at arm's length in front of him. His eyes took her in. "I love your body, your breasts." He moved his hands to her breasts, and he gripped them like they were two balloons he was trying to pop. Then he let go and stripped off his clothes and pushed Hester not-too-gently down on the sofa. He was on top of her, in her, his hands beneath her buttocks raising her up and into just the right spot. Hester whispered, "Yes, yes, yes," as she felt Al about to come. But as soon as it was over, she was disgusted with herself. She wasn't going to lie to this man for another minute. "Al, I have to tell you the…"

"Shush," he whispered, "Hester Randall, we're getting married right away. No arguments." He was still on top of her, and he pressed his forehead into hers in such an intimate and sincere way, she couldn't ruin it.

Al got off the couch, picked his suit pants up, and pulled a small black box from one of the pockets. He was naked, his penis still erect. He handed Hester the box. In it was a thin gold band with a diamond so small it was hard to see. Hester didn't want to be petty about it, but as elated she was about marrying Al, this token of his intentions sorely disappointed her. Nevertheless, she put the ring on her finger, which made it look even smaller.

Almost immediately Hester, uncharacteristically, thought a rather selfish thought, *what if this pathetic little ring gets lost before the wedding? Al will have to take me shopping, and in front of the sales person and me, he'll have to buy a ring that is much more suitable for the wife of the vice principal of Sourland High School.*

The problem of the too-small ring, along with the other larger problem of the lie, Hester solved two weeks later with another stroke-of-genius lie—an absolutely necessary one, Hester told herself.

After Al and she booked the banquet hall at the country club with a sizeable non-refundable deposit, mailed the invitations, took her dress to the seamstress, and rented a large apartment near the high school, she called him up at school to tell him the bad news.

She was crying genuine tears because it was truly tormenting her to have such a falsehood between them.

"I'm so upset, Al. It started with cramps and I just started bleed-ing. It got bad, and, Al, I passed the fetus."

"What do you mean, you 'passed the fetus'?"

"Into the toilet. Our baby went into the toilet."

"Hester, call an ambulance!"

"No, Al, I can't. It was just a blob," she told him in a voice wracked with what was true sorrow because she was thinking of her baby that wound up in the garbage can, "a huge blob of nothing. I stopped bleeding right away after I passed it. It was awful, though, and I felt so bad, so I reached into the toilet to touch it, and…Al, my ring slipped off my finger. I tried to get it, but I couldn't find it, and it was making me sick feeling around in all of that blood. Al, I'm so sorry, I just flushed everything down."

Fourteen

Hester was satisfied with the way the patio looked for now, and for the first time in days, felt hungry. She went inside and unwrapped the low-fat zucchini bread she'd baked for Al before the storm. She cut off a slice and stared at it, trying to decide if ingesting it would be a mistake since her stomach was still a little queasy. Just as she took a bite, someone tapped on the slider. She jumped and choked down what was in her mouth. It was Dee and Eve.

They looked like two middle-aged misfits peering through the glass. Hester knew they'd seen her sitting there, so she had to let them in. They were both pretty disheveled, which seemed par for the course for Dee, but totally out of character for Eve.

"Wanted to come by and tell you the good news. No fatalities! Isn't that just the best news, Hester? And already the cleanup crew is all organized, the Dumpsters are on site, all of that's been done." Eve was so alive with energy, she was out of breath.

No fatalities, huh? That's what she thinks… Hester tried to act interested in the details about the clean-up, but she wasn't, considering the mess she had on her hands. Al's mess. How could she think about anything else?

"Come on, we need you." Dee was already cutting herself a piece of the zucchini bread.

"What about my roof? I've got to get ahold of the insurance guy." It was the only excuse Hester could come up with. What did she give a shit about the roof for now? The damn roof was the least of her worries. It, at least, could be fixed.

"Hester, honey, Dee told me about your roof. How awful you got hit so hard; but let me tell you, they never cover hurricane damage," Eve said as she moved into the chair opposite Hester and sat staring at her like she was a lost child. "They cover wind damage, they cover flood damage, but they don't cover hurricane damage, which is really wind damage and flood damage rolled into one. It's so unfair, I know, but you have to read the fine print on everything these days. Nobody will tell you the truth, especially insurance people. They're the worst. You can't believe a thing they say. Right, Dee?"

Dee nodded. Her mouth was full.

"But more importantly, Dee told me all about Al. How awful. You must be so worried about him," Eve whispered, and her voice was so soft, it felt like a kiss to Hester. Hester wanted so much to smile at Eve and say, *oh, he'll be just fine*, but she knew she'd choke on the words.

"How are your units?" Hester, desperate to get these women out of her trailer, changed the subject, when she really wanted to blurt out, thanks for stopping by, but I want you to go away, to get the hell out of my house, I mean, my half-destroyed trailer, or rather my totally wrecked life—the one in which my perfect husband screws my former beloved student, who by the way is dead. And, you see, I'm trying to pretend it was all an accident, a freak of Nature accident.

"I lost two screens. I was lucky." Dee was leaning against the counter, brushing crumbs off the large shelf of her breasts.

"Great, that's great." Hester tried to sound sincere. She looked back at Eve.

"Nothing, no damage at all. All of Coconut Palm Drive is completely intact."

"Good for you, Eve. That's great. I'm glad it wasn't a total disaster for everyone."

"Nothing around here is ever a total disaster. We'll have this park fixed up in no time. Right, Dee?" Eve winked at Dee, "It's the Pleasant Palms way!"

Hester feared she might regurgitate the mouthful of bread she'd forced down if these two didn't stop with the affirmations.

"Believe me," continued Eve, "I've been here off and on winters since I was a little girl back in the sixties, when my parents bought into the park. Pleasant Palmers stick together and get things done. Some trailers may not be worth much, but the land they're sitting on is worth a ton of money. Marvin says sooner or later, some big developer's going to come along and make us an-offer-we-can't-refuse for this place."

Eve Bridgeford, fit, cute, with hair dyed the color of pennies and cut into a short, straight page boy, was passionate about Pleasant Palms. She was married to Marvin, an older man from their hometown in Flint, Michigan, who started a business decades ago manufacturing hot-water heaters.

"Hot water is a red-hot business," was how Marvin put it the first time Hester met him. "Don't know a son of a bitch alive who likes a cold shower. Do you?"

Eve was pretty subtle about it, but every season Marvin and she arrived in new Town Cars, his navy, hers cherry red. You never saw her in the same bathing suit twice. She talked endlessly about their three kids who went to posh private schools and on to Notre Dame and into the family business. Four years ago Eve and Marvin bought the old mayor's 1953 West Wind on the Intracoastal at the end of Coconut Palm Drive. They had it shredded and carted away and put a brand-new Destiny prefab in its place. Hester never saw a trailer like it, granite countertops, stainless steel appliances, a crystal chandelier, Jacuzzi tubs in both bathrooms, and a gas fireplace.

If Eve's trailer was the palace, then Dee's was the pits. Dee Larson, a retired state worker from Connecticut, had been a secretary in the accounting department, which to Hester's thinking must've been a rather dull way to spend forty-three years of your life. But to hear Dee talk, the people she worked with were fascinating. She had wild stories about outrageous liaisons. Accountants, it seemed, screwed around more than college kids on spring break in South Beach.

Before Hester accepted Dee's stories as gospel, though, she had to consider the fact that once you got to know Dee, you learned she would say or do just about anything to be the center of attention. It was obvious by the neglected appearance of her dark and dingy 1982 Vagabond trailer that she'd rather be out somewhere gossiping than home cleaning. Why, to even get from the doorway to the kitchen, you had to navigate stacks of *Sun Sentinels* and *Star* magazines, and boxes and bags full of yard-sale finds or things she swore she was getting ready to take to Goodwill. The once-olive sheers on the windows were as old as the hills. Orange-brown faux-wood paneling made the space look even smaller than it was. The counter in the kitchen was obscured with open cans of food, a grease-encrusted toaster oven, and an array of dingy Post-it notes Dee had obviously written to herself a while ago. When Hester went to visit her a couple of days before the hurricane, Dee ushered her past the disorderliness to the bedroom, where two twin beds were hinged to opposite walls. Thankfully, nothing was on them. Dee made Hester sit on one while she propped herself up with pillows and reclined like Jabba the Hutt on the other and told her a half-dozen stories.

"Eve, you know what?" Dee said now, "Marvin's not the only one around here who thinks some developer wants to get his hands on the park. I heard the other day…"

"I hate to interrupt, girls…" Hester didn't hate to interrupt at all, but she said it anyway. "I had a rough night last night and I really need to rest. So do you mind…"

"Hitting the bottle again, old girl?" Dee had a twinkle in her eye, but Hester felt herself stiffen at the comment. Really, Dee hardly knew her well enough to make such an accusation.

"Come on, Dee, my place is a mess. I've got to get somebody over here to put a tarp over the bedroom and…"

"And her poor husband's in the hospital," Eve added. "Leave her alone, Dee. Can't you see she's upset?" Eve turned to Hester with a serious look on her face that reminded Hester of the way her mother frowned at her when she got her first period. It was an expression that meant, "You poor thing." It made Hester miss her mother, again, for the millionth time.

"Hester, you should've gone in the ambulance with Al last night. You want me to drive you to the hospital now? How is he anyway? He was barely conscious." Eve reached across the table, put her hand on top of Hester's, and patted it like she was trying to tamp down dough.

Dee was rooting in the refrigerator for some milk. Her large buttocks in her bright-red sweatpants looked like a giant inverted heart. She was mumbling something about fat-free milk and how gross it was. Hester slipped her hand from under Eve's and started feeling worse about everything. She knew Eve meant well. They both meant well. They were damn nice women Hester was lucky enough to have met; but nice or not, she needed to be alone. She figured she'd throw them a bone of information and then maybe they'd leave and not be offended.

"Look, thanks for coming over, and Eve, thanks for offering to take me to the hospital. Al's okay. He had a concussion, broken ribs, slight heart attack…"

"A heart attack!" they said it together.

Dee spun around and her thick lips hung open in amazement. "Hester, jeezus, so it was a freaking heart attack!"

Why didn't Hester just keep her big trap shut? God, she was furious with herself. Now she'd have to listen to them say how upset they were about poor Al. In an hour all of Pleasant Palms would be at her door with everything from garlic hummus to key lime pie. By noon tomorrow all the details about poor Al's condition would be in the goddamn "PP Newsletter."

"Dee, Eve, I'm exhausted. Don't tell anyone anything. Let's just wait a few days and see how Al does. Please, I just want to lie down and take a rest now."

"Okay, we can take a hint. Right, Dee?" Eve got up, locked eyes with Dee, and jerked her head toward the door, but before she took a single step toward it, she said, "Oh, I forgot to ask about your young house guest. What's her name? Nina, was it? Where was poor Nina when all hell broke loose?"

Hester's cheeks turned red hot. *Yes, where the hell was Nina when all hell broke loose? In bed with my husband!* How she wanted to say it, to tell the truth. *There was a fatality. Almost two fatalities. I wanted to kill my husband. I almost did.*

But what she said was, "Nina was on the beach. Can you believe it? She was looking for shells, but she saw the storm coming and ran back here to the trailer. Thank God she had enough sense to get out of danger. Thank God she's alright. She was pretty shaken up."

"Poor thing. Maybe she can help with the clean-up. Keeping busy might help take her mind off things. She can come with us. It'll get her out of your hair, and you can have some quiet time to yourself."

"Well." Hester could barely think what to say. "Well, I'll tell her when she gets up. You know how young people are. They could sleep forever."

As soon as Dee and Eve left, Hester lowered the bamboo shade and the mini blinds. She lay on the couch in the dim room and put her feet up on the throw pillows. The wound on her calf throbbed. She closed her eyes. She hated telling lies, but she told them anyway. To her parents, to Al, at some point, to just about everybody. And now the lying was going to have go on and on and on. What was the alternative? If she told the truth, her future with Al would go down the drain.

His words rang in her head. He'd been emphatic. "Hester, I did not do anything wrong."

Maybe it wasn't what it looked like. Maybe Nina was scared. Maybe... bubbles of thought burst inside of Hester's skull and disintegrated. She could not sustain the process of putting two and two together. It was as though her brain had shrunk to the size of a pea.

Nina's dead body was in one of those thoughts. Hester tried not to let it burst open inside her head, but it did, and she saw the plastic bag in the hole beneath the bo tree. It was useless to try to stop the thoughts. Another burst. She could see the outline of the young woman's features against the black plastic of the garbage bag. Maybe, Hester, had made a mistake, and Nina hadn't been dead and maybe even now the girl was trying to squirm out of the sheets and the bag and the earth.

Old Chet's kitchen light, probably a hundred and fifty watts, shone like a beacon and backlit Hester's shade. What was in her medicine cabinet that might anesthetize her—K-Y Jelly, saline spray, Visine, Tums, Tiger Balm, Benadryl? Benadryl. Maybe a handful would work. She rolled over and turned her back to the light, but it seemed to be everywhere and penetrated her closed lids. She was too exhausted to get off the couch and get the pills so she lay there letting her memories torture her.

Fifteen

At their wedding reception Al was at one of the tables telling a joke to a couple of school board members. Hester stood by the next table waiting for him. Her colleagues Janine Apgar and Frances Middleton were seated not far from where she stood, and bits and pieces of their conversation drifted into her hearing range.

"They didn't know each other that long. Hell, Frances, she just got hired in September. You know that, and I'll bet everything I own, they didn't know each other before she got here. Did they?"

"I don't know. I don't think so, but I think they make a nice couple." Frances took a sip of her drink.

"Yeah, a nice couple of hypocrites."

"Janine, you're just jealous." Frances laughed.

"Well, to tell you the honest-to-God truth, I am jealous and why shouldn't I be? I liked Al. Hell, I still like Al, and before Hester was hired, he was coming on to me all the time. He just never asked me out." Janine sounded terribly disappointed.

"He didn't take Hester out either, that I know of. He never took anybody he slept with out. All Al Murphy ever wanted out of anybody was sex."

"Really? So who else has he had sex with?"

"Well, let's see." Frances's eyes shot up toward the ceiling, and she started silently counting on her fingers before she looked back at Janine. "Everybody on staff under the age of forty."

"Get out of here. Even Dr. Vanguard? I don't believe you!"

"Oh, Janine, under that heavy sweater and behind those bifocals is a tigress. Why, she knows more about the reproductive habits of whales than the president of *National Geographic*. She shows this video of them doing it, and you can see the male whale's enormous penis. It's six feet long, and all of the kids go wild when they see it. They say she just stands in the back staring at that screen. Personally, I think it's creepy, the way she exposes her students to such suggestive things."

"She's just plain weird."

"An understatement."

"Then Mr. VP Murphy must be even weirder to screw around with her."

"Oh, he's harmless really, just completely insatiable. You know how some men are just oversexed."

"So why's he marrying Hester?" Janine sucked the last of her drink through the straw.

Frances lowered her voice and Hester lost what was said. Then Janine said, "Huh? I can't hear you."

"Maybe she's…you know," shouted Frances.

"No way, no way, she's way too thin to be, you know." Janine's voice was full of authority.

"Okay, so if she's not pregnant, then she must know some tricks nobody else knows. Or maybe she's just able to keep up with him. They used to do it every day in Stalmeyer's old office."

"What? You've got to be kidding."

"No, you've got to be kidding, you didn't know that? Everybody knew that. Even the students knew that."

"I'd heard it, but I didn't think it was true."

"You didn't want to think it was true, but just ask Gladys. Every day, ninth period, Hester would come looking for him and pretend they had to discuss something. Murphy would always be down at the gym, and she'd go down there. They'd lock the door, and, well, you know."

"That's disgusting. What a little tramp. How could Al marry someone like that?"

"Because he's a bigger tramp." Frances fiddled with a speared maraschino. "What do I know? Maybe he's in love. Whatever that means. Like I said, they look like they make a nice couple."

"Nice couple, my ass. She's a..." Janine looked up. Al and Hester were walking toward where she and Frances were seated. She sat back quickly and folded her arms beneath her chest, which pushed her large breasts upward and deepened the *V* of her almost totally visible cleavage even more. She smiled up at newlyweds.

Hester had assumed Janine was nice, had even hoped they could be friends, since they were the same age and taught the same subject. *Not now, not ever*, thought Hester, trying not to get upset; but it bothered her—and she couldn't deny it—that Janine might have been with Al. How could he? Look at her. Her hair was over-processed, bleached, probably with straight peroxide, and teased on top in a lame attempt to get it to look fuller. To Hester it looked frizzled and ratty. And her makeup was an even worse disaster—thick foundation a shade too dark for the skin on her neck, red-orange lipstick a shade too bright for the dark foundation, too much eyeliner, and even though she couldn't see them now, Hester knew Janine had humongous thighs, chubby knees, and skinny calves. In a dress or skirt her legs looked like upside-down triangles. The worst, though, was the way she acted when she wasn't in the classroom—naive and stupid, like a girl instead of a woman. No, there would never be any friendship here.

Well, at least old Frances, the math teacher, had stuck up for Al and her. Boy, had Hester misjudged her. To look at Frances, you would have thought she was as uptight as an algebraic formula. She had this look about her that made you think she was always thinking a zillion steps ahead of you, like she had a brain the size of a water-melon, a brain that could burn rubber as it sped through a secret series of logarithms at the same time she was talking about the latest movie she'd seen or what she'd had for dinner the night before. She wore her hair short, and never completely brushed out the perfect circles left by her small sponge rollers, as though their geometric perfection outweighed any aesthetic consideration on her part. She wore her eyeglasses around her neck, attached to a chain with links made up of plus, minus, multiplication, and division signs. She always wore a white shirt, a box-pleated skirt. She wore thick panty hose and brown walking shoes. Her one nod to whimsy was a patch with the face of Einstein on it which she'd stitched on the breast pocket of her navy blazer. Although everything she wore was crisp and clean, she still looked astonishingly frumpy.

But Hester was feeling warm and fuzzy about Ms. Frances Middleton and thought at the moment that she looked just right, uniquely herself, almost classic. Hester studied her lovingly as one might study an old masterpiece in a museum when she realized that beneath all the dowdy trappings was a woman who wasn't all that bad looking, a woman who wasn't all that old, a woman who had probably only recently turned forty.

Holy shit. Another woman Al might've done it with.

"Ladies, it is so great to see you here. There's nothing like being vice principal of a place where the whole staff supports you." Al was schmoozing the women. "Frances, I love your dress. Why, I barely recognized you without old Einstein close to your heart." Hester knew if they'd been somewhere else like in the faculty room, what Al would have said would've been something more like, without old Einstein sucking your tit. He was vulgar, but he made you laugh, sometimes. "And Janine, Janine, I haven't seen you much lately. How's that Shakespeare festival going? Doing *The Taming of the Shrew* this year?"

"Oh, Mr. Murphy, you really do have such a charming sense of literary humor, but you know me better. I'm playing it safe and sticking to *Julius Caesar*. All war, blood, and guts, lots of corpses and no sex, unless you count the scene where the boy plays the harp."

"You mean lute, don't you, Janine?" Hester pounced.

"Harp? Lute? Who cares, Hester? You know what I'm talking about."

"No, I don't. What's sexual about what goes on in that scene? Have you even read it?"

"Of course I've read it! What are you trying to insinuate?" Janine still had her arms folded, and as she wagged her head at Hester, the mounds of her breasts jiggled nearly out of her plunging neckline.

"Now, now, ladies, calm down." Al was smiling, staring at the mounds.

Janine took the chance to talk to him directly. "You know, Al, I really want to get tenure, and the English classroom is a minefield. You say the wrong thing, and people start thinking and talking, and then everything gets blown out of perspective. Now everybody wants to put *Catcher in the Rye* in the curriculum. Can you imagine? All that cursing, and there's even a character, Sunny, who's a prostitute."

Hester wanted to jump in, *yeah, Janine, but Holden only gets beat up, he never gets laid, you goddamn phony, you!* But she didn't want to make Al mad, so she smiled a fake smile—the kind that makes your lips go stiff—and envisioned endless hours of English department meetings stretching out before her, where her sole purpose in life would be to disagree with anything Janine Apgar said.

"Your invitation came as such a surprise, Murphy." Frances was speaking with a genuine lilt in her voice. Al leaned over a little in her direction.

"I know, Fran…"

Fran! Hester never heard anyone ever call Frances, Fran. Christ, maybe Al really had done it with her.

Hester listened as Al continued, "But you know when it's right. You know when you've found the one, and Hester is the one for me."

Al looked up at Hester with those dark eyes of his, his smile natural, easy, his straight white teeth perfect. Hester inhaled and reached for his hand. It warmly encircled hers. This is what she'd wanted all along—Mr. Wonderful, a wonderful man. The kind of man other women wanted, but who only wanted you. Hester, who'd been dumped by a long-haired hippie, who'd done the worst thing she'd ever done for him, and who'd been deserted by him in her hour of need, was now, thank God, Al Murphy's wife—till death do them part.

Now she could stop missing her mother, her sister, her father. Al was her whole family now rolled into one. Hester happily contemplated her good fortune. She let her eyes drift over the heads of the seated guests, let the music the DJ was playing wash over her.

"Will You Still Love Me Tomorrow?" by the Shirelles was on, and Hester thought, *yes, yes, I know he will still love me tomorrow and forever. I'll make sure he will.*

Al suddenly squeezed her hand hard. She looked at him, thinking, *poor Al, he doesn't know his own strength.* She saw him look back at Frances and Janine. Hester tried to pull her hand away, but his hand tightened around hers. Her rings pressed into the soft flesh of her fingers.

"Al, you're hurting me." Hester whispered it as quietly as she could. He looked at her blankly, as though he didn't recognize her, then looked away. Maybe he hadn't heard her. There was so much noise. Maybe he'd had too much to drink. He didn't loosen his grip.

"Al," Hester said louder and closer to his ear, "you're hurting me."

He acted like he didn't hear her. Hester wanted to wrench her hand away, but they were right by Frances and Janine. What would they think if she made a scene? She didn't want to ruin her own wedding, but why was Al hurting her? Really hurting her. She thought her fingers might bleed; the larger diamond was pressing into bone. The DJ was playing "Love Me Tender."

"Al, dance with me," she shouted above the din, took her other hand, and grabbed the wrist of the hand he had clenched around hers. She dug into him with her fake nails. She didn't care if they all broke off.

He looked at her, looked down at her nails digging into his wrist, smiled stupidly. She let go.

"Your wish is my command, wife." The stress he put on the last word made Hester wince. Al chuckled, let go of her hand, and ushered her onto the dance floor.

"Love me true…never let me go…" He pulled Hester close, his chin warm against her temple. Everyone on the dance floor backed away and watched them. Hester could feel their eyes on her and knew they must be thinking how in love Al and she must be, how there was such chemistry between them, such a special spark.

Elvis's voice was sweet and sexy. It made Hester want to cry, she was so confused. *He's got to be drunk*, she thought. *What else could it be? I'll have to monitor how much he drinks, pay more attention.*

"Never let me go…" Al was singing along with Elvis, the sound of his voice lovely. It filled Hester's whole head, made her feel like he was inside it. He seemed happy and oblivious about what he'd done. He held Hester gently.

Maybe, he was only fooling around. It couldn't have been on purpose. She wanted to ask, but was afraid to draw attention to the incident, afraid to hear how he might answer her. He probably didn't realize how delicate her fingers were.

She began to let herself relax into his arms, and by the end of the song, Hester had almost forgiven him entirely for hurting her. When the music stopped and Al leaned in to kiss her, she let him. Everyone clapped, and they both took a corny bow.

After they cut the cake, Al took the garter off her leg and threw it over his shoulder to one of the single men; Hester threw her bouquet to, of all people, Janine Apgar.

It was time for the last dance, Johnny Mathis's "Wonderful, Wonderful." Hester had requested it in advance because in her mind it expressed perfectly the way she felt about Al. He was "oh so wonderful." The DJ put it on, and Al started spinning her around too quickly, ahead of the music. They were off the beat, but Hester was happy now, enjoying herself and anxious to go home to their new apartment and make love. Everything finally seemed as perfect as Johnny Mathis's pitch.

Then Hester remembered a small thing she heard and let slip by. It was what Frances had implied about Al marrying her because she was pregnant. It made her feel bad. Honestly, she hadn't wanted to trap Al. Once in her life, being pregnant had ruined everything; she couldn't let not being pregnant ruin her life now.

She knew a good thing when she saw it now, and Al Murphy was better than good—great job, great personality, great in bed. If somebody like Janine would've gotten him instead of her, it would've driven her crazy. It would have been all downhill from there. She pictured herself bludgeoning Beth Humbolt to death with a stapler the next time she tried to correct Hester in class or stabbing Robby Pherson with a pair of scissors. That's how she would've ended up: insane.

And if she ever did reconcile with her parents and her sister, wouldn't they be so happy that she'd made a good life with someone stable like Alexander Murphy?

Hester looked up at her new husband, and the priest's word came back to her from the morning service: "You are no longer two separate people. By the grace of God, you have become one. What one of you does, so also does the other."

Odd way of putting it, like one of them had to disappear into the other in order for a perfect union to exist. She knew enough about Al already to know he wasn't about to fade away the least little bit. So what was left? Adam would take back his rib.

Stop it, stop overanalyzing, she told herself. But the terrible idea that she'd be the one who would have to give in, would always have to give in, had already taken hold of her.

They were still dancing, but for Hester the magic of the moment had passed. Two spots on her fingers were sore. She spread them apart on Al's back, tucked her head into his shoulder, and tried like hell to get even a small bit of happiness back.

Sixteen

A month and a week after the hurricane, Hester was in the kitchen chopping parsley and basil for a salad. She looked out the window in time to catch the sun burst from behind a thick slab of gray clouds.

Al was on the patio sipping a Miller Light. In the shadow of what remained of the bo tree, he looked like he didn't have a care in the world. He wore a faded pair of surfer trunks and an old Sourland High basketball shirt. His hair had grown long and was wavy from the humidity. His *Best of Italy* CD was playing on his boom box. He sang along to "Santa Lucia Lutana."

Al's injuries required four weeks of rehab, and his insurance paid for him to stay at the rehab center. While he was gone, Hester slowly returned to the land of living. There was nothing she could do to change things. Her feelings toward Al ran cold and hot. She missed Nina, but not as intensely as she had at first. Hester, lately, found herself thinking more often than not that there was a chance, though slim, Al hadn't done anything wrong.

Eve and Dee nagged Hester into getting back to water aerobics. On Friday nights they invited her to play pinochle at the clubhouse. They even dragged her to shuffleboard, and that's where she met Barb Hendleman.

After a tournament Barb won, she invited Hester back to her place to celebrate. Hester thought there'd be other women there, but discovered when she arrived, it was only the two of them.

Barb lit the tiki torches that lined her patio and bought out a bottle of Gallo zinfandel—the white kind that Hester was not at all fond of.

"You know, Hester, my husband, Cliff never bowled in his life till we came down here. He comes home from recycling the trash and tells me he joined the bowling team, which didn't sit well with me. 'What about your back, Cliff? If your back goes out again, I'm the one who suffers. Remember when you couldn't get out of bed and had to pee in a jar? Who jumped up and got the jar, held the jar, emptied the jar? Me. No way, Cliff. I won't allow it,' I said to him. Quite frankly I was a little sick and tired of his back going out. He was such a big baby about it."

Barb took a sip of the zinfandel and Hester did too, and almost gagged on it.

Cliff, of course, totally ignored Barb and started bowling every Friday with the Pleasant Palms team. He promised to be careful, and it seemed he was, about his back anyway, because soon he was out four nights a week practicing. Barb began not to mind because she had the remote control to herself and got to watch her own shows. At the end of the season, when the bowlers held a banquet at the Ocean Club House, Barb was surprised to learn the team was coed—seven men and Lola Matson, a tall raven-haired woman with milky skin, who looked to be in her early fifties.

"I thought, no wonder Cliff can't wait to go bowling. He's been bowling with goddamn Snow White. Of the seven stupid dwarfs, Cliff must've been Dopey. Hester, you should've seen those men falling all over this Lola. Anyway, each member got a gag award for things like gutter balls, splits, and so on. I was sitting with Cliff, having a pretty good time despite being annoyed with him for not telling me about Lola, when it was announced that Cliff was getting the award for the biggest flirt!

"Everybody laughs. Then I catch Lola staring at Cliff, and Cliff raises his glass of Scotch in her direction and smiles this suave smile. I was furious, but decided to let it go until we got home. DJ Janet started the music with Carol King's 'It's Too Late.' Clifford doesn't say a word to me, gets up, goes to Lola's table, and asks her to dance. Right in front of me, like I wasn't even there.

"I tell you, Hester, if I had a gun, I would have shot him. They were the only ones on the dance floor, and the whole place got real quiet. They were doing the cha-cha. I never saw Cliff do the cha-cha! They were staring into each other's eyes and had these silly smiles on their faces. Cliff spins Lola in toward him. The song was over, and right in front of me, he kisses her."

Tears glistened in Barb's eyes. "That was it for me. Cliff came back to the table, sat down, and looked at me, but before he could open his mouth, I picked up the bottle of his Johnny Walker and poured what was left in it over his head. Then I threw the empty bottle at Lola. It missed and shattered against the wall behind her into a thousand pieces.

"Hester, we'd been married forty-two years, and it was over in one night. I threw him out, and he moves in with her on Queen Palm Drive. I've never spoken to either one of them since, and I never will. They could be right behind me in the blood pressure line, and I act like they aren't there. I've gotten pretty good at pretending they're both dead."

Hester didn't know what to say. It was a terrible story, and the cheap wine was making her head spin. She felt sorry for Barb, but she also felt trapped in the circle of torches and the miasma of the woman's sadness.

"And you know what, Hester, the worst part is I'm totally alone now. None of the men around here even look at me. If they're widowed or divorced, they want someone younger, a lot younger. Even the men who are ten years older than me and on their way out want someone young. That horrific bowling banquet may well have been the last time in my life I was out to dinner with a man. And now Cliff goes around acting like a teenager in love, and I'm drying up like a forgotten old prune."

Hester, trying to make Barb feel better, blurted out, "Barb, you look great for your age, and everybody loves you. I just met you, and I think you're a wonderful, vibrant woman. How can you think about yourself like that?"

But the truth was Barb did look like a dried up prune, and her situation was depressing. Hester was tired. She didn't want to be alone with Barb any longer. She didn't want to hear about how lonely she was, or about how Cliff walked away from that bowling banquet with much more than a gag trophy. He'd bowled his way into a whole new life for himself. And Barb, well, Barb was left behind; and because she was a woman, an older woman, the same kind of second chance would never come her way, and that was just the painful truth.

Barb spoke up before Hester could excuse herself, "You think I still look okay? You know, Hester, I wanted to ask Stanley Upshure over for a drink, but the last time I talked to him told me he thought the old billionaire who married Anna Nicole Smith was the luckiest old bastard in the world. He called Anna Nicole the hot blonde with the double D's. It's disgusting to listen to a seventy-year-old man talk about a young woman's body like that, but you know what? Maybe I'm too sensitive. Nobody's perfect, right?"

Hester felt like saying, *damn, Barb, you can do better than Stanley Upshure*, but she didn't. The least she could do was leave her with a little hope. It did no good to let on to the world that you're bitter or your feelings are hurt or your confidence is sagging right along with your aging body. Barb's nice-sized boobs probably used to look sexy. So what if they now looked like hanging papaya. So what if her arms were flabby, and her wide calves were covered with sunspots and purple veins. She'd put on pink lip gloss and penciled in her eyebrows. Even with her mascara smeared from her tears, Hester could see that at one time she had been attractive, and desirable.

"Barb," she said, "you may not be Anna Nicole Smith, none of us are, but I like you, a lot, if that makes any difference." It was easy for Hester to see she made Barb feel better. The woman leaned toward Hester and stared into Hester's eyes. The zinfandel-fueled look of admiration made Hester uncomfortable, so she added jokingly, "Not that I'm a lesbian or anything," and then felt stupid for doing so.

Walking home on the deserted lanes of the little trailer park and thinking about Barb Hendleman brought Hester to tears. Then she remembered Rachel Rizzo who had roomed next to Hester at Glassboro. After curfew when everyone else was asleep, they'd sit in the dorm hallway smoking and talking. When Hester was going through her crisis with Arty, Rachel kept telling her not to give up on Arty.

"Hester, the smart woman stays. The smart woman stays." Rachel missed the whole point, which was that Hester had no choice. Arty was the one who dumped Hester.

But Rachel was right, though, if you looked at Barb's situation. Barb had every reason to dump a cheater like Cliff, but now Barb was the one who was alone. If she handled things differently, held back and let the dust settle, maybe she could have reined Cliff in. Maybe if she put all those years of being together on the scale before she blew her cork, she wouldn't be stuck now being the unwanted one.

Al kept calling Hester from the hospital, and when she finally did talk to him, Hester decided to act like nothing was awry and tell him exactly what she told everyone else—Nina had gone back to school in New Jersey.

She knew it was a tremendous lie, but the fact of the matter was that it was a necessary one. Again, Hester wasn't ready to end things with Al; and besides, as she kept telling herself, she didn't know how Nina died. She couldn't blame it on Al if she didn't know.

But Hester could see where the police might come to the conclusion Al was guilty, and how horrible would it be if innocent Al was found guilty of a murder he didn't commit. She didn't want him to go to jail for the rest of his life, and she especially didn't want him to lose his pension, their pension. Her pension was a pittance and would never be enough for her to live on. If Al's was gone, she'd be broke.

And other men? What hope did she have of finding a man at her age? If she did happen to find one, he'd probably have a ton of baggage, new baggage. *Better to deal with the devil you know, than the one you don't.* Someone had said that to her a long time ago…probably Rachel.

Life with Al, when she reflected on it, wasn't all bad.

The timer went off. Hester tossed the herbs into the salad. She took the eggplant out of the oven and put it aside to set. She shook olives out onto a small glass plate shaped like a fish and shaved thick curls of sharp provolone over them. She dressed the greens and herbs with oil and vinegar, poured herself a glass of pinot noir, took a sip, and looked out the window again at Al. He was staring at the bo tree, his beer in his hand.

All for Love by John Dryden. Hester closed her eyes and thought of the comparative thesis she'd done in grad school. Dryden's seventeenth-century reworking of Antony and Cleopatra versus Shakespeare's sixteenth-century play. One part of a line came back to her. She'd quoted it near the end of her paper, thinking at the time how pathetic Cleopatra sounded, trying to blame someone else for her own mistakes; and, yet, it was undeniable, the Egyptian queen had been taken in and fooled by Antony.

"I would reason more calmly with you. Did you not overrule and force my plain, direct and open love into these crooked paths…" Hester sipped her wine again and thought, *Al, you son of a bitch, you are forcing my open love into a crooked path.*

Hester knew Al would never bring the subject of Nina up again. If Hester didn't bring it up, they would never talk about it. Al had a sixth sense about when it was best to remain in the dark. And he liked to keep others in the dark when it worked to his advantage. He'd been well suited for the job of vice principal of a school like Sourland High because he was good at sweeping things under the carpet, and leaving them there. But Hester knew that beneath his non-confrontational exterior, there was a manipulative genius at work, constantly striving to control everyone and everything around him.

On that balmy December night, Hester couldn't begin to realize exactly how voracious her husband's appetite for dominance really was, how ruthless he could be when it came to his survival.

Looking at him through the window, she wondered if he wasn't only pretending that everything was fine, that Nina was fine, that she, Hester, was fine, that the whole world was spinning correctly on its axis. What was going on in that handsome, scheming head of his? She'd be damned if she could figure him out.

She picked up the antipasto, and singing along with "Funiculi Funicula," joined him in the rosy twilight on the patio.

Al smiled at her. "How's that dinner coming along?"

"*Perfecto mundo!*" Hester's Italian accent was laughable, and she gave the appearance of being happy. She was becoming almost as good as Al at keeping people in the dark.

Seventeen

Hester was outside her classroom door waiting for the bell to ring when she saw Janine Apgar come out of her room backwards. She appeared to be talking to someone who was still inside. It was freshman orientation, the start of a new school year, and Hester hadn't yet been able to forgive Janine for what she'd said at their wedding several years ago, so Hester was still on the look-out for some way to make things unpleasant for Janine.

Janine had her hands on her ample hips, and in her blue straight skirt the cheeks of her rump looked like bowling balls. She'd recently started dying her brown hair orange. "Not orange, Hester, auburn," she adamantly corrected, when Hester commented on it. Janine had it parted in the middle today, and curls hung on either side of her face like links of hot sausage. At least with the orange hair, Hester concluded, Janine's red-orange lipstick didn't look as garish, and that was about the nicest thing Hester could think of concerning Janine's current appearance.

Janine seemed to be flirting with whomever Hester couldn't see. Her orange head bobbled on her thick neck. She shrugged her shoulders, her breasts jiggled. *Who is she talking to?* The suspense was killing Hester.

Hester was beginning to think the bell was never going to ring, the malfunction on purpose. Freshmen teachers were never happy about orientation day. Everyone else on staff worked quietly in their rooms while they had to orient the freshmen. Hester begged Al, who was in charge of scheduling, not to assign her any, and he didn't; but he assigned five whole sections to Janine. Hester felt triumphant. Al knew Janine wasn't a favorite of hers.

But how had Al convinced Janine to take all those freshmen sections without Janine going ballistic? Janine personally told Hester how much she "hated the whiny little bastards" and how "all the books the freshmen read were nothing but drivel." Those were her exact words.

The bell rang, Hester could go back into her room now and dig out her plans for *The Immoralist*. She couldn't believe it was still in the world lit curriculum. An older man, who is ill, travels to Africa and hires young boys to wait on him while he tries to find some meaning in life. He's too distracted by the intense Saharan heat, and the distracting beauty of the boys, to be able to draw any conclusions about anything. What a depressing story.

Work could wait, though. Hester wanted to see who came out of Janine's classroom. According to good old Frances Middleton, who kept Hester up on the gossip, Janine hadn't had a boyfriend in a long time. Maybe she'd found someone on staff to hook up with over the summer.

Hester watched as Janine disappeared into her room. Nothing happened. Hester almost turned away to get started on the Gide unit, when who comes out of the room but Al. He had his clipboard in his left hand, but his right arm was stretched out, and his hand was still inside the room, holding on to something. Then Hester saw it, Janine's hand in his, her bright yellow bangle catching Hester's eye like a caution sign.

Janine reappeared in the doorway, and Hester watched as her husband pulled Janine toward him and whispered something in her ear. The sound of the woman's laughter drifted down the hall to Hester, and pierced her through the heart.

Eighteen

The whirring of chain saws woke Hester, and her first thought was, *where am I?* She leaned up on one elbow. Dust particles quivered in the light that came in on either side of the shade. She was on the couch in the living room. Al was on the La-Z-boy. They'd had a calm, uneventful dinner together last evening. Even watched an episode of *The Sopranos,* but Hester drank too much wine, passed out on the couch, and now she was feeling pretty fuzzy. The noise outside wasn't helping, though it wasn't waking Al up. People were shouting and hammering things. Hester listened to the sounds of glass shattering, metal scraping against metal. The humans were trying to fix what Mother Nature had jumbled up.

Though she hadn't been there long, it seemed she'd heard the history of Pleasant Palms a hundred times. It began with the Great Depression and the misfortunes of a family named the Banfords. They were broke and freezing to death in Michigan, so they packed up and headed toward Florida. They ended up in Destination, which was not a true town, just a store and gas station next to a dairy farm on the only road leading south out of Palm Beach. The Banfords pulled off the road and asked the farmer if they could pitch their tent in the pasture in return for working on the farm. They ended up staying the whole winter. In the spring when they returned to Michigan, they were happy and full of hope.

Back up north times got better, years passed, and their children grew-up and moved away. In the 1950's when Mr. and Mrs. Banford decided to retire, they bought a sleek new travel trailer and drove to Destination, Florida. They wanted to thank the man who'd helped them out when they needed it. The farmer, happy to see them, invited them to park their trailer in the pasture by the beach and stay on for the winter.

It wasn't long before other tin-can tourists joined them. The farmer herded his cows across the road to another field and charged the Northerners a small fee. The pasture filled with Chateaus, Vagabonds, and Tropicaires. The strangers became friends, and the farmer made more money than he ever had.

The next year the travelers asked if they could leave their trailers in the pasture during the summer while they drove their cars back. Then maybe the farmer could build them a modest clubhouse or a small restaurant or a bathhouse? The farmer got worried. What did he know about clubhouses and restaurants? He still had another twenty acres to farm, and he was getting old and tired.

Eventually the friends got together and asked to buy the pasture. "Name your price," they told the farmer, and he did. And that's how Pleasant Palms Trailer Park came to be.

In 1990, Al and Hester Murphy flew down to Palm Beach on spring break for a conference on technology in the classroom. Al was eager to jump on the computer bandwagon, and he was good at scheduling school business in vacation spots so they could travel "on the district's dime," as he liked to put it.

As soon as they checked into the Breakers, barely ruffled by their business class flight, Hester reflected, and not for the first time, on the advantages of being married to Al, even though she'd insisted on buying her own airline ticket. She didn't really like Al fudging the travel voucher.

When the meetings were over and Hester's skin was just getting that caramel glow, Al decided they should stay on. He wanted to rent a convertible, explore a bit, and get a tan too. Hester had no objections, not that it would've changed his mind if she did. She called for a substitute and faxed some plans to her supervisor before they checked out of the Breakers and headed south on A1A.

"Al, it is so sexy to play hooky at our age." Al was driving down A1A, and Hester had her hand on his thigh. She looked over at his profile, and even though his eyes were hidden behind his tinted aviators, Hester could tell by the set of his mouth he was pleased with himself. He looked at her and smiled. She knew she looked pretty good in her tight, white capris and low cut silk top. Her hair, mousy from the long winter in New Jersey, was sun streaked now. Her skin glowed. Al reached over and tweaked her closest nipple through her top. It made her jump, but she liked it when Al touched her like this. It made her feel connected to him. It made her feel young, and in love. At a moment like this, Hester's biggest regret evaporated. At a moment like this, a child would only have been in the way.

They drove past mansions and stretches of beach. On the radio Jimmy Buffet sang about Margaritaville. They eased around a curve. Emerald lawns led to meticulously trimmed hedges and Belgium block driveways to gilded gates. Yachts as big as houses, with names like *High Note* and *Octopussy,* drifted majestically down the Intracoastal.

Then suddenly, they were driving through the middle of a trailer park. Five narrow lanes of pale-blue travel trailers stretched east and west from A1A.

"Did you see that?" Al hollered over the music.

"It was a trailer park!" Hester shouted back.

"No kidding."

"Turn around, Al. Please! Let's take a look."

"Cut me a break, will you, Hester? I was thinking the same thing." He made a sharp U-turn, parked in front the Pleasant Palms Trailer Park Office, and hopped out. Al had an athletic body, a perfect body, except for that one bad ankle of his.

"Your Royal Highness, welcome to your new kingdom," he said as he opened Hester's door. The way he looked her in the eyes made her blush.

It took Al only a few minutes to set his mind on buying the 1978 Chateau trailer on Fish Tail Lane. But the way Al told it later, it was Hester's decision. Al said it was up to her. He stood by the sliding door repeating what a great place it was, but it didn't matter unless his beautiful wife was happy too. He did make her feel like a queen sometimes.

So, although it was more expensive than she thought an old trailer should be, and monthly fees were high, and taxes would be more because they weren't homesteaded in Florida, and insurance had to be figured in, and Al would probably want to fly down as much as possible, even if Hester couldn't go. Despite all of this, Hester nodded eagerly and said, "If you think we can afford it, Al." After all, he did handle all their money

Al gave her a big kiss right on the lips right in front of the manager, while simultaneously and secretly grabbing her ass. "How's it feel to officially be trailer trash?" he teased.

"Great! Just great!" Hester was bursting with excitement. It was so great to be with Al when he got his way.

Nineteen

"Theo, if you're not busy, would you take this box into Mr. Murphy's office? I finally got the lit mag done." Hester dressed carefully this morning thinking about newly-hired Theo Ottinger. She looked stylish in her black tailored pantsuit, her favorite leopard print scarf loosely wrapped around her neck.

"Sure, no problem, Mrs. Murphy." Theo turned toward Hester. The copier room was cramped, and they stood only a couple of feet from each other. Hester could see the soft brown freckles on the bridge of his nose.

"Please, Theo, call me Hester. We're colleagues, and it makes me feel older than I am when you say 'Mrs. Murphy.'"

"Hester? Okay, Hester, sure, no problem." He put down the stack of papers he was holding and picked up the large box.

"I hope I'm not keeping you from something."

"Not really. Just trying to run off the one-act plays my freshman performing arts students wrote last week."

"I'm glad to hear you're having them write something. It seems like the English teachers are the only ones who make students write, and as I'm sure Al told you, at Sourland High every teacher is supposed to be committed to teaching reading and writing across the curriculum. Al will be thrilled to hear about what you're doing."

Theo smiled, and the dimples Hester admired the first time she met him, appeared. Handsome, vibrant Theo seemed pleased by what she said. He seemed like the kind of young man who wanted to get ahead in life, and would. Hester liked that about him.

Al wasn't in his office when they got there, and Hester stalled for time by asking poor Theo a million questions. She wanted Al to walk in on them, but the bell rang, and Theo quickly excused himself.

The next morning Hester fussed with her hair, blew it out, set it on electric rollers, and brushed the hell out of it to get it smooth. *Eyeliner, mascara, lots of lip gloss. The gray pantsuit or the navy skirt and vest? Definitely pumps. They give my calves good definition...so the skirt and vest.*

As soon as the last bell of the day rang, Hester headed to Theo's classroom. She could hear the music as she was coming down the hall, Roy Orbison, "You Got It." She caught her reflection in the glass as she opened the door, and thought she looked pretty good. Theo was standing on a student desk stapling posters on the bulletin board singing his heart out to the record. From the back his lanky body looked almost feminine, his long sandy-colored hair pulled back into a neat ponytail. Hester walked over and handed him the next one in the pile.

He almost lost his balance. "Oh, thanks, I didn't hear you come in," he shouted over the music, flashed those dimples, and jumped down. "Want to dance?" he laughed and sang another line of the song before he turned the record off.

"I just came to offer my services. Al told me last night he put you in charge of the Shakespeare festival." This was a lie. Al and Hester didn't say two words to each other last night. She caught him walking Janine to her car and was so annoyed, she took her dinner, her copy of *The Inferno,* and her pride, and spent the night in the guest room. She found out about Theo directing the festival that morning from Gladys.

Before Theo could answer, Hester added, "I know Janine Apgar always assists whoever is in charge and likes making the extra money, but Al thinks she deserves a break, so he suggested I see you about your plans." Another lie.

"I haven't thought about the festival yet. I mean, it's only October, so that leaves two months before rehearsals."

"Theo, believe me, December will be here before you know it, and you have to cast the performance before the break, or the kids will never know their lines. Look, why don't we get together after school for a few days and plan it all out?"

"If you say so."

"Come to my room after the last bell tomorrow, and don't be late. We've got a lot to do." And without thinking, Hester winked at Theo, and she was startled by the way he blushed.

That night while she was cooking dinner, Hester told Al, Theo Ottinger asked her to help him with the Shakespeare festival. He was in a panic, so she couldn't say no, even though she knew Janine would be upset because she usually assisted whoever ran the festival.

"Please, Al, can you explain it to Janine. If I try to tell her, she'll accuse me of taking money out of her pocket. You know how she can be with me. Coming from you it'll be easier for her to take, especially since the two of you seem to get along so well." Hester let the dig hang in the air between them before she went back to chopping her onions and imagining the look on Janine's face when she learned Hester would be working on the festival.

Theo and Hester sat in Hester's chilly classroom one afternoon trying to decide *Midsummer Night's Dream* or *Much Ado About Nothing* when Al walked past. Hester caught him craning his neck to see what they were doing. He was checking up on her, and it was about time, she was enjoying Theo's company more than she expected.

A few days later they held a casting call for *Midsummer.* The day before the break, the last part given out, Theo asked if Hester would meet him for dinner one evening during Christmas vacation to "flesh out some ideas for costumes and sets."

The word "flesh" sensuously tumbled out of Theo's mouth.

"Al and I are leaving for Florida on Christmas Day," Hester said, "but I could squeeze in lunch on Christmas Eve."

"Lunch. Christmas Eve. It's a date, Mrs. Murphy, I mean, Hester." They walked into the hall together and in the distance but heading in their direction was Al. Hester grabbed Theo's hand forcing him to turn toward her and away from Al.

"Wait, Theo." She went up on tiptoes and kissed him, hoping he'd kiss her back. Theo didn't hesitate. He took Hester's chin in his hand, looked into her eyes, and kissed her, an opened mouth, hot tongued kiss. Hester sensed Al getting closer and closer. By the time she wriggled free from Theo, Al was standing six feet away, the look on his face not a happy one. His deep set eyes shifted from her to

Theo and hardened. What had she done? She didn't give a damn how mad Al was with her. She wanted him to be furious with her, but she hadn't thought about the possibility that Theo would get caught in the crossfire.

Twenty

"And up and split and up, together…keep those arms going…"
Joyce Valducci shouted commands to the grunting people
in the packed pool. "Dueling Banjos" blared from her boom box. Hester was in the shallow end behind Dee and Eve trying to do jumping
jacks while simultaneously making circles with her hands in water
that barely came up to her hips.

Who dreams up this stuff? She wondered as she headed around
Dee and Eve and got out of the pool.

"Is there a problem, Hester?" Joyce shouted.

"No!" Hester shouted back, "just going to the ladies room!"

She didn't have to go, it was an excuse. When she got inside the
stall, she put the seat down, sat on it, and stuck her fingers in her ears
to block out the loud music. During the one week that Nina spent in
Pleasant Palms, Hester insisted she go with Hester to water aerobics.
Nina jumped into the cold water, and Hester was stunned by how
quickly the girl's nipples hardened and how visible they were through

the thin fabric of her bikini top. Hester was tempted to tell Nina to go home and get changed into something less revealing, but she couldn't figure out how to say it without embarrassing her.

Before the hour was up, Nina concluded that she hated water aerobics. "It's stupid, Mrs. M," she whispered to Hester between routines, her voice edgy, "besides it hasn't done you any good, has it?"

Hester was a bit wounded by what Nina said. It wasn't fair. Hester worked hard to stay fit and trim, and here was Nina, doing nothing and every inch of her body looked lean and sculpted. Al would've said, like a brick shit house. Hester had heard more than one man besides her husband, say, this woman or that was built like a brick shit house. Hester knew it meant that the woman being referred to had a great body, but why brick? Why shit house? Really, the comparison confounded her.

Another comparison, the one between herself and Nina, didn't confound her, so much as depress her. When Hester was around Nina in Florida, it made her feel old. She could do water aerobics all day, every day, for the rest of her life and never again look like Nina did in her bikini. Hester would continue to age, her muscles would continue to take on adipose tissue, her bones would turn brittle, her skin sag and wrinkle. Being fifty something was what it was, and Nina was right, water aerobics were stupid. Hester could step it up, though. Start running again. Running was something Hester did briefly in the past, but stopped because Al said it took up too much of her time, and she was going to ruin her knees. And, as he warned her, he wasn't going to be the one to push her around in a wheelchair; but now she could see, no matter what the downside was, jogging would get better results than jumping around in a pool.

Finally the music stopped and Hester came out of the ladies room. Joyce was toweling off, telling everyone, "Good job! Good job!" and pulling on a bright red T-shirt that had printed on it, "I *WINE* A LOT. I DON'T KEEP THINGS BOTTLED UP." That made Hester smile. It felt good to smile. Maybe she'd end up liking Joyce Valducci more than she'd ever like water aerobics.

Dee and Eve were going to do some more pool walking. Since everyone else left and the music was gone, Hester, not wanting to be alone, decided to join them. She would jog tomorrow morning, early. For now walking around in the pool was better than nothing.

The women follow each other in a big circle. After about ten laps, they stood in place and bounced up and down. Sarah Kettinger breast-stroked over. Her round white sunglasses hid her eyes, her long nose was covered with zinc oxide and beneath her small mouth her first chin disappeared into a fat second one which jiggled as she spoke, "You won't believe it when I tell you."

"What won't he believe?" coaxed Dee.

"The Daniels got a call around midnight last night." Sarah jerked her head from side to side. Her greater chin followed the lesser one as she checked to make sure no one was within earshot. "Their son Matt, the one who lives in Oregon with his wife and new baby, was arrested last night. I tell you my heart goes out to that family. You know how close Oscar and I are to Sandy and Dave Daniels. They are good people, the salt of the earth. I tell you I don't know what this world is coming to. Matthew must've been on drugs. Drugs will be the death of this—"

"Sarah," Dee, who had little patience for tangents, interrupted, "just get to the point."

"Alright, anyway, their son Matt put his new baby in the micro-wave and turned it on."

"What? You've got to be kidding." Hester honestly thought she was kidding.

"Girls, I swear on my sainted mother's grave. He did it. He put his two month old baby girl in the microwave oven and turned it on! Judy, Matt's wife, went for a walk and left baby Sharlene home with Matt. Matt told the police Sharlene wouldn't stop crying no matter what he did. He tried everything and then he thought, maybe she's cold, so he stuck her in the microwave and turned it on for a couple of seconds."

"What the hell happened?" Dee gasped.

"Well, baby Sharlene is badly burned, in intensive care, criti-cal condition. Matt's in jail. But you should've heard Sandy on the phone, 'My son would never do anything to hurt anyone. He loved that baby. He would never hurt her. You know Dave and I didn't raise him like that. He's a good boy. Really he is.' Well, I'm thinking, is she kidding? A 'good boy,' a nutcase is more like it. Then she claims, 'He's never done anything wrong in his whole life.' Right?"

Hester was sick to her stomach. She trudged away from the wom-en to the ladder and climbed out of the deep end. *More fodder for nightmares*, she thought as she grabbed her things and walked home.

Al was polishing the used golf cart he'd just bought. He looked up at Hester as she was draping her wet towel over the lounge. "There's something on the counter for you."

"Oh yeah, what?"

"A surprise."

"What kind of surprise?"

"Oh hell, Hester, just go in and look."

He's frustrated with me? If he only knew, Hester was tempted to tell him the last thing she wanted from him was another surprise, but thought better of it and went inside the trailer. A small gift box was on the counter. Under it was a card. She opened that first. It was one of those thinking-of-you Hallmark cards. There was a little man on the front with a thought bubble over his head. In it, it said, "Thinking of you…" Inside the card it said in big letters, "…always makes me happy!" Al signed it, "Al."

Hester couldn't ignore the narcissistic subtext of the message. *I get a card from him telling me how damn happy he is. Well, what about me? Am I happy? Will I ever be again?* She took a deep breath and tossed the card back on the counter, rather than in the trash, which is where she really thought it belonged.

Hester halfway already knew that whatever was in that box, it wasn't going to make her feel any better. Bringing Nina back to life, or being able to prove Al was innocent, or calling the police and telling them where Nina was buried, or ending her marriage, or all of the above might make her feel better.

Hester picked up the gift. The wrap was sparkly silver, the ribbon pink. It looked like a gift for a much younger woman, not for old Hester Randal Murphy, who felt like she was drifting away on the tide of time, her existence becoming more vapid and miserable by the minute. Al, though, thought Nina was still alive, back in New Jersey, back in college, partying with kids her own age. If Hester didn't have the backbone to tell him the truth, turn him in, leave him, then she deserved to live in torment.

She had no backbone. There was no way out. She invested the best years of her life in being Mrs. Murphy, and she didn't have the strength to start over, to try to be somebody else, to try to be who she really was.

Hester wasn't surprised when she unwrapped the box and it was a ring box, but she wasn't prepared for the wide, brilliant diamond encrusted band. It was so beautiful, it made her cry. She looked up, and Al was watching her from the doorway.

"It's a belated Christmas gift, and…" He hesitated. "Thanks." But he didn't say for what, and Hester didn't ask. She wiped away the tears as Al came into the kitchen and reached for her hand. Hester watched him as he took the ring and put it on the third finger of her right hand.

"I saw in one of your magazines about how women are buying their own diamonds for their right hands to show the world that they feel good about themselves. I knew you would never splurge on something like this, so I did it for you. You should feel very, very good about yourself, Hester."

He sounded like he was reading advertising copy. Hester didn't know how to react. Al's hand was on her wrist, his touch warm and familiar. Hester leaned back against the sink. Al tilted his head and tried to get her to look into his eyes. She did. He had wonderful, intense eyes. Al ran both his hands up Hester's arms to her shoulders. He massaged them and reach around to the back of her neck and massaged the stiffness out of it. Then he was stroking her décolletage, his hands just above her breasts. Each motion lifting them, almost imperceptibly.

Hester didn't move. She looked down at Al's hands. They seemed as though they were touching someone else. Why was she letting Al put his hands on her? Hadn't she resolved never to let him touch her again? Hadn't she drawn a line in her mind that she wouldn't cross?

She'd live with him because she couldn't live without him, but that would be all. He would pay for things, he would take care of her, and get nothing in return. That was the way she wanted it. Yet here he was, slipping one strap of her bathing suit off her shoulder, then the other. The top of her nipple was showing. As he leaned forward, she felt his breath on her face. His lips were warm on her neck.

For nearly two months, Hester had not once touched, nor been touched by her husband. She believed, in fact, she'd been permanently cured of her prior physical obsession for him. Since their bedroom roof still had not been fixed, she slept on the couch, and he moved into the guest room and was sleeping in the same bed, on the same sheets, for Christ's sakes, Nina slept on.

So what was happening now? Why wasn't she pushing him away? Squirming out of his arms? Running for her life?

But Al had Hester's face in his hands, ran his fingers through her hair, down her back. His tongue traced a wet path from her neck to her cleavage as he pulled her suit down to her waist. He cupped her breasts in his hands and rolled her nipples between his thumbs and forefingers, tugging on them, staring at them.

Hester was paralyzed. *Stop him. Make him stop.* She closed her eyes. *It's not Al. It's someone else.* It felt so good. Al's mouth was on her nipple, sucking it. He stopped and yanked her bathing suit to the floor. She stepped out of it as if in a daze, and he lifted her onto the kitchen counter. He spread her legs and kissed her between them. When he put his tongue in her, her orgasm was so swift and powerful, she thought she'd been struck by lightning.

Al eased her down from the counter and hugged her. His body was hot, his thin shirt damp with sweat. He lifted her head and kissed her gently, sucking her lower lip between his lips. He forced his tongue into her mouth. Hester was jammed against the counter. Al's penis was hard as a rock. She reached into his pants and found it.

When it was over, Al took a step away from her, and Hester, not sure what to do, put her swimsuit back on. They looked at each other, but Hester didn't know what to say, and as time passed, she began to feel bad. Al looked so satisfied, so relieved, but she only felt guilty. Hester could barely hear the sea pound the shore because blood was rushing through her head making it throb. It had felt unbelievably good, yet she broke the promise she made to herself. She was disgusted with herself.

Damn it. She walked past Al, grabbed her cover-up from the arm of the couch and the car keys from the hook in the hallway, and headed out the door.

"Hester, what's wrong? Where are you going?" Al was tying the string to his sweatpants. He tried to follow her, but she shouted over her shoulder.

"To Home Depot."

"I'll come," he was behind her.

Goddamn you, Al, you already did, is what popped into her head.

"I don't want you to come!" She got in the car and drove away.

Hester didn't know why she went to Home Depot. Either here or a sleazy bar, she figured as she wandered up and down each aisle. She was desperate to distract herself from what had just happened. It was too much for her to sort out at the moment.

She started in lumber and checked the price of a length of crown molding, turned down the plumbing aisle, and looked at tub faucets, continued on to hardware and counted six different kinds of chain saws. A pink tool kit caught her eye. She thought about purchasing it. She'd never fixed anything around the house in her life, but maybe she should start to learn. She leafed through wallpaper catalogues and inspected the large area rugs that hung from ceiling rods. She ran her hand along the tops of the granite counters in the sample kitchens. In the paint department, she read the names on the paper swatches of all of the green paints. Sage, shamrock, lime, roller-coaster... In electric fixtures she spent a good deal of time picking her favorite ceiling fan, and in seasonal she sat in one of the outdoor bar stools and watched a couple argue about how much to spend on a gas grill. The man won, and they got the most expensive model: rotisserie, three burners, warming tray.

Hester saved the garden section for last; it was the only part of the store she really liked. When she came here with Al because he'd gotten temporarily fired up about fixing something himself, she would head for garden and tell him to find her when he was done. She liked to look at the flowers and the small trees in large black plastic pots, and smell the stacks of mulch and topsoil, and think about which patio block would look the best if they ever had a big house with a big yard again, which wasn't likely.

An empty flatbed sat next to the gallon containers of ginger plants, so on an impulse, Hester lifted three of the containers onto it, pushed it up and down the aisles, adding to the cart impatiens and gardenias. The tags said they would grow in shade. She paid, loaded up her car, and drove to the Boyton Inlet. She wasn't ready to face Al. She parked by the fishing dock and turned the car off.

She needed to figure out why she'd given in to Al so quickly and how she was going to act toward him now. It was a sick dance they were doing. She knew Al was a weak man, in constant need of attention, especially from other women. It drove her mad, but she knew it, and married him anyway.

Then there was her insatiable need to be loved by a man. Would she ever get over it? At her age why couldn't she be happy just to be alive? She knew it went back to her father, the way he cut her off completely. The last time he spoke to her his voice was hard as stone, his face so empty. He haunted her memory and showed up in her dreams, but he would never be in her waking life again.

Al was her family now… Al was all she had.

But she wasn't proud of the lengths she'd gone to keep him. All those times she tried to make him jealous, tried to make him feel the pain and humiliation she'd felt. She forced herself to flirt with other men. She used other men. And it worked. The minute Al thought another man was interested in her, he was hot for her again.

How pathetic, she thought now. *What a fool I've made of myself.* She watched a fishing boat head for the inlet, a pelican land on the sea wall. The sun blazed as it hung just above the Hypoluxo Marina, its fat golden tail trailing across the water.

Hester sighed. She turned the car on, pulled out of the lot, and headed toward Pleasant Palms. The plants needed water. She better get home and get them in the ground.

Twenty-One

Nina had on a tight, almost mid-riff T-shirt and even tighter jeans. Her hair, the color of peanut shells, was pulled up on top of her head in a frizzy ponytail. The skinny fifteen year old stood in the doorway of Hester's classroom looking more like a ten year old, except for her large breasts and the silver ring in her navel that pulled Hester's eyes reluctantly to the gap of flesh between her garments.

"I gotta tell you something, Mrs. M."

Hester looked from Nina's bare abdomen to her face. "Okay, Nina. Come in."

Nina shuffled her way over to Hester's desk and stood picking the chipped polish off one thumbnail with the other. "Well, you know last week when I finished reading *To Kill a Mockingbird* to you?"

"Yes?"

"Well, remember I told you it was the best book I ever read?"

"Yes?"

"Well, I lied."

"I see. And what did you lie to me about?"

"About it being the best book I ever read. What I should've said was that it was the only book I ever read."

"Really? I never would've guessed," Hester said. "Quite frankly, you did an excellent job for never having read a book before."

"Hell, I can read, Mrs. Murphy." Nina looked up at her teacher.

"Watch your language, Nina."

"But it's true. I can read. It's just that I never sat down and read a whole book."

"Why not?"

"Because…I guess, because of the way things were."

Hester wanted to get home early to catch Oprah's book club show with Toni Morrison. She stayed awake half the night rereading *Beloved*, but Nina seemed on the verge of telling Hester something important, and the girl's eyes glossed over like brown sea glass and tugged at Hester's heartstrings.

"Alright, Nina, sit down and tell me about the way things were."

Nina sank into the chair next to Hester's desk, leaned back, and tucked her thumbs into the belt loops of her jeans, which resulted in her inadvertently pulling them down enough that Hester found herself looking at a few strands of Nina's dark pubic hair. But Nina seemed oblivious about how much of her body was showing.

"I watched T.V. I watched it all the time when my mom was working." But that was later, Hester learned. When Nina was a little girl, they were on welfare, and her mom was always home, always reading to her, and teaching her how to read and do math and figure things out. But then her mom got a good job at the Twin Towers, but it was shift work and every other week she had to work nights. Nina was alone until midnight then.

"So see," Nina said, "I totally know how to read, but because I was by myself I never bothered to. The T.V. made me feel like I wasn't alone."

The high rise in Queens where they lived was a terrible place, and Nina wasn't allowed to go out of their apartment without her mother. Nina never disobeyed, because she was scared to death of the hallways that reeked of urine and trash, and where men lurked in dark corners.

Nina had a few friends at school, but none came to the apartment, so she really couldn't call them friends. She didn't really know what it was like to have a real friend. All she had was her mom. Then one day her mom went to work early in the morning and never came home. Nina stayed in the apartment and watched the Towers implode, over and over again. After eight days, a woman Nina had never seen before, knocked on the door and said she was Nina's aunt. She had papers to prove it and was taking Nina to her home in a place called Moretown, New Jersey.

Nina had been Hester's student now for over two months, so why hadn't Hester been informed by Nina's guidance counselor or Mr. Heck or even Al that the girl had been orphaned by the 9/11 attack? It seemed Nina didn't know what happened to her mother, didn't know this aunt who had somehow gotten custody of her. It was a heart-wrenching situation, a lot for a fifteen year old to handle.

Hester started to reach toward Nina to pat her on the shoulder, but let her hand drop on the desk. She'd been conditioned not to make physical contact with her students, but Nina, who was struggling to hold back her tears, unhooked her thumbs from the belt loops of her jeans, leaned forward, grabbed Hester's hand. "Mrs. M, it's just awful. I miss my mom so much, and I hate my aunt. She's hardly ever home, but when she is, she's horrible to me. She hollers at me and curses and never lets me do anything. She's not anything like my mom. I don't even think she's my aunt."

"I'm sure she is, dear, and I'm sure she's doing her best to look after you." Hester was trying to gently extricate her hand from Nina's grip, but the girl began to cry and only tightened it and pressed her teacher's hand to her warm chest. Hester, uncomfortable with where this was going, said more sternly than she meant to, "Calm down, Nina. I know you've been through something terrible, but I'll help you work it out."

Nina eyes brimmed with tears. She let go of Hester's hand, hugged herself, bent over, and cried harder. Her shoulders heaved. Hester watched the girl, feeling both pity, and misgiving.

Is this a kid who's been through hell, or a little actress who wants some attention?

Though they'd spent a good deal of time together, Hester wasn't sure. The teenager seemed to have no substance. She was, Hester realized now, whatever Hester wanted her to be. Nina was like a hollow chocolate bunny, a thin shell of sweetness with nothing inside.

Nina took a deep breath, and in one swift motion leaned forward and grabbed Hester's thighs. Her hands felt like the small hot claws of a frightened animal. It was as though no boundaries existed between them, and Hester wondered how she'd let Nina touch her again. This was the kind of thing that if anyone saw it, anyone like Janine Apgar, it could be blown out of proportion, totally misconstrued. Something like this could be a teacher's downfall.

Hester peeled Nina's hands off her thighs and held them. Nina resisted, sobbing, "Work it out? Mrs. M, how?"

Hester stood up and Nina did too, her head barely came to Hester's collarbone.

"Nina, listen to me." Hester's voice was firm. "You're in Sourland High now, you're safe, and I'll see what I can do to help you. Maybe I can talk with your aunt and try to get her to go a little easy on you."

"No, please, you can't tell my aunt I told you anything about her. You can't," she pleaded.

Hester stepped back from Nina. The girl's eyes were red from crying, her nose was wet, and her mascara was all over her face. Hester thought, *God, she looks pathetic; but what more can I do?* And, as if in answer, Nina threw her arms around Hester and hugged her tightly. Hester smelled the cloying scent of Nina's mango shampoo and felt Nina's tears dampening her new beige sweater. Hester kept her arms down, her hands at her sides. But the girl's neediness was palpable. Reluctantly at first, Hester put her arms around Nina. Their bodies against each other grew warm, and Hester was surprised to find herself really hugging Nina, hard. They embraced for what seemed to Hester an eternity, until Nina stood on her toes and whispered into Hester's ear, "You won't tell my aunt, Mrs. M, will you?"

"No, Nina, I won't. Don't worry, dear, I won't." As Hester felt Nina go soft in her arms, she remembered a line from Robert Browning. It went something like, our interest's on the edge of dangerous things…

Twenty-Two

Finally, Jefferis Roofing showed up and put a new roof on 23 Fish Tail Lane, and Eliot Carruthers, a retired plumber who lived in the park and did handyman work, put in a new window and floor, and repainted the bedroom.

Hester met Eliot Carruthers years ago when Al and she came down for the holidays. Eliot, sloppily dressed in dirty work clothes and smelling of beer, stopped by and gave Al his business card. Al hired him to spray WD-40 on the sliding door, replace the air-conditioner filter, and power wash the patio while he went golfing.

When Eliot finished the jobs, Hester offered him iced tea, and Eliot told Hester about his first wife, his second wife, and his four children, two with each ex. He hadn't seen anyone in his family in years. "I left my whole life behind in Ocean Pines, Maryland," he said sadly, "and it's a long story, so enough about me. What about you, Mrs. Murphy?"

"Call me Hester, Eliot."

"Hester...hmmm, love that name. How'd you wind up with a name like that?"

"My mother liked it because it means star, but Hester is also the name of the main character in—"

"*The Scarlet Letter*," he interrupted. "Hawthorne. Damn good read."

Hester couldn't deny she was a little surprised by Eliot Carruthers' enthusiasm for Hawthorne's rather dense novel. She guessed his intellect belied the grease under his nails, his unshaven face, wiry and neglected mustache, crummy shirt, paint-splattered cut-offs, and sneakers full of holes. Or maybe, he'd really only seen the Demi Moore movie.

Their conversation turned to literature, and it seemed Eliot knew what he was talking about, indeed. His favorites in the American canon were Twain and Emerson; Hester's were Hawthorne, Fitzgerald, Steinbeck, and more recently Oates.

"I got a lady friend down here," Eliot said, "who used to teach English; she's the one who got me started, and now I can't stop. Not interested in any of the new stuff, only like those dead guys. Anyway, old Hester Prynne, she was a great person, but I wanted to beat the crap out of Dimmesdale and Chillingworth. They were like tits on a bull, totally useless. She had to make her own way, Hester did, and she showed them all, didn't she?"

Hester laughed, "Well, in the end, she did."

When Eliot left, Hester put new sheets on the bed, hung curtains, and rewired two lamps she found years ago at a consignment shop and had stored in the closet. That night she went into the bedroom while Al was still watching television, and shut the door. The next morning she was shocked to wake up and find Al snoring gently beside her. He must've snuck in, in the middle of the night. It was the first time they'd slept in the same bed since the night before the hurricane. Just as she was about to get up, Al rolled over and his arm almost touched her. *No way*, she thought. She slipped out from under the sheets, put on her robe, and went to the kitchen.

From the window over the sink, Hester admired the ginger plants beneath the bo tree, which seemed only slightly improved, the scar where it had split still sappy. As she plugged in the coffee pot, a siren blared in the distance then grew louder and louder until it sounded like it was right next door. The emergency was in Pleasant Palms. Hester rushed into the bedroom and changed.

"What the hell's going on?" Al was sitting up in bed raking both hands through his hair. Hester ignored him and rushed out. Beyond the hedge of ixora, she could see flashing lights and people's heads. She ran through the Cantwells' patio to Plumbago Lane. Two EMTs were pounding on the door of the Timms' unit.

Garret Timms was a slight middle-aged man with a disturbingly asymmetrical face. His left cheek was twice the size of his right cheek. He had unusually large teeth, a small upturned nose, close-set eyes. His hair was red, his skin pink. He worked security at the Marriott up the road, but came home every day for lunch.

His wife Ginny was a recluse. It'd been close to two years since anyone remembered seeing her. Everyone might have concluded she was dead if it weren't for her eternally blaring television.

The Christmas before last was the only time Hester ever saw Ginny Timms. Garret and Ginny unexpectedly attended a Beach Club happy hour. Ginny, an obese woman, wore a red muumuu with Santa faces for pockets. Her hair was teased up into a beehive. Her earrings were miniature Christmas trees, and she had on a battery-operated necklace of small white bulbs that flashed on and off when she moved. Ginny sat on the clubhouse deck next to Garret, pouring herself one whiskey sour after another from an old thermos.

Hester sat in the empty chair next to her, and they struck up a conversation. Everything was pleasant until Garret left to go to the men's room, and Ginny started complaining, "You'll never guess what my disgusting husband's most disgusting little habit is, Garret picks his ear wax and eats it!" Her revelation of this family secret caused her to laugh so hard her body shook, and the lightweight aluminum chair she was in, collapsed.

Those nearby who saw her go down gasped for a second, but it being well into the happy hour, and people being what they are, a few laughed. Even Ginny laughed at first, shouting, "I'm alright! Goddamn it, I'm alright! I got lots of padding!" Hester hurried to help her, but she was just too big to pull up. She pushed Hester's hands away and started crying.

"Come on, we can do it," encouraged Hester, but Ginny's face changed, her big blue eyes widened, her tongue slid back and forth across her plump lower lip like she was about to say something. A few men tried to lift her but to no avail. Ginny nervously shook her head, no. "Go to hell, you sons of bitches."

The men backed off. Hester stepped forward again, took both of Ginny's hands, and leaned back as far as she could to counterbalance Ginny's weight. Slowly, miraculously, Hester was able to pull Ginny up enough for her to get her footing. Ginny smoothed her dress. Hester picked up one of the Christmas tree earrings Ginny lost when she went down and handed it to her. Ginny took it, shoved it in her pocket, and walked down the wheelchair ramp in the direction of her trailer. Sadly, from the back she looked like a giant red M&M. Hester, sure the woman must've been hurt, felt sorry for her.

When Ginny was about a hundred yards away, she turned and with her hands on her hips, hollered, "Garret Timms, get the hell home."

Garret was still inside. Hester found him on the rim of the crowd around the snack table. When Hester finished conveying Ginny's message, he downed what was left of his Coors Light, shrugged his shoulders, and left.

A few days later when Hester spotted Garret at the gas station, she pulled in, lowered her window, and asked how Ginny was doing.

"Never been better," were his exact words.

But now, the EMTs were pounding on the Timms' door and no one was answering. Two policemen arrived and one easily pried the trailer door open. Bang! It swung back against the railing. Just as the officers stepped into the dark living room, Garret pulled up, jumped out of his car, and screamed, "Don't go into our house! Get the hell out of our house!"

Garret's face was flushed, his jugular pulsing. He burst into the trailer yelling and cursing. The police shouted back at him. Then, someone slammed the door shut and it got quiet, even the T.V. wasn't on anymore.

It was getting hot. Hester moved under the Cantwells' awning. About fifteen people were still hanging around. Hester decided to wait. Her curiosity was piqued, that was all it was because what did she care about Ginny Timms? She didn't really know the woman, and the interaction they had at that happy hour hadn't gone well. Ginny, too self-absorbed and too drunk for her own good, hadn't thanked Hester one bit for helping her.

Hester squatted and began deadheading the Cantwell's petunias. She thought she heard whining, but it could've been the wind whistling its way between the trailers.

The door of the Timms' unit opened. One of the officers came out and asked if there was a plumber in the park. Eliot Carruthers, whom Hester hadn't noticed, stepped from between the Mitchells' and Hardings' places with his hand in the air.

"Go get your Sawzall, and hurry up," the officer shouted before he shut the door again. Next, another officer came out and told everyone to go home. Hester had no choice but to go back to her trailer. From her steps, though, if she leaned over the railing she could see almost half of the Timms' front door.

Eliot knocked on the door, somebody let him in, and in minutes Hester heard the buzz of the Sawzall. There was a lull. The door opened again, and the cop who made everyone leave stepped out, looked up and down the lane, and gave the thumbs-up to someone inside.

The EMTs appeared, disappeared, and returned with a stretcher. Minutes later, they were both trying to pull the stretcher back out through the doorway. Whatever was on it was too big to fit through the door. Eliot came out and started cutting through the frame with his Sawzall. He cut into the wall at the top six inches, then cut down the side and pulled the section loose.

The EMTs guided the stretcher through the larger opening. On it was a giant mound covered by a white sheet. As they rolled it down the lane toward the ambulance, the wind blew the sheet off before either one of them could grab it. It took Hester a minute to make sense of what she was seeing, but there was Ginny. She was on her side. Her rear end had what looked like a green toilet seat stuck to it.

Hester didn't want to stare, but couldn't stop herself. It seemed Ginny's backside had grown over and around the toilet seat. Her white puckered flesh formed a wreath around it. In the middle her inflamed privates looked painfully distended.

Hester gagged at the sight. Eliot Carruthers came out, his Sawzall hanging at his side like a spent weapon. He was shaking his head. Hester wondered if he ever read Sherwood Anderson, and if he had, would he agree that Anderson could never have imagined anything this grotesque.

The ambulance drove away. The officers returned to the trailer. Hester was about to go in and rummage for some Pepto-Bismol to calm her stomach when the policemen emerged with Garret between them. He was handcuffed, his head was back, his eyes barely open. He was crying, hard.

Hester was stunned by what she'd witnessed. She went into her trailer. Al was in front of the television, staring at the flickering screen, holding the remote in the air and clicking it like if he did it enough, it would propel him into another galaxy. *Too bad it can't,* she thought. If Al were gone, she'd have no choice but to make her own way.

Hester didn't have it in her to tell Al about the Timms. He might laugh, and that would put her over the edge. She looked at Al and felt nothing but aversion. She didn't want to wake up tomorrow morning and find him next to her. She had to keep Al out of her bedroom.

Menopause, the perfect excuse. *I can't sleep. I don't want to keep you awake. Don't you think you'll be better off in guest room?*

Twenty-Three

Hester went straight to Al's office after finding out Nina's mother died in the Twin Towers. Why hadn't she gotten that information ahead of time from guidance? It was their job, wasn't it?

Al half listened to her, his eyes glued to the computer screen. Hester, curious to see what was so interesting, began to walk around his desk. He clicked the mouse.

"Nothing you'd be interested in, honey. Just putting another fire out over that bus incident. Mr. Hudson wants to sue us for suspending his boy, when that kid was the one mooning people out the back of the bus. The old man wants to know how we identified his kid. He's calling it an invasion of privacy, and me, a pervert. Can you believe it? He thinks I made the kid pull down his pants so I could make sure it was him. Screw Hudson," Al said as he leaned back in his chair a nd cupped the back of his head in his hands. "Anyway, I'm swamped right now, but, I hear you. Elsie and Lisa dropped the ball. What's new with guidance?" He looked back at the computer. "I'll talk to them and set something up."

"Please, Al, don't forget. I want you to schedule it so Lisa Lambert realizes this is serious. It's important to me to find out what's going on with Nina Tattoni. I really like this kid."

"Come on, Hester, you like them all."

"No, I don't. Remember Humbolt and Pherson and…"

"That was decades ago. Now you're a better teacher so you have better students, and you love them all."

"Nina's special."

"What's so special about this Nina kid?"

"I can't really put my finger on it. She just is…special."

A few days later, Hester was early for the 10:00 a.m. meeting Al scheduled for her with Nina's counselor. Lisa Lambert showed up ten minutes late with a Starbucks latte in hand. She sat across from Hester and avoided making eye contact. She studied the cover of Nina's folder and sipped her coffee. It left a foam moustache on her lip. Hester watched her lick it off. "Mrs. Murphy, I'm so happy you could make our little meeting," she finally said.

Happy I could make our little meeting? I'm the one who insisted on it, you moron. Hester was about to lose her patience, but she controlled herself and said calmly, "Well, Lisa, I thought it was due time I got the facts about Nina Tattoni. She transferred in, in January, right after the break. Now it's the end of February, and I've been told nothing about her extremely disturbing situation. Quite frankly, I think this meeting should've taken place before she…"

"Quite frankly, Mrs. Murphy, I think we should wait until Ms. Gunter gets here." She flipped her long auburn hair off her shoulder and took another sip of coffee.

"Elsie doesn't have to be here."

"Yes, she does, Mrs. Murphy, because I invited her to join us, so I think we should just sit and wait until she arrives."

So this is how it's going to go. Mrs. Murphy? Ms. Gunter? Where the hell does she think she is? Buckingham Palace? They were all on the same team, all in the same trenches, so why the high and mighty act? Hester felt like wringing Lisa's scrawny neck. It wouldn't do any good to complain to Al about her either. He hired her. Her resume was "top-notch" and, according to him, she was just what the Sourland High's Guidance Department needed.

Hester started grading papers. If you're an English teacher, you don't waste time on idle banter. Chatting with Ms. Lambert fit right into that category, so Hester ignored her and concentrated on one more attempt at analysis of "The Lake Isle of Innisfree."

"Hester Murphy, how nice to get together with you!" Short, square, department supervisor Elsie Gunter walked into the conference room.

"Not nice, Elsie, but necessary. Let's cut the bull and get to the point—Nina Tattoni's problem. Give me the facts." Hester scooped up the essays and put them aside.

"Slow down, Hester. I explained all this to Al, and he understands completely. We are so overworked down here in guidance that it's taken us this long to get to Nina's folder. We were just about to e-mail you about a meeting when you pushed the panic button."

Nice job covering your collective asses, thought Hester, *and smart to have already done damage control with Al.*

Elsie sat down next to Lisa. "Look, Nina has had a tough time."

"No kidding, Elsie, why do you think I'm here? I've got a sixth sense by now for sniffing out damaged goods." Hester knew Elsie used to too. She'd been a damn good counselor, but becoming an administrator had changed her. The old Elsie would've been on top of a file like Nina's, would've jumped at the chance to make a difference. But in her present capacity, it slipped by her and landed on young Ms. Lambert's desk, where cluelessness or laziness, or both, were in abundance.

"From what her counselor at her old school told me, it seems her mother was living a pretty isolated existence, and there was no record of who Nina's father was. Father - 'unknown' is how it's listed in her file. Nina's school didn't find out about her mother's death until a secretary happened to spot her picture in the *New York Times* obituary and showed it to Nina's counselor. Nina hadn't been to school for several days, so the counselor went to the Tattoni apartment and found Nina there alone. Nina told her she was fine. Her mother wasn't there, but her grandmother had come to stay with her, but she was at work now. It seems Nina didn't know her mother was dead, and the counselor had to break the news to her. She showed Nina the obituary. The girl read it slowly and studied the photograph the custodial company had submitted to the paper. 'That's not my mother. My mother was a stock-broker, and the lady who died…it says she was a cleaning lady. So, you see, it's just someone who looks like my mother, and the company made a mistake.'

"It took a while to convince Nina that in fact her mother was the woman in the obituary. It was sad because Nina knew the Towers had come down, but she was hoping her mother was just lost or something. The school got Nina into counseling with other kids who'd lost relatives in the attack, but it seems nobody checked her story about her grandmother. Nina must've been alone in that apartment for quite a while. Think about it, she was only fourteen then, taking care of herself, no money, nothing, her mother dead. It's just terrible.

"Then a woman shows up at her door and tells her she's her aunt from Moretown, New Jersey. The aunt tells Nina that her sister, Nina's mother, ran away fourteen years ago, and no one in the family had seen or heard from her since. She told Nina she saw her dead sister's picture in the *New York Times,* and it said in the obituary that she had one daughter, and that's how she found out about her. The aunt goes down to the school and raises hell about Nina being alone for weeks and nobody doing a goddamn thing about it. She threatens to sue, signs Nina out of her school, and brings her back here to Moretown and us."

"What's the aunt's name?"

"Linda Connefry. She lives on Delaware Ave. with her husband. I don't think they had any kids, because we never had any by that name that I recall, but I know she went here back in the early eighties, because she said so when she enrolled Nina. She had Nina's birth certificate, but no adoption or guardianship papers. She said they had a lawyer who was handling it."

"Did you check Connefry out?"

"I didn't see any reason to."

"Well, I'll give you one. If Linda Connefry is married, Nina hasn't seen her uncle yet. Nina says when her aunt is home, which isn't often, her aunt doesn't talk to her. Nina claims her aunt acts like Nina isn't there. Could be neglect. Linda Connefry might not even be Nina's aunt. She might be after money. Eventually the survivors might get some kind of settlement. Nina begged me not to tell her aunt what she told me, and that's a red flag."

Elsie was shaking her head. "Connefry seemed so normal. No lie, Hester, the woman was together—nails done, makeup on, nice jewelry, expensive clothes."

"Looks can be deceiving. I think we should contact child protective services to be on the safe side."

"We don't have any evidence, anything solid to go on. Did you see any bruises on her?"

"No. Nina didn't say anything about getting hit."

"Nina could be lying."

"She didn't give all the details, but she wasn't lying about her mother's death."

"I'll call her in and talk to her, and if I think we need to go further, I won't hesitate to go to the authorities."

Hester knew Elsie was right, but she also knew Nina probably wouldn't tell Elsie a thing.

"Thanks." Hester shook Elsie's hand and got up to leave. Lisa extended her hand, but Hester ignored it. Being inexperienced was no excuse for not doing the basics. Meet with new students, read the files. And look at the meeting; Miss Lambert might as well have stayed at Starbucks. She contributed nothing because she knew nothing, and she knew nothing because she did nothing. At the last minute, though, Hester decided to give Lisa a bit of guidance.

"As soon as you finish that latte, dear," Hester said, "make sure you get Nina Tattoni into a bereavement group, pronto!"

Just what Sourland High's Guidance Department needed, my ass.

Twenty-Four

G arret Timms was charged with neglect. Ginny had been sitting on that toilet for months. The news made the headlines of the *Palm Beach Post,* accompanied by a photo of Garret, who looked like a deer caught in headlights.

Hester put the paper down. There were weeds to be pulled. Keeping busy was better than sitting around feeling badly about Ginny Timms. The soil in the bed of ginger plants needed to be loosened and fertilized. Hester knelt down and was hacking at the dirt with a hand rake when the Hampton family stopped by the hibiscus bush in front of her trailer. Lila Hampton had one son, Phil, and he was visiting with his wife and their three kids. Lila was explaining in a lilting voice about how it's warm enough in Florida for plants like hibiscus to bloom year-round. The young granddaughters, two year old triplets, sniffed the flowers and giggled.

The girls, though all the same size, were not identical. Two were plain girls with straight brown hair and brown eyes. The other sister had platinum curls and eyes the color of new grass. She reached forward and plucked the biggest flower and toddled over to her father Phil, a slim, handsome, young man. He stared down fondly at his sweet daughter. She stopped short of him and threw the blossom at him with all her might. It hit his pants and fluttered to the ground.

The father's pleasant face fell into a frown. The child looked at him, tilted her head quizzically to the side, then ran to him; but Phil didn't bend down to embrace the toddler. Instead, he let her cling to his thighs. She tried to hide her head in his crotch.

Lots of children do that, the thought crossed Hester's mind as she watched. *With their mothers, it's like they're trying to crawl back into the womb.*

Lila Hampton was commenting to her son and daughter-in-law about the intoxicating scent of gardenias, but Hester wasn't listening. She couldn't stop watching that small head, the soft white curls. It was starting to make Hester uncomfortable because the child's face seemed stuck in the triangle of her father's pants right where his penis was. Then Phil reached down without looking and patted the girl's back, while his mother kept talking, now about how many gardenias grew in Pleasant Palms. The mother of the triplets, platinum and beautiful like the one daughter, seemed enthralled by her mother-in-law's botanical musings, and unaware of what her husband was doing to her beautiful little daughter.

Lila was so animated, it was hard not to listen to her. But Hester was getting more nervous by the second about the platinum one and where her poor little face was. She watched as Phil stopped patting his daughter's back. His large hand moved to the head of curls; and, Hester would swear to it, he pressed so hard on her head that half of it disappeared into him. Hester feared he was going to suffocate the child right in front of everyone. She looked at his face and his mouth fell open and turned up into a half smile. Behind his sunglasses, Hester imagined, his eyes rolling up into their sockets.

This was too much. Hester put down her tool and walked over to them.

"Hey, Lila, how would those triplets of yours like some cookies?" She shouted the word "cookies." The little blonde head slipped out from under her father's paw, and she ran away from him in Hester's direction.

Hester scooped her up in her arms and hugged the little beauty. Before she turned to take the child into her trailer, Hester lifted up her sunglasses and stared at Phil. He still had his on and she couldn't see his eyes, but she wanted him to see hers.

"You better be more careful with a child this age. You were pushing on her little head so hard, you could've snapped her little neck." She said it loud, enunciating every syllable, so his wife and mother could hear it too. Even with a bit of a sunburn, Hester saw his skin redden and sensed his rage. So what? She'd rendered him speechless.

It was Lila who spoke, "Oh, Hester, he was only playing with her."

"Don't be such a fool, Lila." Hester left with the child without seeking permission, took her into the trailer, and got some cookies. When she brought them out, Phil and his wife were gone. Lila was waiting with the two plain sisters and took the blonde one from Hester. As Hester handed the cookies out, and the children greedily bit into them, Lila angrily whispered to Hester, "Mind your own damn business," and left.

Twenty-Five

Hester never met Theo for lunch over the Christmas break. She didn't need to. Thanks to him, Al was seeing his wife in a new light. As soon as vacation began, Al turned his attention to Hester. They flew down to Pleasant Palms a few days earlier, opened up the trailer, and had so much sex, Hester was happily worn out. On New Year's Eve, Al poured them each a snifter of cognac. He handed a drink to Hester and made a toast.

"To the year we have our first child."

Hester nearly choked on the cognac. She'd waited more than a decade for Al to want to have a baby. Now at thirty-five, she was going to get pregnant. Finally, she'd be able to right the terrible wrongs of her past. Finally, the lie she told Al when she was twenty-two, letting him think she was pregnant when she wasn't, pretending to lose the baby after they were married, could be erased. Finally, a baby, their baby, to have and to hold, would make up for the one her seventeen year old self left in that garbage can.

When they finished their drinks, they took the rest of Al's stash of condoms to the mail room and slipped them one by one into random mail slots. They laughed the whole way to the beach where Al managed to keep the blanket over them while he came twice before they heard a golf cart drive up. It was only the Dunnes probably checking for something they'd left up there.

"I hope this works, Hester." Al was on top of her, holding himself up on his forearms, whispering. His boozy breath was warm on her face.

"Me too."

"We weren't ready back then, but now it's different. I want a child of my own."

"Me too."

"I'm tired of other people's kids."

Hester was about to say, me too again, but it wasn't true. She loved other people's kids, she wanted to tell him, but he was hard, and inside her again.

"Al, wait. Al, the Dunnes, I can hear them talking. Can't you?"

"Fuck the Dunnes, Hester. I'm trying to make a baby." Al went for broke, humping hard into Hester. She was pinned under him. His body was heavy, and the pounding hurt. She wanted to ask him to stop, but she told herself, *bite your tongue till it bleeds. You want this.*

By the time they got back to New Jersey, Hester was so full of baby dreams, so sure she was pregnant, the thought of that kiss with Theo disgusted her. What had she been thinking? Now she didn't even want to be alone with him in the same room. In desperation she went to Janine and begged her to work with Theo on the festival.

"It'll cost you, Hester Murphy." Janine didn't even look up from her grade book, like she knew it would come to this.

"Fine, Janine, whatever you want." Hester imagined her saying, *your husband naked for a weekend.* It would almost be worth it to not have to work with Theo again.

"Senior honors, all of them." Janine leaned back, twirled a lock of her orange hair around her finger. The cherry-red polish on her long nails made them look like bloody daggers.

Senior honors? That's ridiculous. It would mean Hester would have to take the freshmen. Hester decide to call Janine's bluff.

"Never, no way. Forget it, I'll work with Ottinger. After all, it's not like he's ugly or anything. Besides he's a good…no, a great kisser."

"I'll tell your husband he's married to a pervert. Theo's young enough to be your son."

"Almost, and don't waste your time running to tell Al, he already knows. He watched."

"You're a sick puppy, Hester."

"Forget I ever asked you for anything, Janine."

Hester turned and went back to her classroom. She wasn't bluffing any longer. She didn't want anything from Miss Pain-in-the-Ass. Hester would figure out a way to keep Theo at arm's length. And who was Janine to call her a sick puppy?

Hester started erasing the boards when a wave of nausea hit her. What was happening? Suddenly, she felt sick, like she was going to pass out. *No, it can't be.* She was cramping up. She leaned on her desk to keep from collapsing. When the pain passed, she grabbed her purse and hurried across the hall to the lavatory.

She got in the stall and got her pants down just in time. Another cramp seized her, and the toilet bowl filled with blood.

Hester put her head down. Why the hell had she gone anywhere near Janine? Janine was bad luck. Hester so wanted to blame this on Janine, but the truth was, she couldn't. Yes, Janine upset her. *But some sins can never be forgiven*, she thought. What did she expect? A miracle? Not for her. Not today. God had turned a deaf ear on her prayers. Who could blame Him?

She pounded her fists on her thighs. It took a lot of toilet paper to clean herself. When she was done, she stood up, turned, and looked down at the disaster. Oh no, something was really wrong with her.

Twenty-Six

One Monday afternoon in January, Hester joined Dee and some people at the marina for their weekly cocktail hour. Flo and Ned Nance were sitting in their folding chairs, holding hands and staring silently out at the water, so Hester sat by Eleanor and Fred Bateman, who were talking about when the next full moon would rise. Jean and Cap Forenti pulled up in their golf cart just as Dee came huffing down the boardwalk yelling, "I swear, I don't believe it! Some people have such nerve. You know me. Do I ever tell anybody off? Well, do I?"

Ned, a nice-looking man for eighty-three, snapped out of his stupor, put his glass of Chablis on the plastic table next to his chair, and said, "Dee, calm down and tell Uncle Ned what happened. I can't imagine anyone getting under your thick skin."

"I do have thick skin, Ned, but there is this person who just moved into the park, and I'm about to give her a piece of my mind," Dee reached in the cooler, extracted a can of beer, popped it open, and took a drink.

Jean and Cap, martinis in hand, sat on the bench of the picnic table. Cap asked, "What happened, Dee?"

"Do you know Anita Jackson? She just moved into 15 Royal Palm. Well, she's sitting by the pool in her black tankini, running her fingers through her bleached blonde hair, and she yells across the pool to tell me to stop taking ice from the machine. She says if I want ice to take to the marina, I have to get it from the ice machine in the boating and fishing Quonset. Now come on, I've lived here for years, and I always get my ice from the ice machine at the pool. And how did she know where the hell I was going with my ice anyway?"

"I see your point," said Eleanor as she put her glass of wine down and reached into Dee's cooler. She took a beer and looked at Dee. "Do you mind? I can't drink that cheap wine Fred bought."

"Absolutely not, help yourself," said Dee.

Eleanor popped open the beer. "I met that Anita the other day at the hobby club meeting. The president was talking about replacing the old Singers with computerized machines and turning half the room into a display area. So Anita says to me, 'Why should we do all that if this place is going to be sold?' And I said, 'That's just a stupid rumor. No one would ever vote to sell Pleasant Palms.' And she says, 'You'd be surprised what a person would do for a million dollars. That's what I heard the offer is, one million dollars each!' So I said, 'You just moved in last month, Anita. How come you know so much?' She didn't answer me and turned to talk to somebody else, and I thought, this lady is going to be nothing but trouble."

"You've got that right, Eleanor. Nothing but trouble." Through her T-shirt, rings of sweat were visible around Dee's armpits. "I tell you, folks, when she was yelling across the pool at me in front of everybody, I wanted to stomp over there and yank those sunglasses off her Botoxed face."

"Dee, darling, your fangs are showing," Cap said. "You're usually kinder and gentler than this."

"You're right." Dee sat back in her chair. "Life is too short to spend it being mean. Live and let live. Right?"

"But I still don't like what she said about a developer buying Pleasant Palms," said Eleanor. "Do any of you think it's true?"

"No! It can't be true," Hester said.

"No," they all agreed.

Across the Intracoastal, the orange sun was disappearing from the sky. The group grew quiet and watched in silence as it sank behind the plateau of condominium roofs. The clouds thinned out and turned purple. Fred lit the tiki torches. The scent of night jasmine drifted in on the breeze. Ned tried to tell a joke about a Frenchman and a black man riding on a bus to work. He couldn't remember the punch line, but his attempt at a French accent made them laugh. Dee seemed to be over Anita for the time being, Fred put his arm around Eleanor, and Jean clinked her glass against Cap's. Hester looked around at the small circle of friends and concluded that although they were far from perfect, she was grateful to be with them. She stared up at the stars, smiling as she listened to Flo gently and diplomatically try to help her husband recall the end of the joke.

This is the best I've felt in months. Hester watched the moon rise over the palms.

"Somebody's coming," Jean whispered. They all turned to look up the boardwalk, but it was too dark, even with the moonlight, to see much.

"Looks like two people," Cap observed.

"I think it's your hubby, Hester," said Fred, "I wonder who's with him."

Dee stood up to look beyond the flames of the torches as Al stepped into the circle of light with a woman whose firm body looked trim in a black tankini. "Hester, look what I found by the pool."

"Son of a bitch," Dee said under her breath.

Hester picked up her empty wine glass and walked past Al and Anita into the darkness. Halfway down the boardwalk, she turned and looked back. Anita was sitting next to Al in the chair Hester had vacated. Her blonde hair glowed in the firelight. Al was staring at the newcomer and laughing. *The devil in his own little ring of hell,* thought Hester, *nothing but trouble.*

Twenty-Seven

Yesterday, after getting her period, Hester went straight home, showered, took a couple of pain pills, and passed out—guilt and self-pity ameliorated, for the time being. She didn't hear a thing when Al came home. The next morning he was gone before she woke up, which was unusual.

The first person Hester ran into when she got to school, was Theo. He stopped her outside the main office, "Hester, so many rumors are flying around, what really happened yesterday?"

"I don't know a thing about what happened yesterday."

"Didn't you talk to Al last night?" Theo seemed confused.

"Theo, if you must know, I was asleep before Al came home, and he left before I got up this morning. So no, I didn't talk to my husband last night. Look, I have go, and I really don't know a thing about any rumors."

Hester tried to get away from Theo. She didn't feel all that great, and she wanted to talk to Al before she lost her courage; but Theo blocked her way and insisted on filling Hester in on all the details.

There had been trouble, bad trouble. It was the new biology teacher, Cyril Banks. He did something terribly wrong.

Most staff members thought Cyril was weird. He looked weird. His head was shaped like a light bulb with a high forehead, his small eyes, nose, and mouth compressed into the bottom third of his face. He kept an embalmed two-headed squirrel in a jar on his desk and a live ferret named Mama in a cage on top of his file cabinet.

Cyril Banks loved his ferret. He told his students about the Chinese belief, ferrets are the reincarnations of departed human spirits, which makes them wise creatures. If Mr. Banks became annoyed with a student who wouldn't listen or do what he asked, he'd say, "Let's go see what Mama thinks your punishment should be." He'd make the student stand in front of the ferret, confess his or her crime, and ask for just punishment. Mr. Banks, arms crossed, foot tapping, watched Mama and waited for her decision.

"There, see, Susie, see how Mama is thinking it over."

The ferret never did anything unusual, but after a few minutes, Mr. Banks said excitedly, "There you have it, you must clean out Mama's cage after school."

Needless to say, after a while, no one misbehaved in Mr. Banks's room because no one wanted to touch Mama, let alone clean her cage. The students thought Mr. Banks was nuts, but his quirkiness was tempered by his innate good nature, so nobody minded being in his class. In fact, he was beginning to develop a bit of a cult following.

Something, however, went amiss yesterday in Mr. Banks's room. When Cyril opened his door in the morning, long before Ben, the custodian, turned on the hall lights, he knew something was not right. A foul stench filled the room. Mama was in her cage stretched out like a slender boa of white and black fur. She didn't move and Cyril, upon closer examination, saw that her bodily fluids had pooled on the newsprint in a wet ring around her small corpse. She was dead. When Ben was passing Mr. Banks' classroom, he smelled the odor and went in to investigate. Cyril was filling a large specimen jar with formaldehyde into which he gently slipped Mama. He placed the jar on his desk next to the jar that held the two-headed squirrel.

"This is all my fault," Mr. Banks told Ben as he cleaned the cage with peroxide, "and I will have to be punished for it."

Ben didn't know what to say, so he mumbled, "Sorry about your ferret."

Cyril didn't respond to Ben's comment, but went to the blackboard and wrote in large letters, "Mama is dead. Please, no questions. Thank you very much, Mr. Banks."

Ben and Cyril left the room together and Cyril went to the office to pick up his mail.

Unfortunately for Cyril this was the day he was supposed to start the new unit on reproductive systems. The board of education approved the curriculum last summer. Human sexuality, birth control, safe sex, and so forth were now all part of his eleventh-grade biology course.

Cyril, who never questioned his superiors and always did what was required of him, argued bitterly with Jim Hawson, his supervisor, over the changes. He did not want to talk about sex. He would certainly cover the biology of the reproductive systems, but he would not deliver instruction on sexual behavior. Wasn't that covered in health class? Wasn't that bad enough? His students were children. He preferred to think of them as innocent.

Being raised Christian, instructed in his faith at Shiloh Baptist in Trenton, Cyril lived his religion. Besides, what would his mama, dead almost thirteen years now, think of him talking about such sinful behavior in front of young unmarried people? Jim Hawson didn't seem to care about Cyril's personal beliefs.

"Just do your job and don't take it personally," is what Hawson told him.

But Cyril did take it personally. He'd struggled to become a teacher. It had taken him ten long years to finish college. He hadn't started until the September after his mother died when he was twenty-eight years old. Mama had depended on him. She wasn't married and never had been. Cyril was all she had, except for her brother, Uncle Tad, who only came around once in a great while. How could he leave her alone and go off to college like other young people? No, he stayed with her and took care of her and did whatever she wanted him to. It was the least he could do to pay her back for raising him right.

So when she died, he had plenty of time on his hands. He worked days as a security guard at Quakerbridge Mall and went to classes in the evening. He tried not to feel lonely, but he missed his mama. In his mind he could picture her rheumy eyes, the palms of her hands the color of sand, the broad flat feet he rubbed with lavender cream before he tucked her in at night. He remembered how good her warm breath felt on his forehead when he leaned over for her to kiss him there. He loved Mama more than any girl he ever met, and many girls, especially at Shiloh, had tried hard to please him.

He told Al all of this without being asked. It was an odd interview for sure, but Al hired Cyril twenty minutes after he met him, in spite of the way he rambled on about his mother. Sourland High desperately needed to diversify their staff. The state was putting pressure on the "Crisco" districts to hire teachers of color. Cyril was in his early forties and not what you would call dynamic during the interview, but he'd graduated from college summa cum laude and he was certified, and that was good enough for Al, who was always willing to do cartwheels when it came to guaranteeing state funding.

Cyril, upset over the death of his ferret, bumped into Theo in the office. Cyril, uncharacteristically, launched into a nervous monologue about his extreme reservations about starting the unit on human reproductive systems that day.

When questioned later, Theo said Cyril was talking fast and appeared to be very upset. Theo, who tried to ease Cyril's worries by telling Cyril his students were probably having a lot more sex than he was, admitted in hindsight it probably wasn't the best thing to say.

Ben was back in Cyril's classroom cleaning the windows when Cyril returned, went to his desk, and opened the jar that held the two-headed squirrel. Uncle Tad, the only father figure in Cyril's life, shot it in the woods along the Delaware River last year. He brought it right to his nephew Cyril, whom he considered a great scientist. It was a remarkable specimen. The two heads were perfectly shaped, and both had two clear eyes the size and color of small almonds. Each nose had two pinpoint nostrils and identical silver streaks across the bridges of their noses. The single neck was thick, the body was muscular and lean, despite all the eating the two mouths must've been capable of. Uncle Tad shot it cleanly through the abdomen with a small bullet, so neither of its heads had been disturbed. According to Cyril, which head was dominant was impossible to tell. Uncle Tad had pointed the testicles out to Cyril. They looked like small gray olives on either side of the creature's tiny penis.

Now Cyril held the squirrel in his gloved hands like a minister might hold an undersized infant for an emergency christening. At this point Cyril looked up at Ben and asked him to leave.

"What could I do? I left," Ben told Al later.

When Mr. Banks' eleventh-grade biology class arrived, they were curious about what was on his desk under a white sheet. Many of the girls gasped and sighed when they read the news on the blackboard about Mama. Some of the boys snickered, but stopped when they saw the sad look on Mr. Banks's face. His skin was ashen, and his lips were drawn together tightly. His wire-rimmed glasses magnified the wary look in his eyes that glistened like wet stones.

As several of the students later described the incident, Mr. Banks did not seem to be himself. He said nothing to them. He waited for the bell to ring, went to his desk, and gently lifted the sheet. Many of the students gasped at what they saw. Mama's small limbs were pinned down to a wooden specimen board, her belly sliced open, her skin stretched back and tacked down. Her thumb-sized heart was muddy brown. Her lungs were like a pair of tiny earlobes with no head in between. Her uterus, ovaries, and fallopian tubes seemed oversized and prominent in the small cavity that held them.

Next to her the two-headed squirrel was similarly arranged on another board with one head facing toward Mama and the other toward the door. His testicles and penis rested limply atop his damp tail that pointed downward. Mr. Banks began to talk about the reproductive systems of the squirrel and the ferret. His lecture started out fairly normally, but somewhere in the middle of it, he got off track. It was reported by the students, who claimed to have been interested in the lesson, that he began talking to the dead animals instead of to the students. Then Mr. Banks began hollering at the specimens as though they were real people. He started calling the squirrel Uncle Tad.

"I never told Mama, never, Uncle Tad, never. But it wasn't her fault like you said. You old bastard. Damn you. Damn you."

Mr. Banks started crying and hollering things that ceased to make any sense, until Anna Porter, a smart girl and a good student, went up to him and whispered, "Excuse me, Mr. Banks, but I'm going to get Principal Heck. I'll be right back." She left quickly, not waiting for Mr. Banks to respond. She came back with Al instead of the principal.

Cyril had his back to the class and was hunched over the two dead animals, staring blankly at them. Al put a firm hand on Cyril's back and led him out of the classroom and down to his office, where Al spent a long time talking to him.

That was all Theo knew, because he left the building around four thirty, and Al's door was still closed, but the gossip about the incident spread through the school like dust on a dry, windy day.

Hester went right to Al's office when Theo had finished.

"Oh God, what happened, Al? Is it true Cyril cracked up?"

"Apparently so, but I did damage control, and I think I got through to him. I made him promise to get counseling ASAP. How about you, honey? I didn't wake you up last night because it was late, and I know you need your rest now. How are you doing?" He was getting up from his chair to kiss her when his phone rang. He picked it up and put his other hand on her arm.

"Really? Are you sure? Yeah, I'll be right there."

He hung up. His expression turned somber. He kissed Hester tenderly and whispered in her ear, "Bad news. Cyril shot and killed his uncle last night. They've got him in custody at the municipal building. He's asking for me before they take him to Trenton State Prison. Sorry, gotta go. Love you, and our baby."

She didn't have the heart to tell him at a time like this so she blew him a kiss and said, "We love you too."

Twenty-Eight

After Hester stormed off from the happy hour, Al came home much later humming "The Night They Drove Old Dixie Down." Hester was trying to sleep so she put a pillow over her head to block out the sound of his voice, but it didn't work. She waited for her husband to flop into his chair and turn on the boob tube. His humming was replaced with muffled electronic chatter. Hester rolled over and thought about the rumor that the park might be sold. The possibility made her shudder. *If it is, the trailers will be demolished, the whole place will be dug up. Dug up?*

Dear God, why hadn't she immediately picked up her cell phone when she found Al and Nina? Why hadn't she dialed 911? Hester knew she was in for another sleepless night, and, unfortunately, she was right.

In the morning Hester moved her chaise lounge under the bo tree and laid in it for the better part of the day. She studied the tree. It was like an old friend to her. New bark was growing over the scar, and new branches were budding out around the broken stumps. Fresh leaves were quivering in whatever air there was.

Why couldn't she bounce back like the old tree? Why wasn't time healing her wounds?

But being so close to where Nina was buried, Hester imagined she was keeping the girl company and decided to start reading aloud. Perhaps the ghost of Nina was hovering, lying right next to her on the lounge, wanting desperately to hear the sound of Hester's voice. It didn't make a bit of sense, but imagining Nina's presence eased Hester's inner turmoil. The first book Hester chose, probably since Eliot and she had discussed it, was *The Scarlet Letter*. She hadn't read it since college, but it was a novel she always wanted to teach, and it was the kind of story that would be right up Nina's alley.

After a week of listening to what Hester was doing, Al informed his wife that he hated listening to her read aloud, to her precise pronunciation, her dramatic intonation, her breathy delivery. It reminded him of her schoolteacher voice, which wasn't like her real voice at all.

When Hester ignored him, a few days later he lowered the volume on the television and hollered out the trailer window, "Hey, wife, would you please cut that bullshit out. You're killing me. I can hardly hear myself think."

Later, after a few beers, he brought it up again, asked her why she kept it up.

"I like to read out loud," she serenely answered.

Al laughed and warned her that if she was getting wacky, he'd put her in a nursing home. Hester smiled weakly; she wasn't going to fight with him. After that, when he was around, she whisper the words so quietly she looked crazy, like she was talking to herself. So she was glad when Al began getting involved in Pleasant Palms business, because then he was around less, and that was fine by her.

The third Wednesday in February, an important community meeting was scheduled. Al said he wasn't going to miss it for the world. The bulletin was direct: "All shareholders are strongly encouraged to attend." The gossip mill was still churning out the rumor about a big real estate development company purchasing Pleasant Palms. The offer was supposedly incredible; but since everyone who owned a trailer in the park also owned shares in the Pleasant Palms Corporation, the majority would have to vote to sell. It they did, supposedly they'd become millionaires.

Al planned to get to the community room early to get a seat. He was up at six, showered, wolfed down his hardboiled eggs and toast, and was about to leave when he turned to Hester and said, like it was an afterthought, "Do you want to come?"

"No thanks, I couldn't think of a bigger waste of time," Hester said, but the truth was she didn't want to find out the rumor was true. She looked up from her coffee at Al, and behind him through the window, she saw the tops of the palms swaying in the breeze like giant feather dusters. Al leaned down and brushed her cheek with his lips. It wasn't exactly a kiss, but Hester hadn't expected it, and where he'd touched her, her skin tingled. *Now why did he have to do that?* She put her hand on her cheek and pressed to stop the sensation. Most of the time they were like two planets in the same galaxy, but thankfully relegated to distant orbits. They talked back and forth about what was for dinner or what had to be gotten at the store, but the only important thing they'd said to each other lately was about the sale of the park.

Al asked Hester whether she would vote to sell since they only had one vote between them. And Hester, knowing that selling Pleasant Palms would mean she'd have to do something with Nina's body, almost shouted, No! Never! But thought better of it, saying only, "Al, who needs a million dollars when we're already living in paradise?"

"Exactly, Hester, you are exactly right." Al agreed with Hester so quickly and easily, she didn't believe him. At first, she thought, *maybe he's trying to make me happy,* but Al wasn't the type to say anything just to make someone happy. No, Alexander Bruno Murphy was blunt when it came to offering his opinion, and stubborn when it came to getting his way. There was no limit to what Al would do when he wanted something, and no limit to what he wouldn't do if he didn't want something. In other words, he was Machiavellian with the moral grit of a barnacle.

Hester got up and went out to the patio. Through the top branches of the bo, the moon in the sunny sky was an incongruous, transparent disc. *What dat moon doin' up in dat sky?* Her mom use to make her laugh saying this whenever they noticed the stubborn moon hanging on into the day. Everything was topsy-turvy. Hester's life was topsy-turvy, one slow-motion bad dream. She walked to the beach. Still in the sweats and T-shirt she'd slept in, she rolled her pants up and waded into the surf. Her feet sank into the cool sand. She watched shells tumble in the tide and looked for whole ones.

"Hey, there!" Hester recognized the voice and looked up. Dee was walking toward her.

"Hester, you should've been at that meeting!" Dee said breathlessly. She smelled of coffee and coconut lotion.

"Why, what did I miss?"

"Holy shit, it was a sideshow, and your husband was the two-headed cow. I never knew he was like that."

"Like what?" Hester took the bait.

"I'll get to that in minute, but first let me tell you what happened. Russ Trotman—you know him, the board president read the letter from the attorneys, Ripsome & Newton. When he finished, nothing but dead silence for about two minutes. Then Bing Fagan, the treasurer, says, 'Folks, you know what this means? If we sell this place for three hundred million dollars, and there are three hundred units, then we'd each walk away with one million dollars.'

"The arteries in Bing's neck looked like they were going to burst. He could hardly talk. 'One million dollars each, people, we can't turn this down.' Well, practically everyone stood up and clapped and cheered, 'Sell! Sell! Sell!'"

Dee threw her arm around Hester's shoulder. "You should've been there."

Hester, in an attempt to extricate herself from Dee's grasp and compose herself, bent down to pick up a shell. When she stood up, she said, "Wow, so it wasn't just gossip? Wow."

"No, praise God, it's true!" Dee was jubilant.

Hester, knowing it would be futile to try to change Dee's mind about something she was obviously in favor of, reluctantly asked about Al, "So what did Al do to come off like a two-headed cow?"

"Jesus, Hester, I don't know how you put up with him."

Hester felt like saying, *tell me about it*, but didn't. "What did he do now?" She tried to sound light-hearted.

"Well, he waits till the hoopla dies down and gets on the microphone. 'Not so fast, let's calm down and take a look at this thing,' he says. But Clayton, the project manager from Sea to Sea Development Corporation who's on the stage with the board of directors, says, 'Listen, folks, you've got a topnotch board of directors here, some of the smartest people I've ever dealt with. They've gone over the contract with a fine-tooth comb, and so has your law firm. So there really is nothing else to take a look at. Sea to Sea has made deals like this all over the world. We are the largest ocean-front development corporation in the world. We know what we're doing, and I can tell you, you can trust that we are offering you the opportunity of a lifetime. How many of your friends would've ever lived in a trailer park? I'll bet a lot of them looked down their noses at you, called you trailer trash behind your backs. You stayed here anyhow and now it's going to pay off. This deal is going to be national news. You are going to be national news. So enough talk, let's celebrate. The vote is scheduled for next Monday; but at this point, it's clearly only a formality...'

"Al, whose face is as red as a beet, hollers into the mike, 'Excuse me, what in the hell are you talking about, only a formality? This whole thing stinks. Listen, people, we're being railroaded. Think about your shares. Not everybody is going to get a million dollars. In fact, nobody is. What about taxes? What about capital gains? What about...' Then Clayton says, 'Now, now, why don't you and I—what was your name and unit number, anyway?—sit down over a martini or something, and I can answer all of your questions privately, so we don't waste everyone else's time here. Remember, I've been down this road before and it's very simple, very...' Then Al screams, "Simple, my ass, this place is a paradise and you know it and that's why you want to rip it out from under us. Is there another place on the planet like it? No. Will a million dollars buy us what we have here? No. What's your answer to that, asshole?'

"That's when Trotman started pounding his gavel, telling Al to leave the meeting if he's calling people names. So Al gives him the finger and walked out."

"No kidding? What did this guy Clayton do?" Hester looked back down at the water swirling around her ankles.

"He invited the whole park to a cocktail party on Friday night at the clubhouse. And he told us to dress up. We're all going to be rich and famous so we might as well look the part now. The press will be there too." Dee looked in Hester's eyes. "You've got to get Al to get off his high horse about not selling. Hester, this the best chance someone like me has ever had to be rich."

Hester thought. *She wants to get rich, and I want to...stay out of jail*. Al, who knew he'd be on the same side as she was? Al might not be found guilty of anything, might walk away scot free if Nina's body were discovered, but not Hester. Hester was the one who put it where it was. Hester was the one who lied, who was wrong.

"I'll talk to him, Dee." Hester wanted Dee to drop the uncomfortable subject. She extended her hand to help the large woman maintain her balance as they walked out of the waves and across the hot beach.

When they stepped into the shade by the clubhouse, a golf cart pulled up, and Dee shrieked, "Clayton!" She rushed ahead of Hester, who could see even from a distance that Clayton was young and handsome. His blonde hair was parted on the side, the bangs swept across his forehead. His blue eyes sparkled like the ocean he was surveying. His pale pink Oxford had a crest embroidered on the right pocket, mother-of-pearl buttons. An alligator belt circled his thin hips and held up his perfectly pressed linen slacks. He wore a pair of kidskin tasseled loafers, no socks. When he saw Dee charging at him, he stepped out of his cart, spread his feet wide, and folded his arms across his chest. *Probably to steel himself for the blow*, thought Hester.

Dee was running and panting and waving both hands in the air, like she was batting flies. Hester reluctantly followed her.

"Clayton, oh, Clayton, yoo-hoo!"

Slowly, coolly, he turned his face in her direction. His expression at first was contorted, almost, Hester thought, full of dread; but as Dee got closer, it change into a purposeful gaze, until he was beaming at her, his smile, full of chalk-white teeth, at once gorgeous and intimidating.

Dee placed her fat hand on his bare forearm, as though she were claiming him. She smiled up at him. *She's flirting*, thought Hester, who'd never seen Dee act like this, who sometimes wondered if Dee went for men at all, but here she was fluttering her eyelashes. Hester watched as Dee squeezed Clayton's arm, and it hit Hester—*it's not Clayton, Dee cares about, it's the money...she'll do anything to get it*. Clayton placed his well-manicured hand patronizingly on top of Dee's. *He could care less about Dee, it's her shares he wants.*

Hester turned and headed back toward the ocean, which she really felt like drowning herself in now...again. And for the first time in a long time, she had Tom Buchanan on her mind.

Twenty-Nine

Seemingly undaunted by the news of their failed attempt at getting pregnant, Al turned into a determined rabbit, ready and raring to go every night. This time when Hester got pregnant, she would quit work, stay home, and take it easy. They would have a baby and to hell with the money.

But after almost six months of trying, who could blame him for growing weary. Al started getting on Hester about seeing a specialist, but Hester had a big problem with gynecologists. Some people hated dentists; she hated men who made their living sticking their hands inside a woman's body. The thought of an internal exam sickened her. She couldn't fathom why any sane man would want to spend his life with his face between a pair of strange female legs. She didn't believe they wanted to help women, only that they were perverted. Look at what that quack did to her.

But she couldn't tell Al. He'd be devastated if he knew she'd had an abortion. He wouldn't expect that from her. He didn't always show it, but lately he had put her on some kind of pedestal. And he might conclude what Hester feared he would for a while now, she couldn't carry a baby to term because of the damn abortion.

She tried like hell to get out of going, but Al wouldn't budge on it, so she tried to find a woman gyno. She'd have to go into Philly or New York to see one.

"Get over it," Al told her. "What's the big deal? They're all doctors, aren't they?"

When she had no further recourse, she made an appointment to appease Al. Then as if it wasn't bad enough that she had to go at all, he insisted on going with her. The more she begged him not to, the more adamant he became. "No way are you going alone. You need moral support, don't you? And that's what good husbands are for."

It only took Dr. Harris at Mercer Hospital's Fertility Clinic about two seconds to determine Hester had an abortion.

"So, I see you took the easy way out at one point," he quietly and slowly said as he raised his head and shot what seemed to Hester to be a vile glance. Then he lowered his head and began sticking things up inside of her. The nurse, who looked like a young Joan Rivers, clucked her tongue judgmentally against the roof of her mouth, looked around the room, studied her nails, and never once looked down where Dr. Harris was doing whatever. What kind of protection was she? Harris could've been fouling Hester up even more for all Hester knew.

When the doctor finally surfaced from between Hester's legs, he curtly told her she could get dressed. They'd discuss his findings in his office. The nurse handed Hester a half-crumpled tissue, told her to clean herself up, and followed the man out.

When Hester opened his office door, Dr. Harris was sitting across from Al. Al was leaning forward in his seat, sketching something with the tip of his index finger on the black surface of the steel desk. The doctor was nodding in agreement. They looked like two generals planning their next attack. Hester felt like their target.

"Come in, Mrs. Murphy. I thought it would be easier for you to have Al here so you wouldn't have to repeat things to him later and maybe get things wrong." He sounded like he was talking to a child, and Hester noticed the doctor was already calling Al by his first name. He nodded knowingly to Al. If he nodded one more time, Hester was afraid she'd grab his head by his fat ears and shake him silly.

Panic was beginning to grip Hester. She'd left Al in the waiting room. She expected her conversation with the doctor would be private. Now here they were ganging up on her. If Harris said anything about the abortion, she knew Al would fly off the handle. He would kill Hester for not telling him years ago, for embarrassing him, for... everything. Well, not really kill her, but he might leave her. That would be the worse for Hester. She'd rather die.

Hester almost turned to walk out, but that wouldn't help. It would only create a scene. She tried to control her emotions. The doctor knew about patient-doctor privileges. Wouldn't he respect her right to privacy? Women had rights now. Al was her husband, not her master. Harris was being courteous inviting Al into his office. She had to trust he would talk only in general terms. She regained enough composure to sit next to Al across the desk from the doctor, and hope for the best.

"Now, Hester, the news is not good. You're in your thirties, and that alone would work against you in terms of getting pregnant, but the adhesions are the real problem. You have so many, conception is difficult for you and carrying a fetus to term, unfortunately, impossible." He paused, his eyes riveted on Hester's face. She took a deep breath. Bad news for sure, but at least he hadn't mentioned the cause of the adhesions, the big sin.

"Thank you, Dr. Harris, that's bad—" Hester tried to end the conversation.

But Al interrupted. "What in the hell are adhesions anyway, Doc?"

Hester was dead in the water. The two men started talking about her as though she wasn't there.

"Plain and simple, Al, adhesions are scar tissue. Your wife should've known she'd get them after such a risky procedure."

"What procedure? She's never even gone to a gynecologist before."

Hester held her breath. This was bad, this was the end.

"Maybe not a gynecologist, but she certainly did have something done, and it caused the adhesions in the first place. Up to that point, she was probably a healthy, fertile female who would have had no trouble having a baby, but somebody—and I'm positive whoever it was, wasn't a doctor—really butchered her insides so that now the weight of the growing baby is too much for her damaged uterus. Regretfully, there's nothing we can do now to fix the damage caused by her abortion."

There it was. The A-word hung in the air, hummed inside Hester's head, seemed to raise the three of them up toward it, such power it had.

And then the atmosphere in the office deflated. Al turned red in the face. Hester cried. The smug doctor led them to the door, mumbling about an adoption agency he could recommend.

Thirty

Rather than listen to Al rant about how stupid everyone at Pleasant Palms was, Hester got in the Odyssey, drove to Saint Maximillian's, and lined up for confession. How long had it been? She couldn't remember. Two people were in front of her, and damn it, they were both from the park. She hadn't wanted to run into anybody she knew.

Norman Colter stood behind Elizabeth Hanky. They were waiting for whoever was in the confessional to come out.

Elizabeth was married to Hurley Hanky, who was the guy who invented the automatic pin replacer for bowling alleys and then sold the patent. He bought a chain of roller rinks and managed them until he retired ten years ago. The Hankys lived a few rows over from Hester on Royal Palm Way. Elizabeth kept to herself, but Hurley was always out and about, always into somebody else's business. He was the type who couldn't resist telling other people how they should do things. His totally unsolicited advice forced most people to cross the street to the other side when they saw him coming. Hurley never got the hint.

Norman Colter lived alone in his small unit on Bottle Palm Place. Hester had been introduced to him by Eve, and liked his pleasant smile, his good looks. How could a person like this be alone? Eve didn't have a clue, maybe he was gay. She really didn't know. Well, in Hester's opinion, he was the handsomest old guy in the park, and that was including Al. Hester wasn't finding her Irish-Italian stallion all that enticing these days.

Norman was slender but broad chested, and he still had a full head of sandy hair streaked with platinum. His skin was tan, a little wrinkled, but who at their age cared. He wore board shorts and liked to snorkel. Hester spent more than one afternoon following the yellow crook of his breathing apparatus maneuvering around beyond the break, waiting for him to surface, swim in, and emerge dripping wet onto dry land. It was how Hester imagine Odysseus must've looked when he washed ashore in Phaeacia. The man was a shimmering specimen, and the last time Hester watched him toweling off, she surprised herself by fantasizing about following him home.

Unlike a lot of other people, Norman looked at her when she talked to him, his merry eyes dancing around her face. Gossip had it that he'd owned a car repair shop in Ohio. Hester wondered about that—Norman didn't seem like the type to get his hands dirty.

Hester got in line behind Norman. His verbena cologne filled her nostrils. Somebody came out of the confessional, and Elizabeth went in. Norman turned and smiled at Hester warmly, and the thought popped into her head, *if I do leave Al, I want Norman to want me.*

Elizabeth came out of the confessional and left without kneeling down in a pew to say penance. Norman went in. Hester wasn't purposely trying to listen, but some words reached her ears. She thought she heard "computer porn," but she wasn't sure. Whoever said it could've been saying, "other morn" or something like that. If it was Norman or the priest, she couldn't say, the voice that spoke was muffled.

Then Norman came out, and Hester went in.

As soon as she blurted out her most grievous offense, Hester knew she'd made a mistake trying to confess; but the past kept pounding away at her, and she thought being forgiven for her iniquities would enable her move on. She barely got the words out when the priest rudely interrupted.

"And so you're tellin' me a terrible t'ing, you are." She recognized the Irish brogue of Al's favorite priest, Father O'Hannon. "I regret to tell ya, they'll be no forgiv'n ya, no absolution, not from this priest nor any fine servant of God in the holy parish of Saint Maximillian's. You can count on that, can't you now?"

Hester mumbled, "Yes, Father. Sorry, Father. I just thought…"

"Don't go tryin' to t'ink anyt'ing. Go on your way now and curse the day you sold your soul to the devil by doing such a t'ing to a poor helpless unborn child."

Hester never heard of anyone being denied absolution. Stunned and mortified, she left the confessional, and knelt several rows behind Norman. Her face was on fire. She buried it in her hands and prayed to the Virgin. *Will I never be forgiven? My God, I was young, impulsive, terrified to not do what…* Hester heard the doors at the back of the church open and close. She looked up, Norman was gone. The door of the confessional was opening. Hester couldn't get out of the church fast enough.

A week later Hester, still agonizing over the priest's refusal to give her absolution, still angry that the man robbed her of the comfort she would've derived from knowing God forgave her, was more of an emotional mess than she'd ever been. She hadn't even gotten to her other sins, to what she'd done to Nina. Praying, a practice which had always given her peace, became impossible.

Al was on an overnight fishing trip with guys from the Billiard Club, so in an attempt to keep from slitting her wrists or drinking Drain-o, she put on her swimsuit and went to the beach. It was already after four and overcast. The water was rough, and the sand full of broken shells, but Hester went out where the waves lifted her off her feet. She remembered tomorrow was Valentine's Day; she hadn't gotten Al a card, and she wasn't planning on running out anywhere to get one. *I'll make him one,* she thought, *Happy Valentine's Day, from Hester (your wife with the eternal black mark on her soul). Ha...* So this would be the first time since they were married, she didn't give him a card.

The height of the waves doubled and the wind shifted to the east, but Hester stayed in the water until she was exhausted. An undercurrent pulled her far north of Pleasant Palms' beach. She had to walk nearly a mile to get to back. After showering and putting on her pajamas, she picked up Anthony Trollope's *The Macdermots of Ballycloran* and began to read. Hester was assigned the novel in college, but only skimmed the six hundred and eighty some pages and relied on the Cliffs Notes to write her paper. Reading it now would amend that minor falsehood, at least.

Soon she was wrapped up in the troubles of Thaddeus and Feemy, and forgot her own. But the dialogue was Irish like the voice of the priest, so Hester put the book down and tried to fall asleep. She listened to Chet's too-loud television—*didn't he realize how close the trailers were?*—and the murmur of the ocean beyond until she gave up and put on a pot of coffee. It was still dark, but she filled her mug and went down to the news stand in her pajamas and bought a *Palm Beach Post.* She sat in Al's La-Z-Boy and flipped open the paper.

"Priest Arrested, Charged with Embezzlement of Millions"— the headline took Hester's breath away. Below it was a photograph of Saint Maximillian's Church and Father O'Hannon. *Well, I'll be damned,* she thought. He was accused of skimming cash from the weekly collections for several years. The police estimated the amount to be in the hundreds of thousands. He owned a condo in Ireland and one in Las Vegas. He kept women, young women in both places and possibly a few illegitimate children. The police were checking records. Father O'Hannon denied everything, claimed he was framed, and blamed the missing funds on the parish council.

Hester clicked on the local news. Channel Seven had an exclusive interview with one of the parishioners. Channel Twelve had on a spokesperson from the bishop's office. Channel Ten was interviewing an altar girl.

Hester sat back and felt the hand of God, or maybe it was the hand of the Blessed Virgin, hovering nearby. Inside her head she heard a voice whisper, *you are forgiven.*

Ten minutes later she fell into a deep sleep and didn't wake up until Al came home with two king mackerels and one wahoo, filleted and sealed in Ziploc bags. Sunburned and smelly, he stood between Hester and the television, stretching his arms wide, then wider, showing how big the fish were. Behind him the set was still on, and the evening news was just starting. Between his legs she saw a close-up of O'Hannon trying to shield himself from the camera.

So it wasn't a dream, she thought, and it brought a smile to her face which Al must have thought was for him because he bent and kissed her.

Thirty-One

That night after the visit to Dr. Harris's office, all Al said about the end of their pursuit of parenthood was, "You can forget adoption. I'm don't want any child who is not my own flesh and blood so now because of what you did, I have to suffer too. Serves you right not to ever have a child, Hester Randal."

The way he said "Randal" instead of "Murphy" shook Hester to the core. He stood at the counter in the kitchen, poured himself a glass of vodka, walked past her, and went upstairs. She knew better than to follow him. She should've told him from the start about the abortion, now he was so angry, he might never talk to her again. She deserved whatever punishment he dished out as long as he didn't divorce her, but the silent treatment would be unbearable.

The next day, Hester taught her morning classes on autopilot. The bell rang for lunch. She hadn't slept, her stomach was in knots, but food was the last thing she wanted. She left her classroom and went out the back door nearest the sports fields. She needed some fresh air.

Al and she slept in separate rooms, and this morning he acted like she was invisible.

Now as she walked away from the school and into the stiff wind, she cursed the day she met Arty Kendall, the day she let him inside her. He could go on free as a lark and have as many kids as he wanted, while she was nothing now but damaged goods.

The late-winter sun was doing little to mitigate the cold. Hester sucked in the frigid air, it made her chest burn. She headed toward the dugout so she could get out of the blustery weather. As she rounded the side of the batting cage, she saw two people huddled on the bench. So this is where these kids come to make out, and now she'd have to bust them, send them to the office, write them up later. She didn't need this, not today.

They must have seen her coming because the boy stood up. But, it wasn't a boy. Even from the back Hester knew it was Al. He had on his long camel-hair coat, the collar pulled up around his ears. He took one step back from the bench, and Hester spied the girl for an instant. It was Jennifer Masterson, one of her seniors. She was staring at Al.

"Al, it's me." Hester stopped short of stepping down into the narrow space.

Al didn't turn around but kept his back to Hester. "I've got this, Hester. Just go back to school."

Hester didn't move. She could see that Al was fumbling with something, his shoulders moving beneath the soft fabric of his coat. His body blocked Hester's view of Jennifer. Finally, Al spun around. Hester looked beyond him and saw Jennifer's red face and swollen lips. Hester caught her eye, but she adverted her gaze and stared down at the dirt.

"Well, as long as you're still here, Mrs. Murphy, you might as well walk Miss Masterson down to my office." His voice was steady. "This will be the last time she'll cut class for a cigarette. Right, young lady?"

"Yes, Mr. Murphy." Jennifer glanced at the back of Al's head and smiled serenely. Hester didn't like the look on the teenager's face. It was a brazen, self-assured look. If she got caught smoking, she should at least be somewhat contrite. Then Hester realized, with a sinking feeling, she didn't see, or smell, a single cigarette.

"Al, it is my lunch." Hester somehow found the nerve to challenge her husband in front of the girl. Something wasn't right here, but Hester couldn't imagine Al would ever do anything wrong with a student. Even though it crossed her mind for one microsecond that they might have been kissing, and even though Al was madder at Hester than he'd ever been before, he knew better. He had too much to lose to get caught doing something, anything, inappropriate with a student.

"It'll only take five minutes, Hester," Al said. "I'd do it, but I have to check the rest of the fields. We've got to cut down on this class cutting."

As teacher and student walked back into the building, Hester examined Jennifer out of the corner of her eye and asked, "What were you doing out there?"

"Nothing, Mrs. Murphy, I swear."

"Were you smoking?"

"I hate cigarettes."

"So why did Mr. Murphy say you were smoking?"

"Ask him."

That comment rendered Hester speechless. They walked down the hall in silence, but when they were almost to the office, Jennifer whispered, "I'm sorry, Mrs. Murphy. I shouldn't have done it."

It? Hester felt like she was careening down a roller-coaster. Her heart caught in her throat. She looked at the girl. There was something in those eyes that said "it" had nothing to do with smoking anything.

"Don't do *it* again," Hester whispered back coarsely. She watched Jennifer's pupils tighten to pinpoints. Hester wanted to run back out to the field and confront Al, but after yesterday, after what he said, after what he called her…

Months later, right before graduation, Jennifer Masterson dropped out of school. Since she didn't get a good explanation from guidance, Hester went to her house to find out why she wasn't finishing out the year. Hester, in spite of the incident in the dugout, had grown fond of Jennifer. She was an enthusiastic student and seemed to genuinely enjoy Hester's teaching, and she was creative. There was no reason she shouldn't go on to college and beyond. When Hester knocked on the door, an old man answered. Hester was surprised to find out that he was Jennifer's father. He didn't have a clue where his daughter was.

"She turned eighteen last week and left. Said she's old enough to take care of herself, and I said, fine by me, if that's what you want." There was no way he was filling out a missing person's report. His child wasn't missing, she was stubborn. The girl's mother? She'd been dead for years. Mr. Masterson told Hester, "Mind your own damn business." And shut the door in her face.

Thirty-Two

"Hester, I swear on a stack of Bibles, Lou Latimer bragged to old Chet he was threatened by the police in Minnesota with arrest if he didn't do something about them."

"Dee, come on, has anybody in the park ever seen them?"

"No, but remember Lou lives in the middle of nowhere on the shore of freaking Lake Superior in the summer, so how could anyone from Pleasant Palms actually see them?"

"Well, then people shouldn't talk about something they don't know for a fact is true."

"But Lou himself keeps bringing them up. He told Chet and Chet told the Buchanans and Doris Buchanan told me that Lou said, 'They are over ten feet tall and look so damn real, it's scary.'"

Dee and Hester were sitting on the clubhouse deck the day before the big shuffleboard tournament, talking quietly, when Mrs. Florence and Rosario Domingo slowly walked up the ramp. Miriam Florence, at one hundred and two years of age, was the oldest person in the park, and Rosario, her young, Jamaican caretaker, stuck out like a sore thumb in Pleasant Palms. She was strikingly beautiful and close to six feet tall. She towered over Miriam, who seemed to shrink more every time Hester saw her.

Rosaria's arm was draped gently around Miriam's shoulders. Her long, black fingers looked like a giant tarantula nesting on the old lady's white sweater. Hester couldn't take her eyes off Rosaria, her gleaming skin, broad nose, full lips, her expression as calm as the surface of a dark pond. She wore a white cotton skirt that hugged her hips and a low-cut teal blouse that complimented her willowy neck. Her shiny hair was braided and coiled neatly around her head. She held her chin high, looked at Hester, and nodded, and the huge golden hoops in her ears jiggled.

Mrs. Florence was – rumor had it – the richest woman in the park, and miraculously for her age, still had her wits about her. At least that's what everyone assumed because, since Rosaria came to care for her, no one talked directly to Miriam. Rosaria answered the phone, answered any questions personally put to Miriam, and told whoever might ask that "her" Mrs. Florence was indeed fine, thank you very much, madam or sir. Clearly Rosaria now made all the decisions for Mrs. Florence, from the pair of golden flats the lady wore on her tiny feet, to the pink blush deftly brushed on what was left of the apples of her cheeks. Today the old woman smelled strongly of gardenias, and Rosario had dressed her in beige slacks, a lime green tunic, a white sweater, and a fluffy white hat. If you glanced at her quickly, she looked like a slice of key lime pie.

Rosaria settled Miriam into a rocker and pulled the sleeves down so they covered Mrs. Florence's impossibly thin wrists. She stood behind Miriam and gently pushed her chair, humming, "Don't

Worry, Be Happy." Miriam Florence might as well have been Rosario's little baby.

Hester couldn't help but stare at them; they looked so, well, content with each other. *Lucky Miriam, to have someone like Rosaria,* thought Hester as she was distracted by the flight of a flock of pelicans. Dee watched them too as she said, "That Lou Latimer is playing with fire. The people up in Minnesota won't stand for it. I'll bet it'll be on the national news. Hell, it's probably already on YouTube."

"Dee, I just don't believe it. It's ridiculous. Why would—"

"Shhh! Here he comes."

Lou, the reigning shuffleboard champion, walked past the wheelchair ramp and bounded up the six steps of the deck two at a time. He was a bald, short, slight man, but he had a flinty look about the eyes. He sat in the rocker next to Miriam and put his small feet on the railing. He had on sandals, and Hester's eyes were drawn to his toes, the ugliest ones she'd ever seen. They looked like claws, except for his big toes which stuck out like thumbs.

Rosario kept humming, which helped Hester relax, and she began to plan dinner in her head as she stared at the empty beach and the rolling waves: *vindaloo, the recipe was in that "Curries without Worries" cookbook, now where—*

"Bitch! Bitch! Mother fucker, pick up yo fuck'n phone! Bitch! Bitch! Mother fucker, pick up yo fuck'n phone! Bitch!"

"What in the hell?" Dee jumped up.

Lou struggled to pull his cell phone out of his pocket, while the disgusting ringtone blared, "Bitch! Bitch! Pick up yo..."

Hester shouted, "Lou Latimer, turn that off. That is disgusting, and we don't want to hear it."

Lou laughed and did nothing to stop the noise, but before Hester could say another word, Rosaria flew at Lou, grabbed the offending gadget from his hand, ran down to the water, and heaved it.

"Call the police! Someone call the police! You saw her. That nigger stole my cell phone. She stole my cell phone." Lou was out of his seat, his face beet red. He stomped his ugly-toed foot again and again. Infuriated, he yelled in Dee's and Hester's direction, "You saw what she did! You're my witnesses. If you have a phone, you better call the police."

"Are you kidding me?" Hester lowered the register of her voice like she used to when she was talking to one of her more defiant students. "That ringtone is offensive. You want the police; go back to your trailer and call them yourself. But if I were a cop, it would be you I'd be arresting."

Rosaria walked slowly back up to the deck, looked straight ahead, and kept her eyes on Mrs. Florence. Lou glowered at her but said nothing.

If looks could kill, thought Hester, *poor Rosaria would be dead.*

"None of you has heard the end of this!" Lou yelled as he clomped down the ramp.

Dee went over to Rosario and said, "We're so sorry."

"No mind to you, ladies. You didn't do nothing wrong." Rosaria helped Mrs. Florence to her feet. She put the old woman's hand through her arm and patted it gently like it was the head of a puppy. Hester saw tears in Miriam's eyes. They began to walk down the ramp. Rosario turned and said, "Ladies, no bother to me language like that. Me, alone, I might be laughing too, but not in front of my Mrs., here. No, not that in front of *my* lady."

The next day at seven in the morning, the shuffleboard team met in the community room before the tournament for coffee and donuts. Lou's absence was of immediate concern; they needed him to win. Lois Neiman tried to call him, but there was no answer. She went over to his trailer and banged on the door to no avail. Others fanned out around the park looking for the missing star, but he was nowhere to be found, and the first set started in fifteen minutes.

His car was parked next to his trailer. Desperate to find him, Ted Hunter and Jeff Mickleson jimmied Lou's trailer door open and searched the place. There was no sign of him.

The team headed off to the shuffleboard courts without their best player. It was difficult for the Delray Pines players to hide their relief at the news. The Pleasant Palmers, however, were torn between dismay that something terrible happened to one of their own and anger that perhaps Lou had blown off the tournament on purpose.

"How well," Lois wondered, "do any of us really know anybody else anyway?"

They held the start off as long as they could, but Lou never materialized. In fact days went by, his car still parked next to his empty trailer. When the park manager Harry Stout finally called the police, they didn't want to take the case. Lou Latimer didn't have dementia, did he? Well, then they couldn't put out a Silver Alert.

The next day, though, an officer named Alvarez showed up and asked around about Latimer's activities before he went missing. Eventually, he got to Dee, Hester, Rosaria, and Miriam. The four women and Officer Alvarez sat around a card table in the community room. Alvarez wanted to know if anything unusual happened that afternoon. Dee and Hester looked at each other and then at Rosaria, who was staring blankly at the policeman.

"Nothing happened, Officer. We were just sitting talking. Watching the birds. You know, that sort of thing." Hester was nervous. She wanted to be truthful, but if she said what happened, it would make Rosario look crazy.

"What were you talking about?"

"Dinner, I wasn't talking about dinner, but I was thinking about what I was going to make."

"Did you talk to Mr. Latimer?"

"No. Dee and I were talking. Rosaria was rocking Mrs. Florence in her chair, and Lou was sitting next to Mrs. Florence."

"What was he doing?"

"Nothing."

Dee nodded in agreement. Rosaria eyes locked on Hester's.

"Is that what happened?" Alvarez looked at Rosaria.

Rosaria was as still as a statue, her face finely chiseled obsidian with brown marbles for eyes. Alvarez shook his head, pushed his chair back, and exhaled. "Well, I guess that'll do it for now."

As the week went by, Hester's conscience bothered her less and less. If she told Alvarez about Lou's obnoxious cell-phone ringtone and how Rosaria ripped the phone out of his hand and threw it in the ocean, she would only stir up trouble for the loyal caretaker, whom many people in the park already avoided. *I would have done the same thing if I had the nerve,* Hester thought. *Lou got what he deserved, forget that thing on his phone, he called Rosario the "n" word.*

Several days after the interview with Officer Alvarez, Hester was up before sunrise. She couldn't stop worrying. All sorts of meetings were being held about the sale of the park. The once amorphous rumor was taking on a solid shape. Even Al was being sucked into the whirlwind of speculation.

Hester threw on sweats and flip-flops, and headed down to the marina to see if any boats were going out. The air was cool. The moon was gone already, but the sky was still speckled with stars. Hester could see the outline of someone standing at the end of the dock holding a bucket. The bucket was distinguishable because it was large and bright yellow. The person held it up and tipped it. Plop! Hester heard, but couldn't see, something being dumped into the water. There was another bucket. The person dumped something out of it too. Plop! He or she, Hester couldn't tell which it was, put the second bucket down.

Hester was curious. She kept walking. The sky lightened. It was a woman in a long grey dress. She was between the buckets circling her arms like pinwheels. Hester was about twenty feet away when she realized who it was and watched as Rosario stopped swinging her arms and spit right where she had dumped whatever was in the buckets.

Hester had a bad feeling about what might have been in those buckets. She backed away and left and went home and called Alvarez, and Dee.

Dee called back hours later. She'd been sleeping off a hangover— one Amstel Light too many, she confessed—but she was glad Hester called, because she heard something last night she was dying to tell her—Hester just wouldn't believe it.

"Wait a minute, Dee, me first." Hester cut her off and got right to the point about Rosaria probably killing Lou, probably cutting him up into little pieces, probably spending the whole night dumping his body parts into the Intracoastal bucketful by bucketful. She told Dee she called Officer Alvarez the minute she got home. She almost said one dead person on her conscience was enough, but stopped herself in time.

"Well, you might see things differently when I tell you what I heard from Joan Sampson last night. Joan and Hank Sampson are new here this season and from Minnesota, one town away from Lou's. Anyway, last summer they go for a drive down this rural road with big houses set back on huge lots when Hank sees something that makes him slam on the brakes. Right by the road on either side of this big driveway, instead of urns or pillars or lions, are life-size sculptures of naked slaves, one male, the other female. They have on slave collars and chains, and they have scars from whippings.

"Then down here Hank and Joan are introduced to Lou at some party and after a few drinks he whips out a fistful of photos of the 'magnificent sculptures' he commissioned for his front entrance. The Sampson's go into shock cause Lou's sculptures are the exact ones they drove past. 'Why, now I have a pair of my own,' Lou says. Joan said she was sick to her stomach. She and Hank left the party and swore they'd never go to another party if Lou Latimer was going to be there.

"Hester, now tell me you aren't surprised something horrible like this didn't happen to that jerk Latimer sooner."

Hester was speechless. She didn't know if what Dee told her made her feel better, or worse, and she hadn't clue what she'd say to Alvarez when he got back to her.

Thirty-Three

It took a long time, but eventually Al's rage subsided, and Hester accepted Al's possible dalliance, probably nothing more than a kiss, with Jennifer as a foolish, and potentially ruinous, attempt to hurt Hester back. And so they made peace with each other and the years passed. Hester and Al traveled to, and bought things back from, all the ends of the earth. It wasn't a perfect life, a perfect life would've included a houseful of noisy Murphys; but it was a decent life, and they got along decently, or so it seemed to Hester.

Then Nina came along, and Hester turned into a home body and made the motherless girl the center of her shrinking universe.

One evening, Al was still at school, and snow was falling more heavily than it had all that winter. When the doorbell rang, it startled Hester. She dropped the knife she was using to cut up the chicken and hurried from the kitchen into the hallway. Through the lace curtain on the door window she saw Nina standing on the porch without a hat. Her hair hung in wet clumps on her shoulders, and her nose was running. She wiped it on her glove, inspected the mucous, and began rubbing it into her jeans as Hester let her in.

"Nina, you must be so cold. I told you not to bother to come over, not on a day like this."

Nina said nothing. She followed Hester into the living room, took off her gloves and coat, and plopped them on the coffee table. Hester picked the things up. "I better hang these in the cellar way, they're soaked." When Hester came back, Nina was in the hallway looking up the stairs.

"Mr. Murphy's still at school, Nina, if that's who you're looking for."

"Oh no, Mrs. Murphy, I was just noticing how nice your house is, really nice. It must be nice to live here. I've always lived in apartments, small apartments. Even my aunt's house is small compared to your house."

"Nina, you're acting like you've never been here before."

"No, it's just that every time I am here, I see something I didn't notice before. Like I never noticed that picture over there before." Nina turned and pointed at a painting over the sofa.

"Don't you just love it?" said Hester. "Charles Ames did that painting. He's got a good reputation. Al, I mean, Mr. Murphy and I found it at the Golden Nugget Flea Market and had to have it. It's the Prallsville Mill, up the river in Stockton. Don't you think it looks wonderful over the sofa?"

"Yeah, it looks nice." Nina leaned over the sofa to get a closer look. With her back to Hester, she said, "When will Mr. Murphy be home?"

"I have no idea."

"Do you have to go out anywhere?"

"Who, me? Not in this blizzard!"

"Oh, it's not so bad out."

"It's bad enough. But we'll worry about the weather later. You, young lady, need to get your paper done. I'll put the chicken in the fridge and be right back."

"Maybe when I'm finished writing, I can help you make dinner? Or something?" Nina shouted after Hester.

Hester hesitated. If Nina helped her with dinner, she'd want to stay. Maybe that wasn't a good idea. What would other students think if Nina told them she'd stayed for dinner with the Murphys? What would their parents think? Helping Nina catch up academically one or two afternoons a week was one thing, but spending the entire evening with Al and her—well, that seemed like too much of a good thing.

When Hester first thought about tutoring Nina at their house, she ran the idea by Al. She wanted to make sure she wasn't putting either of their careers in jeopardy.

"Just invite her over, Hester, and don't worry about it," Al said.

"But am I crossing a line with her?" Hester persisted.

"No."

"I just want to be sure I'm not making a mistake," Hester said, then added, "we're not making a mistake."

"Trust me. Don't be so paranoid, Hester." Al was cleaning dirt from under his fingernails with a toothpick. "I'm the VP. Nobody's got the nerve to say anything about my wife, do they? Besides, Nina's a girl, you're a middle-aged woman. It's not like you're going to seduce her or anything."

"Al!"

"You want to seduce her, don't you, Hester?"

"Stop that!"

"Can't you tell I'm joking?"

"Al, you are not funny."

"What the hell happened to your sense of humor, Hester?"

"I have a great sense of humor. It's just that what you are saying is not funny."

"Oh yes, it is, and you know it." His voice was gruff.

And, as if on cue, Hester did start to laugh a little.

"Look, see I am making you laugh." And Al laughed too.

"Al, be serious for a minute. What I'm trying to say is that Nina was in my sophomore class last year, and she'll probably be in my senior class next year. I don't want anyone to think Nina will have an unfair advantage if she's at our house all the time and I'm helping her. Some parents will definitely think I'm playing favorites if they find out."

"Don't worry. You've gone out of your way to help Nina catch up. Hell, you've gone out of your way to care about a student no one else seems to care about. That's all we have to say, Mrs. Murphy."

"Got it, Mr. Murphy." Hester smiled gratefully at Al and turned to leave the room. It was time she got started on their dinner.

"One more thing, Mrs. Murphy."

Hester stopped and turned back. "And what might that be, Mr. Murphy?"

"Before I eat dinner, I want dessert."

"You want the cake before the raviolis?"

"No, I want you before the raviolis. Fuck the cake." Al was out of his seat, and Hester was in his arms laughing like a school girl. See, she did have a great sense of humor.

At first, Nina came to the house twice a week, but as her junior reading selections grew more difficult, she seemed be around almost every night. Once in a great while, Hester went out with some people in her department and Nina still came over and Al worked with her. Before the end of the first semester, Nina was at the top of her class. If Hester had been her natural-born mother, she couldn't have been more proud.

Now it was second semester, the dead of winter. Nina stood by the sink in the kitchen rinsing the potatoes. "Please, Mrs. M, can I stay?"

Hester put the chicken in the oven and smiled at Nina, "Sure, honey, you can stay for dinner, as long as it's okay with your aunt. You better call her now, in case she's expecting you."

"I don't have to call her."

"Yes, you have to call her, or you can't stay."

"But, Mrs. Murphy, please, she's probably not even home."

Hester handed Nina her cell phone. "Call her now, Miss Nina."

Nina took the phone and tapped in some numbers while she stared into Hester's eyes with a hangdog expression on her face as if to say, okay, you satisfied. "Hello, Aunt Linda, it's me, Nina…" She kept talking as she turned away from Hester. "Okay, okay, okay…"

Hester looked over and saw Nina's thumb on the End Call button. Hester said nothing as the silly child pretended to be chatting while she followed Hester into the dining room. *What a little actress,* thought Hester.

Thirty-Four

Turkey buzzards floated like cinders bursting from the inferno of the setting sun. Al and Hester sat in beach chairs on the lawn along the Intracoastal. They sipped their drinks while watching the birds circle and dive for dead rodents between the condos on the opposite shore.

They were discussing what kind of new refrigerator they should buy for their trailer—their old one just conked out. Hester had seen a retro one by Smeg in *Coastal Living*. It was expensive, but she loved it. Al wanted to buy the cheapest one they could find, since the place might be sold, which Hester reminded him was not a fact yet. But Al hammered his point home, "It's not up to me if this place sells or not. Everyone gets a vote, and right about now, I'm pretty sure which way it's going to go, so I am sure as hell not going to sink a lot of money into 23 Fish Tail Lane, Hester. Get your head out of the sand. Stop living in denial. All these people want is money." He took a sip of his Corona.

Hester watched the lime slide down inside the neck of the bottle, wondering if her husband was shifting his allegiance to the pro-sale faction. The thought made her blood turn cold. Maybe if she could convince him to buy the pricey fridge, he'd be more committed to not selling. How much beer would Al have to drink before she had a snowball's chance in hell of getting her way?

Simon Cartright came along with his chair and his gin and tonic in a plastic coffee to-go mug. He didn't wait for an invitation to join them, shook his folding chair open, and started talking about his friend Larry, who had a checkup that morning, his doctor wanted him to try some new drugs to shrink his prostate.

When neither Hester nor Al spoke, Simon shut up, and the three of them stared silently at the parasitic birds.

Eventually Al said, "So, Simon, you've been at Pleasant Palms longer than anyone else, since the late sixties I've been told, so are you going to vote to sell or what?"

Not this again! Hester was sick of all the talk. As bad as things had been these past months for Hester, they could be worse. She thought of Rosaria. Would she have to borrow the woman's yellow buckets? Would she have to buy a chainsaw to saw Nina up into manageable pieces? The police hadn't arrested Rosario. Perhaps they never would, all the evidence having been devoured by the local barracudas. Officer Alvarez interviewed Hester again after her phone call. She told him what she saw on the dock, though she hadn't seen anything clearly, the sun not even completely up yet.

"Well..." Simon hesitated. "Well, Larry and I have been here more than thirty-six years. Larry in his place, me in mine." The man's glassy eyes shifted quickly left, right, left like he was in a foxhole and bombs were bursting all around him. Dee had told Hester the men were partners, but there was a stupid, at least to Hester's way of thinking, park rule: only married couples could cohabitate. But Simon and Larry worked around the rule. They both owned their own units and alternated nights between Simon's place on Screw Pine Way and Larry's on African Oil Lane. Overnight guests were allowed.

"Well…" He started again. "I will vote yes. I love Pleasant Palms, but a million dollars in my pocket means I won't have to live the way other people think I should. And that will make the few years I have left, a whole lot happier."

"And what about Larry?"

"Oh, we are on the same page, as always."

"But what if we don't get a million dollars each for our units?"

"But that's the deal on the table, and I trust Sea to Sea Development. They are a Fortune 500 company, solid. Larry checked them out on the Internet. You can trust them. We'll get that million each." Simon stared at Al as he took a sip of his drink. "What about the two of you? How are you voting?"

"I didn't want to sell at first, but now that I'm talking to people I'm starting to feel a little better about the deal. Yeah, a million dollars would be nice to have, wouldn't it?" Al looked at Hester with a gleam in his eyes, and her heart sank. God, she hoped it was just the beer talking.

Thirty-Five

It was an overcast June evening. The senior class lined up along the football field for the graduation procession. Hester stood in the back entranceway to the school searching the crowd for Nina and thinking about how quickly the years had passed since the girl came into her life.

There she is! Hester spied the peace sign Nina had spray-painted in neon pink on the top of her cap. *What was the girl thinking?*

Hester looked down at her chest. Her T-shirt with the peace sign. She'd worn it that awful day. Peace signs had faded from popularity for years, but now they were everywhere. Every time she saw one it took her back to that moment in time she longed to erase. Ironically, though, she'd kept her T-shirt. Some nights, full of guilt, in lieu of self-flagellation, which knew some saints were known to have done, she wore that shirt to bed as penance. Some cold days even, to remind herself she was far from perfect, she wore it under a sweater.

Nina was standing off to the side. Hester watched as Al walked up to her and they hugged. *At least we have her,* thought Hester gratefully.

Preferring to work behind the scenes, Hester volunteered once again to handle the distribution and collection of the caps and gowns. Dressing up in one herself and marching with the rest of the faculty wasn't her style. Besides, Al needed someone he could trust to see that the two-hundred-plus rentals were neatly boxed and ready to be shipped back to the company the next morning. Hester worked all afternoon setting up tables in the gym and organizing the boxes. With not much to do until the conclusion of the ceremony, she patted the pocket of her jeans jacket to make sure she had the card she'd gotten for Nina. On the front was a drawing of an oak tree. Beneath it was a quote from Coleridge, "Friendship is a sheltering tree." It was blank inside, and Hester had written the following:

Dearest Nina,

It has been a long hard journey. You have overcome many obstacles to be where you are today. But this is not the end, this is only the beginning. College is ahead of you, and I know you will excel. Remember, the love of your mother is with you always and has helped you to survive all that you have gone through. She would have treasured this day, more than even Mr. Murphy and I do. We care deeply for you and will be here if you ever need us, so don't hesitate to call. How proud we are of you!

Congratulations and keep in mind the words of Louisa May Alcott: "Be not afraid of storms for you are learning to sail your ship." In other words, when things go wrong and you are afraid, trust in yourself that you will know the right thing to do.

With much fondness,

Mrs. M

The band started, and the black line of students snaked its way around the perimeter of the field and into the rows of seats. The crowd stood until the graduates were in their places and Minister Norway began with an invocation. Hester stepped out onto the grass and stood on tiptoes, looking for Nina. She saw Al on the stage seated next to Superintendent Law. The faculty, in an unusual seating arrangement Al dreamt up several years ago, faced the graduates and parents.

It had been sunny all day, but now clouds were moving in and it was growing dark. Hester saw Al look up. Principal Glatton, the new principal, was at the microphone giving his speech and seemed unaware of the changing weather. The wind picked up, a flash of lightning bolted through the sky. Thunder rumbled. More lightning. Then the rain came down in sheets and everyone ran for the building.

Hester stood behind the heavy door and held it while the crowd jostled their way through. As more and more people jammed themselves into the narrow hall, Hester was trapped behind the door. It was pressing into her with such force she feared being crushed to death. She shoved against the door with every bit of her strength and succeeded in slamming it closed, unwittingly, right in somebody's face. She tried to open it up again, but she was being swept along by others who were trying to make their way down the hall.

The mass of panicked humanity flowed into the gymnasium, where finally they were able to spread out. Everyone, except Hester and the custodians, who already had mops in hands, was soaked. The people moved the boxes and sat on the tables and flung their drenched jackets about, making themselves at home to wait out the storm.

In a matter of minutes, the room was filled to capacity. Hester was stuck in the midst of a jumble of damp arms and sharp elbows. Noise bounced off the rafters in an incoherent racket. The air felt like it had been sucked out of the room. Hester was trying to maneuver through the crowd in search of a familiar face, someone who might help her impose some order on this chaos, when she felt a hand on her shoulder. Hester spun around.

"My God, Theo! You frightened me."

"Calm down, Hester. It's only me." He was standing so close to her they were almost touching.

"Can you believe this mess?" Hester tried to step back, but Theo put his arm around her.

"It's nothing like the mess your husband's gotten himself into."

"What?" Hester tried to pull away. "Come on, Theo, give Al a break. Just because you don't—"

He put his lips next to her ear. "It doesn't have a fucking thing to do with me liking him or not. I'm only telling you this because I care about you. I've always cared about you."

"Theo, for God's sake, you're married."

"So what?"

"What exactly are you trying to tell me, Theo? That Al screwed up tonight by not watching the Weather Channel or by not being able to predict a fluke meteorological event? Is that what you're trying to tell me?"

"Don't be so naïve, Hester."

"Maybe I'm naïve, but you, Theo Ottinger, are crazy." Hester hated the fact that Theo had been after her for years. She'd tried hard to discourage him, but he just didn't seem to get the message.

"Hester, I am going to tell you something that you can never tell anyone I told you. I don't want to lose my job over this. If it ever gets out that I'm the big mouth, and Al lies his way out of it, well then, I'm the one who's going to be screwed. I know you don't want to admit it, but these administrators stick together, and they're sneaks, fucking sneaks about it."

Theo's breath was hot in Hester's ear. She'd never heard him talk like this. She leaned back and looked him in the eyes. What she saw there, the seriousness, the concern, the—she couldn't deny it—passion, made her feel like she'd fallen overboard in rough seas. Did she want to hear what he was going to say? Did she want him to throw her a life preserver or to let her drown?

"No, Theo, no, I don't want to know anything about Al. Just leave us the hell alone, please." Hester was shaking her head from side to side.

Theo grabbed her chin and turned her face so he could whisper in her ear again, "Hester, it's better to know. I don't want to hurt you, but you have to know so no one else will get hurt."

"Shut up, Theo, just shut up." She knocked his hand away from her face and put both hands over her ears. She tried to get away from him, but they were surrounded by people. Hester twisted her head around, looking for a way out. She saw Al coming toward them. But before he got there, Theo pulled her close again and she felt his erection.

Thirty-Six

The Pleasant Palms auditorium was filled beyond capacity, standing room only, and Alma Alvin was in all her glory. Eve, Marvin, and Hester couldn't get away from her. She was telling them about her young podiatrist who said for seventy-five, she had amazingly young-looking feet. He checked them from all angles, even put them up by his face and seemed to sniff them. Too bad about the one bunion that had become infected, because now he had to remove her little toe, which would ruin the symmetry of her nearly perfect feet.

"If I'd been born in China, he said, the Emperor's eunuchs would have chosen me to have my feet bound." Alma spoke without taking a breath. "My mother would've been instructed to start binding them when I turned seven and to continue tightening the binding until all of the small bones of my feet were crushed, and they curled up like lotus blossoms. And if my feet turned out right the Emperor would marry me. I wanted to ask Dr. Ying why men wanted women to have such tiny feet, but I didn't. Then Dr. Ying said that even though my feet are too big, they do remind him of lotus blossoms. I was so…"

Hester glanced down and saw Alma's gnarled toes as she made her way through the crowd to find Al. She'd be able to pick him out because lately he started wearing clothes in wild colors, things like flamingo pink polo shirts and royal blue shorts. And lately, she started wearing just the opposite, dark somber-looking tops, black pants, a black hat. As flamboyant as Al's fashion sense was getting, he still didn't look as ridiculous as Ralph Trotman, the president of the board of directors, who sported a green madras jacket, a yellow shirt, and robin's egg blue slacks. His comb-over in place, he approached the podium and started the meeting.

"It's Tuesday, February twenty-eighth, 2004, the day of reckoning for Pleasant Palms Trailer Park. For close to eighty years, our small community has worked to create our own little heaven on earth, but it may be time for us to move on to an even better way of life. Secretary Hal Mason and Manager Reed Rush are the only ones who know the results of yesterday's vote. I see they are smiling, so let's turn the meeting over to Hal Mason and end the suspense."

Applause echoed through the auditorium, and from where Hester stood, she watched Clayton's grin widen. Al shifted his weight from his leg with the bum ankle to the other one and mumbled to himself, "Idiots. I'll bet they fucking sold the place." And Hester realized that it had been the beer talking the other night with Simon. She felt relieved to know Al voted against the sale, because yesterday she didn't believe him when he said he did.

Hal with his hanging sack of neck flesh looked in profile like a pelican with a fish in his gullet. He was wearing a flashy Hawaiian shirt.

"Well, here it is…" He waved a large white envelope in the air. "The official results!"

He fumbled trying to open it, and it drifted to the ground like a gliding egret. The manager snatched it up and handed it back to Hal.

"Thank you, we sure don't want anything to happen to this." He pried open the back.

"What the hell is taking the old geezer so long?" Al spoke loud enough for more than a few people to hear.

"Give the guy a fucking break, Murphy." Steve Bearing from over on Screw Pine shot Al a dirty look.

Hal finally got the paper out, shook it open, and spoke into the mike, "There are three hundred shares in Pleasant Palms Trailer Park. Each of the three hundred units has one vote. In order for the sale to take place, eighty percent of the shareholders would have to vote to sell. Two hundred and forty is the magic number, folks." He paused. His eyes skimmed the crowd. "The official tally is two hundred and forty-two for the sale and fifty-eight against! We did it! Congratulations, fellow millionaires!"

Al muttered something Hester didn't hear. The crowd was cheering. Hester moved closer to Al, panic rising in her chest. She gulped for air. It felt like someone was stepping on her windpipe. Al yelled, "What are they thinking? I am so disgusted with this whole place. These people are stupid, stupid fucking idiots."

What the hell am I going to do now? Hester's mind was in a tailspin. *These people are going to dig this whole place up, and I can't stop them.*

Al was still hollering, "Wait until they see what happens! Wait until they don't get half what they think they will!"

Hester was afraid he was going to hit somebody, "Calm down, would you, Al? Try to think positively. Look, I'm not happy either, but at least we'll have a million dollars."

"Hester, you are dumber than all these people put together. Didn't you listen to what I said, we'll be lucky if we get half that!" Al pushed his way through the jubilant crowd. His head was down, his hands shoved in his pockets, his limp more pronounced than ever before.

She watched him retreat and his words echoed in her head, "… you are dumber than all these people put together." Al wounded her before and even rubbed salt in those wounds, but he never before called her dumb. And she was only trying to calm him down so he wouldn't go off and hit someone. She didn't give a damn about a million dollars, no amount of money was worth what she was going to have to do. And she didn't have a plan yet.

Al put the last straw on the camel's back. Hester couldn't take anymore. She stood stock still in the midst of the celebratory bedlam and lost it. She imagined herself in the ladies room on the hundred and tenth floor of Tower One. She was washing her hands, admiring her reflection in the mirror. A good hair day, nice job on her make-up, maybe after work she'd go shopping for a…suddenly there's a crash, a rumble, and the whole building is collapsing, she's going down with it, it is taking her down, she's better than already dead.

Yes, everyone around her was cheering, but she felt dead. Yes, she was "dumber than all these other people." Hadn't she proven it by trying to protect Al's sorry ass. *Now there was a dumb thing to do if ever there was one.*

Thirty-Seven

After the fiasco in the gym Hester was lying in bed in the dark thinking about how odd Theo Ottinger's behavior had been, when Al rolled over to face her and said, "You awake, Hester? My ankle's throbbing. I can't sleep."

She was awake, but didn't answer. Al had been complaining about his stupid ankle for years. She was tired of listening to him whine about it because a bad ankle was a small price to pay not to go to Vietnam. She used to keep reminding him of that. "Al," she'd say, "you know that ankle kept you out of the service and out of Vietnam. Did you forget that if it weren't for that ankle, you would've been the first to go? Did you forget that your birthday was September 14, the first birth date picked in that awful lottery?"

Al could've ended up in a jungle somewhere, addicted to heroin, forced to kill people, sick with some disease, maimed, deranged, or, worse yet, dead. Hester would remind him of all of this. She would tell him about the veteran's hospital in Philadelphia where she volunteered to help with the amputees. They were young guys, handsome young guys, with no arms or legs, with half a face, with a hole in their skull, with their penises blown off.

"It was a blessing, Al, a goddamn blessing you shattered your ankle in that high school football game. It was a true gift from God, and you should be thankful," Hester would add with a sigh.

But tonight Hester was tired, and she didn't want to coddle Al or talk about the war.

When she didn't answer him, he moved closer to her and slipped his cool hand under her pajama top, and began kneading her breast, "I saw that twerp Theo all over you tonight. What was he in your ear about?"

Hester didn't answer, but thought, *what was he in my ear about?* Was Theo trying to stir up trouble or was there something Al needed to tell her?

"Hester, Hester, you fucking love goddess, even the young married men are after you." He rubbed her breast harder.

"Mad at me for interrupting, huh? Well, too bad for little Theodore. You're my wife, and he can keep his pencil dick to himself." Al rolled on his back and lifted Hester on top of him in one smooth move. His hands cupped her buttocks. "You are still so round and firm. It's all of that exercise you get running away from the younger men. How's this for a stud?" He pulled her nightgown up and forced himself into her. Hester propped herself up on her arms to keep her face from touching his. She really wasn't in the mood, but Al certainly was, even after all of the chaos in the gym.

Al had gotten that situation under control by getting on the loud speaker and canceling the entire graduation ceremony until the next day. People were angry about his decision, but Al stuck to it, and finally everyone left. Al and she straightened out the caps and gowns and locked up the building. When they got outside, Nina was standing in the rain alone. They took her with them for pizza. It broke Hester's heart that not one person from her family had been there and probably wouldn't be tomorrow night either. After dinner, Al reached across the table and took both of the girl's small hands in his and told her how important she was to Hester and to him. It made Nina blush, but it filled Hester's heart with joy to see Al acting like a real father. Tomorrow, Hester would order roses for Nina and say they were from Al.

Even though Al had handled the mess in the gym so competently and had been so sweet with Nina, Hester couldn't stop worrying about what Theo said, "…it's better to know…you have to know so no one else will get hurt." What did she "have to know"? Who else "will get hurt"? She should've let Theo tell her.

Al was breathing heavily, his penis thick as a hunk of salami.

"Baby, baby, make me come."

All he needed was for Hester to thrust slightly, and it would be over. But Hester wanted to stop everything and confront him. She wanted to say, "Hey, Al, what was Theo in my ear about? What do I need to know, and who's going to get hurt if I don't?" But before she could get off him, his body went rigid, he hollered something about God, and came. As soon as he let go of her, Hester got up and went into the bathroom.

By the time she cleaned herself up and got back in bed, Al was snoring. No hug, no honey, that was great, no nothing. It was the first time they'd done it without one kiss.

Hester was wide awake. She moved as far from Al's body as she could get and lay watching the shadows on the ceiling and listening to the rain. Had Al hurt someone? Another staff member? He'd certainly hurt her more than a few times. Yes, she knew what it felt like to be hurt, to be young and hurt. She knew what it was to fight your own private war, to stand in a dormitory hallway and bleed like a wounded sow.

Thirty-Eight

Hester didn't go back to the trailer after the meeting but headed to the beach and followed a turtle track from a mound beneath the palms to the water. The path was wide; the flippers had cut deep wedges in the sand. Hester was sorry she hadn't made more of an effort to stand watch one night for one of the behemoth leatherbacks in the act of depositing her eggs.

Not many shells tumbled in the surf, but a long, thin, eel-like fish washed up in front of Hester. Its needle nose was long and hard as a beak, and the thick pale body narrowed to a point like an uncircumcised penis.

"Hey, Hester, great news, huh?" Nancy George came up behind Hester. Darlene Erman was with her.

"Well, I was just thinking about that."

"What's to think about?" Darlene flipped the dead fish over with her foot. "A million bucks, one million dollars each!"

"Well, yes, a million dollars is a lot of money, but Al and I don't want to leave Pleasant…" There she was, doing it again. Always saying what Al thought like she thought it too. Hester corrected herself, "No, Al doesn't want to leave Pleasant Palms, and I'm not sure what I want."

"It's a done deal now, Hester, so chin up," said Nancy. "What kind of fish is that anyway, Darlene? Looks like a slick dick, doesn't it?" She bent over and put her chubby hands on her fat knees to examine the underside of the creature.

"What are the two of you going to do?" Hester asked to be polite.

"I guess it's safe to tell her now, Darlene." Nancy straightened up slowly.

"I would say so." The wrinkles beneath Darlene's eyes deepened as she squinted in the sunlight. "Listen, Hester, Nancy and I have been, well, in love for fifteen years. It's been a strain on us to hide our relationship all of that time. We've never told anyone here about our real lives, about who we really are, because we were afraid we'd be thrown out of Pleasant Palms."

"Darlene and I have had to pretend for too long," said Nancy. "Damn it, I'm seventy-two years old, I spent a lifetime doing what was expected of me. I got married, had children, took care of my sick husband until the day he died, knowing deep inside the life I was living was not the right life for me. It wasn't who I really was. I never did a thing wrong; yet, I felt like a criminal for wanting more."

"And my life, until I met Nancy was a living hell." Darlene took Nancy's hand. "I had two bad marriages, and thank goodness, no children. I made too many other mistakes to mention—back in the sixties, if you can imagine it, I worked for a psychologist as a sexual surrogate for men with impotency problems. Me? Imagine that. And I wasn't even into men, even then I knew I was different. Years later, when I'm turning fifty, with a lousy job at a dental clinic, with no love life, I meet Nancy at, of all places, her son's wedding. He was marrying a young hygienist who worked in our clinic. When we met, Nancy took my hand and held onto it just a second longer than usual. I felt something in her touch right from the beginning."

Hester stood silently for a minute looking at the pair, the tide rising, the feet of the women disappearing in the sand. She couldn't say she was stunned by their confession, that she hadn't suspected they were more than friends. *Odd,* Hester thought, *how the sale of the park seems to be flushing everyone out of one closet or another.*

"I am truly happy for the both of you." Hester meant it. They were a good match.

Nancy extricated her feet from the sand and moved a step closer to Hester. Her teeth were yellowed, and her breath smelled of peanuts, but her eyes drew Hester into their cobalt depths. "When we each get our million, we're moving to Camp Sister Spirit, a womyn's—that's w-o-m-y-n's—land in a town called Ovett, Mississippi. Have you heard of it?"

"No, never," said Hester.

"You probably wouldn't be interested, but the camp is a community of womyn. No men allowed. Get it. No m-e-n. That's why they spell womyn with a 'y' instead of an 'e.' Think of it, no testosterone for miles. The theory is men tend toward confrontation and..."

"Domination," Darlene finished her sentence.

"I was going to say control," Nancy said.

"Well, same thing."

"Not really, Darlene, but that's beside the point. When a man's around, no one listens to a woman, so we're going somewhere where they aren't."

"You bet, honey." Darlene hugged Nancy. Her back was toward Hester, and when the wind parted her short hair, Hester saw scabs in the folds of her neck fat. The scabs reminded Hester of Marge Lampo, a comedienne Al and she saw at a comedy club in New Jersey.

Lampo was a big woman like Nancy, but with a loud mouth and a thick Jersey accent. She was an over-the-top composite of all things female and Garden State, a caricature of the real women who were known for being fast and up-front. Her monologue was irreverent to say the least. She said things like, bad men like fat chicks because their backsides are big enough for them to hide behind when the cops come, or Italian men talk like they're in the mob when all they're connected to is a fork. Hester laughed in spite of herself. Al, on the other hand, was insulted.

The show ended with Lampo saying Courtney Love kissed Marge on the lips one time. Lampo said something to the effect that Courtney was pretty stupid about a lot of things, but she sure knew a hot chick when she saw one, even if she, Lampo, did have scabs in the folds of her double chins.

Hester didn't think that part was funny.

"Hey," Nancy said to Hester over Darlene's shoulder, "talking about testosterone, your husband got pretty loud at the meeting. Is he over it?"

"Good question," Hester mumbled and looked out over the ocean.

The women said good-bye and walked north on the beach. Hester walked south to the jetty and sat down on a smooth boulder. It was close to eighty degrees, and Hester fretted for a minute about not having applied sunscreen, but a more ominous worry arose in her mind. She pictured angry Al storming out of the meeting. She pictured sullen Al sitting in his La-Z-Boy clicking his remote. She pictured naked Al coming towards her, wanting her to make him happy. She didn't think she could, ever again.

Thirty-Nine

Walking into the school foyer was like entering Hades. It was the last week of June, and since only the main office was air-conditioned, the rest of the building was hot as hell. Hester headed drearily down the hall. As she passed the glass-enclosed, climate-controlled, inner-sanctum of the principal and vice principal, she noticed the condensation on the windows and thought, *I hope they freeze to death in there.* Lydia and Diane, the two secretaries whose desks were strategically positioned to barricade the entrances to Glatton's and Al's offices, actually had sweaters on. *Sweaters!* Hester shook her head. *The injustice of it all.*

Hester worked in her blistering hot classroom until noon, when she sat down to rest because she was feeling dehydrated and morose. She thought about it and decided, Theo was a nothing but a drama queen, and Al had a good excuse for falling asleep right after ejaculating. The fiasco in the gym must have taken a toll on him. She'd do something nice for him. She'd go down to his office and invite him to lunch.

Rummaging in her pocketbook for a couple of Kleenex to blot the perspiration off her nose, Hester headed back through the searing heat in the hall. She saw a flurry of activity in the main office. Several top administrators, one board member, and the district's attorney filled the space between Lydia's and Diane's desks. They were gesticulating wildly to each other. Hester pulled the door open; a wave of hotness went in with her and made everyone turn to look. But they all quickly averted their eyes, which gave Hester a bad feeling.

"Let's take this behind closed doors, why don't we?" the attorney said and began ushering everyone into Glatton's office. Lydia and Diane, who Hester was sure knew exactly what was going on, turned back to their computers.

Hester didn't take the hint. "Hey, girls, what's going on?"

Diane tried to sound casual, "Oh, some big meeting or other, probably nothing, nothing they told us about anyway."

"Is Al in his office?"

Lydia swiveled in her chair to face Hester. "No," she said, and swiveled back to rummage through some files.

"Well, do you know where he is, or is that some sort of secret too?" Hester's patience was wearing thin. What was the big deal?

"Look, Hester." Diane got up and came around the side of her desk. She stood close to Hester and whispered, "Honestly, we're not sure what's going on, but Al's in Glatton's office, and something pretty unsavory seems to be going down. Right, Lydia?" She glanced over at Lydia.

"Right." Lydia whispered too. "I think it has something to do with some of the senior girls accusing one of the male teachers of molesting them. But please, don't say I said anything."

"Oh my God, what a mess. Don't worry, Lydia…Diane. I won't say a word about it until Al brings it up. But who do you think it is? The teacher, I mean?" Hester thought of Theo. He'd gotten so bold with her.

"Not a clue, Mrs. Murphy." Diane went behind her desk and sat down.

"Me either," Lydia said as she stuffed papers into a folder.

Hester knew they both knew exactly who the pervert was. Nothing could happen in this microenvironment without them finding out.

"Well, I hope it isn't true, but if it is, I hope whoever the son of a gun is, he gets what he deserves. Right, ladies?"

"Right, Mrs. Murphy."

Hester disappointed she wouldn't be able to see Al and disgusted by this latest scandal, went back to her classroom and licked two melted Hershey bars off their wrappers for lunch. *Why can't these men just keep it in their pants and leave these poor kids alone?* She just didn't get it.

When Al wasn't home by nine, Hester called his cell phone, and as the night progressed she kept hitting Redial. By eleven she was angry and screamed into the phone, "Don't bother to come home!" She went to bed. She was reading *The Winter of Our Discontent*. The fictitious troubles of the married couple in the novel did little to distract her. She heard the front door open and footsteps on the stairs. Al tripped. "Fuck," he grunted and hit the wall.

"I'm retiring. I fuckin' decided. I've had it with that fuckin' place." He stood in the doorway of the bedroom, bracing himself with both hands. He banged his head into one side of the doorjamb. "Do whatever ya want, but I'm fuckin' through." Hester knew better than to say anything when he was like this. He turned away and went into the front bedroom. After Hester heard the thud of his body on the mattress and the sound of his snoring—wind rustling through dried cornfields was what it reminded her of—she got out of bed to look at him.

He was on his back fully dressed. Through the slats of the blinds, the street light ran in stripes across him. His mouth was open. His teeth caught the light like small dull moons. What he said might just be the booze talking; but that something terrible happened in Glatton's office was a fact. Her mind went back to the summer they went horseback riding along the rim of the Yellowstone Canyon. Al was in front of Hester; and for one hour, which seemed more like an eternity, she worried that the old horse Al was on would misstep and Al would plummet off the edge of the precipice. How frightened she'd been—not for herself, she wasn't worried about herself—but for Al.

How would she survive if anything ever happened to him? He was everything to her. Then…and now.

Hester went back and sat on the end of their bed to look out the window. The lights in the shopping center across the river glowed, and the almost full moon cast an eerie white path over the lawn. It was too light out to see the stars. She wouldn't know if one were falling or not.

Forty

Two days later Debbie from the Pleasant Palms office knocked on the door of their trailer. Al was in his La-Z-Boy with the TV blaring—Judge Joe Brown rapping his gavel on the desk, shaking it in the air.

Hester stopped making the coffee and went to the door. She knew Al wouldn't. Debbie handed a paper to Hester. "It's important; make sure you read the whole thing."

Hester thanked her and handed it to Al, who immediately hit the Mute button and started reading. Hester went back to the kitchen and plugged in the percolator.

"Hester, hand me my cheaters." Al was never one to skip the fine print. Hester tossed him his glasses. He put them on and read silently for few more minutes before he exploded. "What the hell? Are they kidding? Listen to this, and I quote, 'Ribsom & Newton are due ten percent, or thirty million, of the three hundred million sale price. The buyers have put down ten million and the board of directors has voted to give the Ribsom & Newton nine-point-seven million of this down payment to assure a smooth closing. Each of the three hundred unit owners in the park will receive an equal share of the remaining three hundred thousand dollars from the down payment, or a sum of one thousand dollars each…'"

His voice grew louder. "As each unit owner must share in the cost of legal representation, the final figure to be equally distributed is two hundred and seventy million, but there may be other costs that may lower the final figure. The sale is contingent on a thirty-day closing, which means all units must be vacated in thirty days from today.' Can you believe this?" Al got up, went into the kitchen, and tossed the paper on the counter.

"Already we're down to nine hundred thousand, and no one has said one word about capital gains. That could be another forty percent. And what are the mysterious 'other costs'? Hester, do you understand what this means?"

Hester was scrubbing the sink with Clorox for the third time. She didn't want to talk to Al, but she couldn't help looking up at him and saying, "No, Al, remember I'm too dumb to understand what anything means?"

"Oh, God, Hester, get over it, would you? I didn't mean that, and you know it. And you know these idiots sold us out. All we're getting before we have to be out of our trailer, is a thousand dollars. Not enough to pay a mover, let alone put money down on a new place. How are we supposed to buy something else if we don't get a decent amount down?"

Al was fired up and pacing the small space in front of the sliding glass doors like a caged tiger. The angrier he got, the more

pronounced his limp. Hester used to see him like this at school outside his office when one principal or another—he had lived through
so many—had pissed him off.

"I'm going to the office. Somebody's got to say something about this,
and I guess it's going to be me, since nobody else around here seems to
have any balls or brains." He grabbed his sunglasses, his hat, and left.

Hester was glad she wasn't Debbie. She stopped cleaning and
picked the notice up from the floor where Al dropped it. *Thirty days is
not much time, and Al's ranting isn't going to change anything.* Hester
put the paper in the basket with other bills and junk mail, grabbed her
laptop, and went out under the bo tree.

She turned it on and Googled "Arthur Kendall." She clicked on
the third listing down. An article from 1980, in *New Jersey Magazine*
about MIAs and POWs appeared on the screen. Ten years had passed
since the men listed had disappeared in Vietnam. There was little
hope any of them would be found. Hester scrolled down and there it
was, highlighted in blue ink, Arthur Kendall, Lodi, N.J., missing since
July 16, 1970. *He's gone. He's been gone.*

Her warped fantasy for so long—Arty finds her to tell her everything was a terrible mistake. They were young and foolish, and in the
end they learned a hard lesson from what they did. It was his fault, all
his fault. He hugs her and says, "Hester, I am so sorry."

Now, Hester saw the truth right in front of her on the computer
screen—Arty went to war and never came back. He would never find
her, never apologize.

Hester logged off. What she wished for was true? Arthur Kendall
had been punished too, severely punished. How many times had she
imagined him with his wife Trish and kids, two or three kids, maybe

more than that? One big happy family, but that's not how it was. If he had a child, he never saw it. Just like she hadn't seen hers, theirs. Many times she hated her life, but now she realized at least she had one. And she'd wasted all that time being jealous of Arty, imagining what Arty's life was like, when he never had one.

In the shade of the bo as the air grew cooler, Hester looked at the weeds between the impatiens. They needed to be pulled. She put her laptop aside and went to work ripping the stubborn invaders out by the roots. She twisted the dead leaves off the ginger plants and picked the shriveled flowers off the gardenia bush. Two feet down was Nina's decaying body, but on the surface, the lush and colorful plants belied death and filled the space with beauty.

Hester knew she had to move Nina, but the thought of it, of digging up the plants, of going down deeper and deeper with the shovel, hitting something, seeing the black bags, seeing the duct tape, touching the bundle, feeling the fat, writhing maggots made her sick and filled her with shame.

Her hands were black with soil. She brushed as much dirt off as she could and went inside to do another thing she'd been putting off. She washed up at the kitchen sink, then went down the hall and into the guest bedroom.

The night Hester buried Nina, she also hid all of her belongings. Distressed as she was, she'd thought to throw whatever was in Nina's drawers and closet into her suitcase and carry-on bag, and shove them under the bed where Nina had slept. Since then, Hester avoided the guest room and only came in to dust and vacuum.

The bright red luggage was cheap stuff from Marshall's that Hester had mailed Nina $40 to buy, along with the $266 for her flight down. The girl had been desperate on the phone, crying about how no one at college spoke to her, how cruel her aunt was, and how she missed Mr. Murphy and her.

Hester sat on the floor, unzipped the carry-on first, and started taking things out. Two small black push-up bras, a copy of *People* magazine with Brad Pitt on the cover, a classroom copy of *The Great Gatsby,*—Hester knew Nina hadn't turned it in—a plastic bangle bracelet, a Hello Kitty address book, a pair of shorts with "Too Cute" written across the rear, a hairbrush, a makeup bag full of cheap cosmetics, a box of tampons, and birth control pills.

Birth control pills? Hester felt her heart drop. What was Nina doing with birth control pills? She never paid one bit of attention to any of the boys at school. This must've started at the community college, or…

Hester lined the items up in a row on the floor in front of her. They looked like artifacts from a lost civilization of junk collectors. Nina had so little, and what she had was cheap and worthless. How insignificant her life seemed if this is what she left behind. Everything there saddened Hester, but it was the strands of Nina's light-brown hair tangled in the bristles of the worn brush that made her go weak inside.

Hester picked up the *People* magazine; the corner of a page was turned down. It was a story about that cop Drew Peterson, who was accused of killing his wives. She put it down and picked up the copy of *The Great Gatsby.* The cover of the paperback was dirty, half the front torn off. Hester fanned through it and was amazed by the number of marginal notations. In the beginning the notes seemed based on class discussions, but further along there were curse words, doodles, small drawings of stick people in obscene positions—a couple having oral sex, a man on top of a woman.

Hester cringed. Her heart filled with dread. There were things going on in Nina's head Hester knew nothing about and couldn't have
guessed, not in a million years. And she clearly had little respect for
school property or for what Hester was trying to teach her.

After chapter six practically every other page was defaced. Midway
through the last chapter, Nina made a list of each character and an
equivalent slur. "Nick Caraway = pansy ass," "Myrtle Wilson = fat
slob." And so on.

This annoyed Hester. It seemed so out of character for Nina, but
clearly it was her writing. Hester closed the book and tossed it on the
bed, and it flipped open to the inside of the back cover, where something was written in big capital letters that had nothing to do with
the novel. "MRS. MURPHY = STUPID OLD BITCH" and "THIS
BOOK BELONGS TO NINA MURPHY"

Nina Murphy? What had she wanted from them? To be adopted?

How could Nina write such things? Hester believed Nina had
loved her. Obviously, she hadn't. Hester put everything back in the
carry-on, threw the battered copy of *Gatsby* in on top, and lifted
the suitcase onto the bed. She remembered throwing a folder full
of papers from the drawer into it. She rummaged through the short-
shorts, skinny T's, and hoodies until she found it. It was packed with
old stuff like Nina's report cards from elementary school, her First
Communion certificate, notes she had written to her mother when she
was a little girl, things like that. She shuffled through the papers and
found Nina's birth certificate.

Nina Alexandra, born—November 11, 1987. Mother—Jennifer
Tattoni, father—unknown.

That date? That year? Hester sat still and counted back nine months and tried to remember what happened in the spring of that year.

Well, Al found out about the abortion. She couldn't forget that traumatic event. She mentally tried to go forward from that awful day. Was that when she saw Al in the dugout with Jennifer Masterson? Then Jennifer dropped out of school and disappeared from the area altogether? Hester couldn't remember the exactly sequence, and she couldn't imagine a connection between Jennifer Masterson and this Jennifer Tattoni, who was Nina's mother. And then there was Nina's Aunt Linda, whose last name was Connefry, but that was probably her married name. Hester remembered teaching another Masterson girl beside Jennifer, but she'd be damned if she could remember if her first name was Linda.

If only she had her old yearbooks, but Al had thrown them away when the whole rush-to- retirement thing started.

What really did happen last June? Al certainly had some sort of breakdown—over what?—she never did get a straight answer from him. Could it have been Al, and not Theo, who was harassing those girls? Was Al capable of molesting students?

Never, he'd never take a risk like that. He's too smart, too cautious. They never would have given him his pension. So, it couldn't have been him.

Hester put the folder down. *That name, Jennifer, just a coincidence, that's all.* She dumped the rest of the stuff in the suitcase onto the bed. Everything smelled like soap. There was a used bar of Zest tucked in a pouch, more clothes. Hester unzipped the lining inside the top and found some photographs. The first one was of a baby on its stomach on a blanket. Obviously, it was of Nina. The eyes had the same wide eagerness.

Baby Nina was bald as a cue ball, but her face was a pudgy miniature of the perfectly shaped one Hester knew. The next one was of Nina as a toddler. Sitting up, laughing into the lens, two little teeth visible in her open mouth. She looked like an angel. An adorable little angel.

Hester heard the slider squeal open. She slipped the photos back in the lining of the suitcase, scooped everything into it, and slid it under the bed. She hurried into the bathroom.

"Hey, anybody home?"

"Yeah, I'm in the bathroom."

"Well, honey, looks like we're moving." Al sounded okay again. "I spent all this time with a couple of the board members, and the upshot is that Pleasant Palms is sold, and they're going to tear this place down. Once we took that first installment, the sale became binding. It would take something huge to stop the closing. So I think we better talk."

Al was outside the bathroom door. Hester flushed the toilet.

"Can you hear me, Hester? Come on, really, we have to talk. We've got to make some plans. We can go back to Lambertville, of course, and check up on Nina. God knows why we haven't heard from that girl. I've tried to e-mail her and nothing, I get nothing back. Have you gotten anything?"

Hester stood in the bathroom thinking, *he doesn't know, he really doesn't know.* Then in her mind's eye she saw the bulldozer plowing down the bo tree, the trunk being pushed to the ground, and the roots popping up, and Nina with them.

"For Christ's sakes, Al, give me a minute." Hester washed her hands and studied her reflection in the mirror. There she was, as she really was, middle-aged, not the young, attractive person she used to be, changed—some would say for the worse. She picked up the brush, ran it through her hair, took a deep breath, lifted her chin, and stared into the small universe of her own eyes. Who would she be without Al? Another old woman, alone. Was she strong enough to endure that?

She could hear Al's anxious breath on the other side of the door. Another decision to be made. The beginning of another chapter in their life together. Maybe they would start traveling again. Hester could hear the drums of Africa calling her. How long had she dreamed of going on a safari?

I'll move Nina's body. I'll do it in the middle of the night. No one will know…

But did she have the strength to dig up the corpse? What would she do with it? She didn't really believe Rosario chopped Lou Latimer up into little pieces and dumped him in the Intracoastal. Rosario and Mrs. Flowers were probably only cleaning out the old food in the freezer. Why waste it? Why not feed the fish?

Or she could leave Nina's dead body where it was. She could let things unfold according to God's plan. Maybe the workers would find it, maybe they wouldn't. If they did, the truth would come out, and set her free. *This little light of mine, I'm going to let it shine…* The words of that old church song. She could hear her mother's voice singing them to her. If Nina's dead body did come to light, the devil would get his due. Hester might go down with her husband, but the travesty her life had become would at last be over.

Oh, how she vacillated between doing something and doing nothing.

Hester came out of the bathroom casually dabbing some lipstick on her lower lip. She hesitated, then said, "Al, there's nothing to talk about. I'll do what you want to do. No need to talk about it, is there? Besides, I'm supposed to meet Eve for a game of euchre."

She applied lipstick to her top lip and pressed them together. When she reached for her jeans jacket, Al grabbed her wrist. "I'm not fooling around here. This is serious business."

Here it comes, she thought. He was just pretending not to know before. She waited for him to ask, to beg her to tell him what she'd done with Nina's body.

"We have to find another place, and we can't fool around about it. Three hundred of us are in the market now. All of the good deals will be gone in a week. You can play games for the rest of your life, but right now we've got to get a real estate agent and start looking." Al slipped his hand from her wrist into her hand and swung her arm back and forth, just like a little kid who wanted to go for a walk.

Hester led him into the narrow kitchen and turned to face him. She looked at him, and he seemed genuinely concerned about just what he was talking about. Nina, in his mind, was still very much alive and having a grand old time somewhere in New Jersey.

"Look, Hester, I figure realistically we'll end up with about five hundred thousand, which is a far cry from the million everybody's been talking about, but with capital gains tax, closing costs, corporation fees, you know, all of that stuff chips away at our profit." He leaned against the refrigerator. "Still, it's a hell of a lot more than we ever had before…"

He kept talking, but Hester's mind was elsewhere, back in the bedroom with those photos. That baby girl was gone forever. *Her once-shiny plump flesh now rotting flesh, her short life a pathetic waste, and Al's worrying about getting a jump on the real estate market?*

And then there were those birth control pills. *Were they for Al? So she could let Al fuck her without getting pregnant? Were they?*

Behind Hester on the counter was the cutlery set, their gleaming stainless steel handles jutting out of the walnut block like so many invitations. The temptation to reach back, to swiftly grab one, to swing it up overhead and bring it down into Al's jugular was extreme. What on earth was stopping her?

Hester forced herself to say, "Al, I'm sorry to interrupt, but I have to get over to Eve's. She's waiting for me." How wonderfully calm she sounded when she really wanted to scream, *fuck you, Al.* But she wanted to get the hell away from him, so she added, "I'll tell her maybe we'll get together later for dinner. Maybe we can barbecue something up by the beach. Or is that too much for me to decide? I mean about dinner and what we might eat. Maybe it takes more brains than I have to figure something like a barbecue on the beach out. Anyway, then you can talk to them about buying real estate because at least they're not dumb...like..."

She was babbling on as she worked her way to the door and slid it open. Right before she stepped out, she noticed Al had a strange look on his face, of befuddlement, mixed with pure anger.

Leaving him standing there looking so bewildered, so bewitched...why, it made her feel better than the damn sparkling rosy-tipped fingers of dawn.

Forty-One

So much had changed since the end of the last school year. One day Hester was teaching English, the next day she was a retiree. The sound of that word, retiree, didn't make her happy. She was too young to be a retiree, but when Al got it in his head to do something, there was no changing it. And he was ready to move on from the old Victorian too.

"Al, I really don't want to sell this house. I love this house," Hester argued.

"You'll love our next place just as much."

"How do you know what I'll love?"

"You love me, don't you? You'll love anything I love, right?" Al smiled.

"I'm not completely sure about that."

"About loving me?" Al's face turned serious.

"Come on, Al, you know better than that."

"Then if you love me, trust me."

271

When the real estate agent came over, Hester signed the papers. A month later the Victorian was sold, and the Lambertville condo purchased. Al threatened to hire an auctioneer and auction off all of Hester's stuff, all of the Victoriana she'd spent decades collecting and that had given the house such an air of authenticity, and all of the souvenirs she'd spent a fortune on, if she didn't get rid of the stuff herself. Promptly and secretly, she rented a storage container in Frenchtown and hired a moving company to clear everything out of the house while Al was away on a golfing trip.

"I don't care what you did with it. I'm just glad it's gone," he said when he returned.

After the Moretown closing, Al took Hester to Split Rock Lodge in the Poconos for a couple of days. It was late August, the hot and humid dog days of summer. The small Appalachian range was primarily a winter skiing destination; and the old resort, a bit past its prime, was nearly empty.

Hester and Al sat alone on the deck in the afternoon sun. A skin of algae grew on the stagnant surface of the lake. Al surprised Hester by renting the honeymoon suite. It came with champagne and chocolates, so last night when they arrived, Al popped the cork and proposed a toast.

"To you, Hester, my loyal and true wife. To our future together as two old lovers and friends."

Now, Hester thought as she raised her glass toward Al, *how could anyone not love a guy like this?* She took a sip and the cold bubbles made her lips tingled.

The champagne gone, Al helped Hester out of her clothes and insisted she lie on her back on the bed. He placed the chocolates in a row down the middle of her torso. He undressed, knelt on the bed next to her, and worked his way south, eating and kissing…

The memory still fresh in her mind, Hester reached over and entwined her fingers in her husband's. "Do you know, Al, how happy you make me sometimes?"

"Sometimes?" He'd been resting with his eyes closed. He didn't open them.

"I'm still not over moving out of Moretown."

"Hester, please, you're not going to start with that again, are you?" He turned his head, opened one eye, and squinted at her.

"It was home. It was convenient to school. What if I wanted be a substitute teacher and go in a couple of days a week."

"You don't need to, Hester."

"But I might want to."

Al opened both eyes and jolted up. "You're not going back to that school," he said sharply.

"Al!"

"Don't argue, Hester. We've got plenty of money. You don't need to work anymore." He put his head back and shut his eyes again.

"Alright." Hester didn't want to argue. "But I just want to say one more thing."

Al sighed, "One more thing, then I'm taking a nap."

"The real reason I didn't want to leave Moretown was because of Nina."

"What's Nina got to do with Moretown?"

"She could walk to our house from her aunt's house whenever she wanted. Now that we'll be so far away, we might never see her. She doesn't have a car. She'll never be able to get to Lambertville."

"I'll pick her up and drop her off, okay?"

"That's a lot for you to do, Al, but you understand, don't you? I want to keep her in my life."

"You don't have to worry about that, honey. I can guarantee she'll be in your life. Now are we done with this topic?"

"Yes, if you can guarantee Nina will be in my life." Hester leaned back, closed her eyes, and dreamt about what Al might to do to her when they got back in their room.

Forty-Two

The night started with mojitos at Eve and Marvin's place. Then Hester, Al, and the Bridgefords went to the beach and fired up the grill by the clubhouse. Hester cooked pork chops, corn, and slices of zucchini. Al opened two bottles of pinot grigio, and the four friends, sitting on one side of the picnic table, watched the ocean and ate dinner. The sun was setting behind them, and when it was dark, they took the wine onto the beach and sat in the sand. Marvin and Al talked about how much gasoline was going to cost by summer and who might eventually replace George W. as president. It was obvious to Hester they were trying not to talk about the sale of the trailer park. That didn't last long. Back and forth they went about it. Marvin was all for it. Al had reconciled himself to the idea. They were like broken records. Hester wanted to shout, *would you guys shut up? It's after the fact.*

The conversation did eventually shift, but now it was about how much money they were going to make. The estimates the two men came up with varied wildly, but by the sound of their voices, the number of digits involved satisfied them.

Eve hit Marvin gently on the arm. "I think the whole thing is a huge mistake," she said, "There's not another place in all of Florida like this. Trailer park or not, those developers—"

"Eve, be—"

"Marvin, would you let me finish?" She smacked Marvin's arm again, only harder. "Those developers know it. I think they stole this place out from under us, and we're just too blinded by greed to notice."

Marvin leaned over and kissed his wife. "Whatever you say, honey." And he began rummaging in her beach bag for something. Al stared out at the only thing to be seen, the whitecaps in the moonlight. The closing was only days away. Hester wondered why everybody wasn't sick and tired of talking about it. She sure was. And, as if there wasn't enough on her mind, Frances Middleton called that morning out-of-the-blue to ask if she'd seen the news, there'd been a stabbing at Sourland.

Al stood up to stretch, and Marvin, having found a cigar, lit it. Eve poured herself and Hester more wine.

"Brandon Lynch stabbed Ernest Colburn to death," Hester blurted out.

"What?" Al looked down at Hester.

"Who are they?" asked Eve.

"Former students," Hester answered. "A lot of kids didn't like poor Ernest. He was a loner, an odd young man, to say the least."

"Odd? Aren't we all odd in one way or another?" Eve sounded tipsy. "But that's no reason to kill…"

"What in the hell happened, Hester? Would you get to the goddamn point," Al insisted.

"Where Brandon got the knife, nobody knows, but they got into a fight over some girl."

"How the hell did you find out, Hester?" Al seemed perplexed.

"Frances called this morning."

"She called you and not me? And you're not telling me till now?"

"Didn't think you'd give a damn. Wasn't sure you knew those two."

"I knew every single kid in that whole goddamn school. It was my job to know every single kid, and I took my job seriously, and you knew that. Who was the girl?"

"Frances wasn't sure. Her guess was Kimberly Ramsay."

"That Ramsay girl was on my radar. She was a regular in my office. Drove her teachers nuts. She was addicted to her cell phone. Couldn't get through a class period without checking it. I threatened to throw it out the window. It was pouring rain, and she said it would be ruined if it got wet. I told her that was too bad, and she burst into tears. Of course, I gave it back to her at the end of the day, and she was so goddamn happy I was afraid she was going hug me. She was alright. I could see Ernest and her together, but Brandon? No, Brandon was out of her league. So what the hell was he beating up Ernest for? Christ, these kids could drive you nuts. They are so fucking stupid, and they make the most goddamn stupid mistakes."

"Don't I know," Hester agreed.

"I think CNN carried the story about the school stabbing this morning, right after the report on Iraq. How about that mess over there? Seems to be out of control, like things were in 'Nam," Marvin changed the subject.

"Vietnam? Were you there, Marvin?" Hester asked.

"He went alright," Eve answered for her husband, "but he doesn't like to talk about it."

"But if it weren't for 'Nam, I would've never been interested in plumbing and hot water heaters." Marvin leaned back in the sand on one elbow. "Found out when I got there, the government didn't draft plumbers. So as soon as I got stateside, I signed up for plumbing school. They weren't going to send me back into hell a second time."

"Wow, I didn't know that." Al sat down, crossed his legs, and massaged his ankle.

Eve noticed. "Is your ankle bothering you, Al?"

"Yeah, old football injury..." his voice trailed off.

They all grew silent, and the sound of the crashing waves seemed to mesmerize the four Pleasant Palmers. Over the ocean a gibbous moon glowed and stars punctured the black dome of the sky. The extraterrestrial light blurred the outer edges of things, made everything colorless, made the earth dwellers appear ageless.

To save the evening from ending, Hester suggested Al tell a couple of jokes.

"You're such a great joke-teller, please?" She said light-heartedly.

So he rallied and did, and, even though the ones he could remember were gross, they all had a good laugh. When the wine was gone, Eve and Marvin went home.

Al and Hester were pleasantly loaded and tired. It was hard to tell which had the greater bearing on their unspoken but mutual decision to stay put. It had been a hot March day, near eighty-five degrees. Now a breeze was coming off the water. All they could see when they looked out were the phosphorescent white caps, dollops of meringue folding again and again into the black batter of the ocean. Hester pushed the warm sand around with her feet and laid back in its lingering heat. It felt like a caress. Al had his knees up, his elbows resting on them, and his head on his forearms. Hester thought he was falling asleep until he said he was still hungry. They went back to the trailer. She rummaged in the fridge and took out some leftovers. Al lit a candle on the patio table, and they sat down to eat. Between them was a platter of cold chicken and two bottles of Corona.

Al took a long swallow of beer. "So why do you think we haven't heard from her?"

"Who?" Hester knew who, asking was a reflex.

"You know who."

"No, I don't," Hester lied. She didn't want to talk about Nina, not now when she was feeling good, and not to Al.

"Don't lie, Hester. You most certainly do know who." He paused from fingering the lip of his beer bottle, and looked up at her. "Nina Tattoni, that's who."

"Oh, Nina? How would I know why we haven't heard from her?"

"The least that girl could do is pick up the fucking phone and leave us a message." Al cursed more than usual when he was drunk, or annoyed. Now, since his mood had shifted, he seemed to be both.

"Yes, Al, she could, but she's probably busy with classes and everything." How easily lies rolled off her tongue.

"That's bullshit."

"Look, she's barely eighteen years old. Be a little realistic, would you? Besides, what makes you think she would call us?"

"Because…" He hesitated and took another swig of the Corona. Before he could finish his sentence, Hester butted in.

"Because she cares? Come on, she has her own life. It's not like we're her parents or something. Don't get so upset. Eventually we'll hear from her." Hester watched Al gnaw off the last little piece of meat from a chicken bone. "Hey, we could go for ice cream. You want some ice cream?" Hester said this the way she would've said it to a toddler. Anything to get off the topic of Nina, anything to prevent Al's temper tantrum from escalating.

"Hester, get real. It's late. You're drunk."

"Speak for yourself, mister." She said this to be smart. The truth was she was feeling no pain.

"It's just that she left in such a hurry. What was the big rush?" Now Al was pulling the skin off a thigh. "You'd think she'd let us know how she's doing."

"We'll probably only hear from her if something goes wrong, so don't waste your time worrying about her."

"I'm not worried. Damn it. Did I say I was worried?" He turned the thigh over and took a bite of meat. A large chunk came loose, so he had to push it into his mouth with his finger. The flickering candle illuminated Al's face and made his nostrils look like someone had shoved olive pits up them. His mouth was too full and half open. Deep lines ran like thin wires across his forehead, his nose had several dark spots on the tip, there were downward creases at the edges of his eyes, and his chin was drooping. For the first time since she'd known him, Hester looked at him and thought, *he might not age well.*

Still tackling the meat on the thigh, he waited until he swallowed and said, "Look, wife, I'm sick and tired of you always telling me what I'm thinking or doing. You don't know anything about what goes on in here." He tapped his thick pointer against his temple hard enough that Hester heard a hollow thump.

Hester wanted to say, *Al, can we please change the subject?* But she knew she wouldn't, because he was already irritated and at this late hour arguing with him wasn't the brightest idea. She picked up a chicken breast, bit into it, and chewed slowly and deliberately. The less she said, the better, but the needle in Al's brain was stuck in a bad groove.

"Look, Hester, by the time I got out of the hospital, Nina was gone. In my mind what happened is a freaking blur. I was hurt pretty bad. I think I remember seeing her lying there, but I don't know how she got there. Shit, all I know is what you told me. Nina went back to school. That's it. That's all you said."

"She'll probably call tomorrow. It's Sunday and she'll probably have some spare time." Hester's voice was nonchalant, while she was thinking, *what in the hell am I saying.*

"Yeah, you're probably right." He reached across the table. Now the candlelight fell on his hairy arm. Next to the plate of cold chicken parts, it looked grotesquely alive, like a giant, hairy chicken leg. He put his hand on top of Hester's hand and squeezed gently.

"Hester, I am fucking lucky to have a wife like you who is so… What I mean is, you could've assumed things. You could've panicked and done something stupid, but you didn't. You believed me and now because of that, because of your trust, we're here together. You knew I could never do anything like that, especially to Nina."

Hester drank some beer and leaned back like the Queen of the Calm Exterior, while inside she trembled with anger.

"Like what?" It hopped out of her mouth like a tiny toad, and as soon as it did, she was sorry.

"What in the hell do you mean, 'like what?' Like you know what. She was like a goddamn daughter to us. You know that." His voice was loud, but earnest, not angry, just emphatic, emphatic enough for Hester to almost believe him all over again. His hand was still on top of hers. It was heavy and warm. He kept it there for a moment longer as he tilted his head to look into her eyes. His were glazing over, but he had the most soulful way of lifting his eyebrows up in the middle that made him look ardent, or maybe, contrite. He took his hand away and crossed his arms.

They sat staring at each other, and it felt to Hester like they were alone in the universe, maybe even falling faintly through it, for all she knew. She forgot about Nina for a second, and since Al had leaned back out of the light and had stopped eating the chicken, he was handsome again. She thought about the way practically every woman they'd met this season at Pleasant Palms Trailer Park had fallen all over him. Nancy Ettinger, who was practically old enough to be his mother, had the nerve to tell Hester she'd better watch out, or someone would snatch a handsome guy like that right away from her. What else was new? After almost three decades of marriage, she was still going to have to fight off other women. It was getting tiresome, and it didn't take a genius to realize that in Florida old women on the prowl outnumbered alligators and pit bulls combined, and were deadlier to a married woman than both carnivores put together.

Al stuck his lower lip out the way Brad Pitt does in his movies, and Hester almost giggled. His toes were moving up and down on her calf, and she could feel the sand falling off her skin. He sank back in the chair, took a sip of his beer, and moved his foot between her thighs, where he gently pushed his heel as far as it would go. Automatically, involuntarily, she slid down toward him, her legs fell open. He bent his foot forward. Hester reached down and pulled her shorts to the side.

The thought of stopping him flickered and dimmed in her mind. She didn't. His face had grown serious and determined. Looking in his eyes was like looking down the barrels of a gun. But Hester just wanted to feel good, drift away, love and be loved. She wanted to escape into what was being done to her, and not think about the fact that it was Al who was doing it. She turned her head, closed her eyes. She had read on a blog about a place in San Francisco called the One Taste Urban Retreat Center where every morning about a dozen women get naked from the waist down and lie with their eyes closed in a quiet room while fully clothed men stroke them into what the group calls an "orgasmic meditation." Well, that was what Hester wanted right now, an anonymous one-sided explosion. She wanted it for once to be all about her.

She rolled her head back, her body tingling down there where Al was pressing. Her arms dropped to her sides. Her eyes opened. Between the two trailers, there was nowhere else to look but up. Stars layered the sky, some close and brilliant, others distant and blurred. It was magnificent, like seeds sown across the blackness, and Hester felt as though she were drifting up toward them. She was aroused, her breathing shallow. She slid forward. Suddenly the stars seemed to be falling, a blow to the head, scattering teeth. Where the distracting thought had come from, she didn't know, but it made her twitch.

Al stopped, pulled his foot away, leaned across the chicken and put his hand around Hester's throat. The move, made so quickly, scared Hester. She tensed until he ran his hand down her neck, over her chest, and caressed her breasts. She was ready now for Al to do whatever he wanted to do, then someone coughed. In the semi-darkness Hester saw Chet's shadow through his screen window. She straightened up, and Al did the same.

"Thought I heard something. Just checkin' to make sure every-thing's alright. You know how we all look out for each other here. I see there's no problem, so I guess I'll just try to go back to bed now." Though Chet claimed concern, the tone of his voice betrayed his impatience with his neighbors. He'd probably been spying on them all night, and he might as well have said, why don't you go inside so I can get some goddamn sleep?

The moment between them over, Hester adjusted her shorts, stood up, and picked up the platter of chicken.

"Wait. I want to tell you something." Al put his hands on her hips and pulled her toward him.

"Go ahead, Al. I'm listening."

"No. Sit down."

What now? Hester thought. It was after midnight. The carriage had turned back into a pumpkin. "Can't it wait till tomorrow?"

"No, goddamn it, Hester. No, there's something I have to get off my chest. I should've told you this a long time ago."

"Jesus, Al. We've been married almost thirty years. What can you tell me tonight that I don't already know? Let's just go to sleep." Hester didn't want to listen to him confess something she already knew, but that he didn't know she knew. There were lots of cans of worms she didn't want him opening up. The creepy-crawly truths, once out in the open, would eat away at her carefully fortified illusions.

"Just sit down and shut up, Hester, and hear me out."

Hester was almost in a panic. Whoever said it was a good thing to lay all the cards on the table must've been nuts. When all the cards are on the table, there's still only one winner. Reluctantly Hester put the chicken back on the table and started to sit down.

"Wait!" Al said it way too loud. "Grab me another beer first."

Damn it, Al, Hester wanted to scream at him, *can't you just leave well enough alone?*

Forty-Three

In Lambertville in late October, Hester and Al walked along the towpath. The geese waddled from the bank of the canal into the water, and the fallen leaves, like tiny empty boats, drifted south on the swift current. The Murphys, officially retired, tried to walk every day. Some days Al did; some days, complaining about his ankle, he didn't. But Hester, who couldn't wait to get outside and away from their new condo, never missed a morning.

Though the development overlooked the Delaware and their unit had lovely views, it wasn't, in Hester's estimation, at all like their Moretown Victorian. It was small, not as small as their Pleasant Palms trailer, but drastically smaller than the Victorian; and though Hester would never admit it to Al, she felt like it was a step down from what they had.

Al, she was sure, assumed she'd sold or given away what he called "her junk"—junk she spent years collecting, scouring flea markets, yard sales, and antique shops to find. Now Al wanted new things for the new place.

"Hester, all it was, was other people's trash," he'd said.

Trash? It wasn't trash. Knowing objects had a provenance, a life before her, made Hester feel rooted. How many people sat in that chair? Who walked on that rug? Who ate dinner off that plate and washed it and put it away? New, unadulterated things weren't intriguing at all. What was there to stir the imagination in a set of Riedel wineglasses from Linen 'n Things?

Hester fought with Al as much as she dared, about how the condo should be furnished, and surprisingly, he agreed to compromise: twentieth-century Modern. Hester was okay with the decision. He could buy his new stuff, but she'd be able to mix in some Art Deco and some of the things she already had, unbeknownst to Al. Would he know the difference between Arts and Crafts, and Modern? Hester doubted it. He acted like he cared, but eventually the real work of pulling the condo together would fall to her. She started at the Golden Nugget Market, purchasing a Haywood Wakefield blonde wood bedroom set, burled maple twin headboards for the guest room, two Eames chairs, and a seventies Steelcase sofa for the living room. Al stayed home and painted all the walls a pale gray. He'd be happy if the place looked monotone.

"Do you miss school?" Al had fallen behind Hester on the towpath so Hester stopped to wait for him.

"Why would I?"

"Maybe because you were there for most of your life?"

"Not a bit." He pulled the collar of his jacket up. "It was time to go. Remember, Hester, at least we got out with my full pension and benefits. Who knows? If we waited for you to have your twenty-five years in, it might have backfired. New Jersey's so screwed up, they could pull the plug on anybody's pension at any time. When nothing's fully funded, public servants can't count on anything."

"You're right, I guess." The wind picked up, dark clouds moved overhead. "Want to turn around? It's getting pretty chilly."

"Fine with me. You're the one who always forces me to come out here. You know me, I'd rather stay home and submit to waterboarding than exercise."

"Ha, ha…you'll thank me when you're old."

"I am old."

"Not as old as you're going to be."

"Old enough."

"For what? Staying home and channel surfing for ten hours a day?"

"Don't start on me, Hester. For Christ's sakes, I just retired. So what if I watch TV all day? Who gives a rat's ass?"

Al was right, so Hester shut up and sprinted ahead.

She was home before him and pushed the button on the gas fireplace. The flames danced their predictable dance while Hester stared at them and thought through a plan for the day. The tight quarters in the condo, and Al's constant presence, drove Hester to plot a daily escape. She'd go to the Kintersville dealer center. Someone at a yard sale said they'd seen a hand-carved Madonna there, probably Mexican, nineteenth century. An old wooden statue like that might add an eclectic touch to Al's uncluttered decor.

Al came in and clicked on the television even before he removed his hat or jacket. Judge Judy was hollering, "Who do you think I am, anyway? An idiot? On your best day, you'll never be as smart as—"

Hester avoided the temptation to stick her fingers in her ears. Instead, she went into the bedroom and lay down on the bed, rolled on her stomach, and looked at the clock: 8:14 a.m. It was already second period at school; she wished she were there. It was too early to drive to the dealer center. She couldn't go online because Al didn't set up the computer, "Why bother when we're leaving for Florida soon?" Al was hell-bent on leaving before it got cold.

She rolled again onto her back and stared at the ugly popcorn ceiling and the sleek blades of the overhead fan. *What is water-boarding anyway? It must have something to do with dripping water, maybe on your forehead.* Hester tried to imagine it. It didn't seem so bad. Drip, drip, drip.

She wished she were tired and could fall asleep for a while, then sex crossed her mind, and the idea seemed like a good one. How many years had it been since they'd done it in the morning? A long time, maybe since they stopped having sex in school, when the brighter the light, the better, when a ceiling full of florescent bulbs didn't bother them one bit.

Hester took off her sneakers and went into the living room. Al was in one of the Eames chairs with the remote poised for action.

"Hey, you? Want to fool around?"

"What? Now?"

"Yes. Now."

"Come on, Hester, you've got to be kidding me."

"No, I'm not kidding you."

He looked up at his wife like he didn't recognize her and sank deeper into the leather. He seemed to be considering it until the television screen lit up with the face of a defendant and his eyes were drawn back to it.

"Maybe later," he said as he totally refocused on the testimony.

Al hadn't rejected her completely—"later" meant later. So why the bad feeling? Maybe because "maybe" meant just that. She couldn't remember ever saying to him, "Maybe later, Al."

Chagrined at her own foolishness for asking him in the first place, Hester looked around the room. Was it the open layout, the obsessive orderliness, the sleek uninviting furniture, the simplicity of it all, or was it Al? But she felt as though she'd fallen into a scary place.

An hour later after a steaming hot shower, Hester, listening to NPR, was driving north toward Kintersville. She didn't give a damn what it cost, she was going to buy the Madonna.

Forty-Four

Hester brought out another beer for her husband and sat down across from him. She was tired and impatient.

Al opened the beer and said, "I want to tell you something I never told anyone, something that happened in college."

College? Hester was relieved. *College was decades ago. Whatever happened then, couldn't possibly matter now—not unless he murdered someone. The statutes of limitations never run out on murder. But Al's no murderer*...again she shoved the whole terrible incident almost completely under the carpet.

Hester could tell Al was totally drunk, and therefore he would be impossible to shut up. She did the only thing she could do, other than run away. She sat back and listened.

Al went to this party one night and left early. The twang of Hendrix's frenetic guitar blared from the stereo in the apartment where everyone was still partying. The sound followed him all the way out to Pitman Road, where, when he turned into the wind and headed back to campus, he could no longer hear it.

Right then and there, Hester wanted to butt in. She was confused because he said Pitman Road, and Pitman Road was in Glassboro, where she'd gone to college. Al always bragged about going to Trenton State College, the best state college, according to him, in the state. She'd have to ask him about it later because he was staring into the flame of the candle and talking like he was in some kind of trance.

It was 1969, he said, and if you didn't dig Hendrix and Joplin and Cream, you weren't with it. He wasn't very "with it," and didn't care if that meant he didn't fit in. Why he went to the stupid party, he didn't know, but he was having a lousy time, so despite the fact that it was a bitter cold December night and he didn't have a ride, he left the party around midnight. Summit Ridge Apartments was a mile and a half from his dorm, and this wasn't the first time he'd made the trip on foot back to the Glassboro campus.

Glassboro! The second revelation, thought Hester. *We did go to the same college, at the same time.* How she wanted to say something smart-assed about who was he to look down his nose at her all these years, but Al kept talking. His eyes wandered from the flame to the darkness beyond her.

That night at Summit Ridge he got drunk and stoned, but he still had enough sense to walk through the dry weeds that grew along the macadam because the road was narrow with no shoulder. There were no streetlights; the moon must've been behind the clouds, because he couldn't see his hand when he put it out in front of him. He had on his black leather jacket, dark jeans so it would've been damn-near impossible for anyone driving a car to see him. He could end up like road kill, smashed, flattened, gone. People hit things, heard the thud, kept driving. He'd seen lots of dead animals left on roads to rot. He'd seen maniacs speed up on purpose, swerve directly toward some confused animal, bang. All that was left were guts and fur scattered all over the place. Things like that disgusted him. He had to admit back then pretty much everything disgusted him. For the past couple of days before the party, getting high wasn't even working for him. He got a buzz for a few minutes and then whatever he smoked or snorted or ingested only brought him further down than he already was.

Snow began falling in small flakes that melted as soon as they hit the ground, but before long thicker flakes mixed with ice were coming down fast. The wind whipped the cold mess into his face. He lowered his head, pulled his collar up, tried not to think about how his face stung or how thin and insubstantial his stupid leather jacket was. He should've put in the zip-in liner. The storm was the beginning of a front pushing through; behind it was an Arctic blast. The velocity of the wind increased steadily, moving through the fields of dry corn-stalks on either side of him. The frantic rattling crescendoed in the gusts, reminded him of crashing ocean waves.

He started humming Mascagni's *Cavalleria Rusticana*, just like his grandfather Bruno Petrelli, taught him. Every summer until his mother's father died, he went with Pop Bruno to Long Beach Island. They stayed in his old dilapidated Nomad in Holgate's trailer park. For two weeks they'd fish all day and fall asleep at night to the sound of waves pounding the shore like a throbbing heart.

Humming the tune brought back these good memories and made him feel almost warm inside, almost okay. He got to the end of the fields. He stopped humming because even that wasn't helping. He was frigid, his face burned from the cold, his hands were numb. It was the worst he ever felt.

Ahead he could see the lights of the Sunoco station. He'd stop there to use the john. A good excuse to go inside and warm up. He walked from the road into the circle of light cast by the florescent tubes. He hurried into the office to ask for the key. The men's room was as cold as a meat locker, colder than it was outside. He wasted no time, and when he returned the key, he looked around for something to do so he could stay in the office near the hot radiator. The man behind the counter hung the key back on its hook, then turned and buried his nose in the drawer of the cash register. There were two oak chairs by the window, and parts of the newspaper were scattered across the top of a low table. He sat down in the chair closest to the sizzling radiator, picked up the paper, and pretended to read it.

He didn't have to look at the headlines to know what they were about. The same thing was splashed across the front of every newspaper from Key West to Anchorage. It was what was weighing heavily on his mind, and the minds of all healthy young American men, that night. They were all in the same boat, and while passing the bong around at the party, Jake, the genius English major, kept up a droning monologue about the perfect antanaclasis. He hadn't a clue what the term meant, but he didn't have any trouble understanding the gist of what Jake was saying: "Tonight we *hang* together, for assuredly, tomorrow we shall all *hang* separately."

Yeah, all the pot in the world couldn't dull the fact that at noon on that coming day, he and every other American male born between 1944 and 1950 would be relying on the fickle finger of fate to save them from destruction.

He put the paper down, stared at the man's back, and thought about how the man looked old enough to be his father. The man's back was broad, but his shoulders were rounded where muscle had turned to fat and he had poor posture. He had on a gray work shirt, and beneath the collar a lump of flesh bulged. Up along his hairline, several red pimples festered. He wore a peaked knit cap that sat on top of his brindled hair like a large blue breast with a twisted nipple. If the man had a son, the son would probably be Al's age, and the man would probably be worried about his son and what might happen to him, if he was one of the unlucky ones. Some would be safe, but not all. Then again, maybe the man had a daughter, in which case he wouldn't give a rat's ass about what would happen in just a few hours or what might happen to a kid like Al.

How could he think of himself as a kid? He was over twenty years old. He was almost through college. All right, he wasn't a kid, but tonight he didn't feel like a man either. So what the hell was he? A big baby. He pushed the thought away.

He would've talked to the guy, if he knew he had a son, but on the off chance the man didn't, he decided not to. He didn't want to hear about how lucky the guy felt about having a daughter, and all that sort of shit. Girls get away with murder. He leaned forward in the chair to stand up. When he did, he felt dizzy. He'd lost track of how much he'd drunk from the keg, and God knows how much from the punch bowl that was a mixture of Boone's Farm Strawberry Wine and Colt 45. He must have taken a dozen or so hits from the bong. He remembered tossing a nugget of hashish from his own stash into its bowl and bogarting the pipe for a while because he knew just how good his own stuff was.

The air in the small waiting area seemed too hot now, and some steam from the radiator set the small valve quaking as it escaped. He didn't want to vomit where he was, so he turned quickly toward the door. Once outside he bolted beyond into the dark and clung to a fence post, where he threw up several times before he got the dry heaves. Eventually, when he felt slightly better, he edged his way along the fence until his hand clamped down on some barbed wire. It hurt in a dull, distant way as though to someone else, yet it made him feel better. It made no sense to him, but he did feel better.

A car approached, moving slowly through what had become an even heavier snowfall. The lights swept across the whiteness in front of him. He raised his arm and lowered his head in anticipation of the glare, and in the flash of light he saw how bloody his hand was. He rubbed it on his jacket, but before he could check it again, he was in the dark.

His mouth tasted like sour beer and throw-up. If only he had a Lifesaver. He felt around in the pockets of his jacket. The blood from his hand was getting all over the inside of one pocket. Damn it, they were both empty. He ran his tongue around his teeth and spit. He passed the diner and headed down Main Street. He entered campus through the Holly Bush parking lot and crossed over the commons to Evergreen Dormitory. No one was at the desk. He signed in and went to the lounge. No one was there either.

They're all out getting blasted. Who could blame them? Even the guys who were against getting high would be in town trying to pick up one of the high school girls. Tonight anybody could get lucky. The girls would be doing it out of sympathy, though, and that would make it sickening and just plain damn disgusting in the end.

Janet, his girlfriend at the time, would be royally pissed at him. He knew this for sure. She'd gotten tickets to see Santana at the Spectrum to celebrate, possibly, his last night of not knowing. Ignorance was bliss for someone like Janet. She'd left him a slew of messages. He didn't call her back. He didn't want to see her. He was getting tired of her. She wanted too much from him, always holding hands, always kissing, always calling each other to talk about absolutely nothing. He'd been sleeping with her for three months, and already it was just a fucking routine. He thought Santana was a decently talented band, but not cool enough to get him over his latent dislike for Janet.

He dragged himself up the stairs to the third floor, all the while keeping his bleeding hand in his pocket so it didn't drip all over the place. When he got to his room, because of his injured hand, he had to reach into the right pocket of his bell-bottoms with his left hand. He had a hell of a time getting his key out, because his jeans were tight, too tight, but he liked them tight. They looked goddamn good on him, and he knew it. He had the kind of body girls liked to look at, why shouldn't he show it off?

As he left-handedly fumbled to unlock the door, he thought about his body, about the way it could kick a ball, throw a ball, hit a ball, about the way it moved to music, about the way it felt when he was with a girl, on top of her, and she looked so small and, well, helpless beneath him. He could see the way his biceps flexed when he held himself up above her, and if he dropped his head a bit and looked, he could see his pectoral muscles bulging and his nipples hardening and beyond that, his healthy penis swelling. They all liked the way his body felt—he didn't want to brag, but since he was fifteen, he'd never gone more than two weeks without sex.

Yeah, he had a great body. In church sometimes he would thank God for such a gift, especially if he was sitting around someone who was too thin or too fat or a little deformed. He'd think about how lucky he was to have what he had, and he tried, really he did, to take care of it. He didn't smoke regular cigarettes, he didn't eat a lot of junk food, he even took vitamins. So he drank a little, smoked a little dope, popped a few pills, so what? He'd stop all that once he graduated. Even though he'd majored in history and education, he could've been a great athlete or phys ed teacher or coach. He'd always been physically fit, and he knew he always would be. That is, if his luck held out.

He hadn't joined the Student Democratic Society because he hadn't wanted to jeopardize his teaching career—everybody knew the FBI was keeping records on all of those freaks—but deep inside he sympathized with their cause. He hated the war; he just couldn't let anybody know how much. He hated Nixon and all the fucking hawks, and in about ten hours, his whole life could be in their hands. It would all come down to the luck of the draw, whether he would live out his life as planned or be sent off to some dumb-ass war that he knew—he had studied it—was unnecessary and illegal. But he had to keep these thoughts to himself. After all, he planned on being a high school principal or even a district superintendent one day, and he couldn't get his name involved with any of those hippy radicals.

When he finally got inside his room, he was glad Steve, his roommate, had gone home for the weekend. Living with Steve was like living with an extra piece of furniture. Steve was quiet to a fault, unable to muster any kind of defensive response despite Al's repeated and ruthless offensive mocking. Steve took turning the other cheek to a whole new level, and Al eventually grew to ignore him just as much as he did the brown water spots on the ceiling or the thick black scuff marks on the floor. He was so used to Steve, though, that he felt sorry for him, for his overwhelming and awkward passivity. What would happen to someone like Steve in a war? He almost felt sick just thinking about it and considered for a second that he'd volunteer to go in Steve's place if he had to. Better Steve wasn't around; this way he wouldn't feel like he'd have to.

He looked around the cramped space at the blank cinder-block walls painted the color of infected mucous, at the unmade beds whose sheets reeked of semen and sweat, at the dirty clothes strewn across the floor in growing piles that reached like living things toward air or light. For about the thousandth time, the thought of cleaning up the room flickered across his mind, but in the next second was gone. Then in the next he was tempted to call Janet, but that idea passed quickly too.

Oh fuck it. He held his hand under the cold water faucet and watched his blood swirl down the drain. He knew what he had to do and that he had to be alone to do it. Isn't that why he left the party? Isn't that why he hadn't called Janet in the first place? Isn't that why he'd broken into the custodian's closet and stole the heaviest hammer there was? Isn't that why right now he was reaching under his bed to find it? Isn't that why he was going to put Leslie West's album on the record player and drop the needle in the groove for "Look to the Wind"? Isn't that why he would turn it up as loud as it would go, so no one, if anyone were around or cared, would hear him scream out in pain when he sat cross-legged on the linoleum and smashed the hammer with all his might into his ankle?

When it was over, he dragged himself to his bed and pulled himself up onto it. He hadn't broken the skin, so it wasn't messy. At first it didn't hurt that much, so he wondered if he really had broken it. His ears were ringing, and he lay on his back listening to both the ringing and the pounding of West's bass. He reached over and turned off the record player. In the morning he'd holler till someone came into his room. He'd left the door open. He'd show them his ankle, which would be so swollen his skin would be taunt. He'd seen enough football injuries to know how it would go. For now he wanted to sleep, but instead he found himself thinking about his mother. She died when he was eight. As much as he loved her, he hated to think about her. It was too sad. When she was alive—his father told him this—every year on September 14, she would say, "Alexander Bruno Murphy, September 14, 1948, was the luckiest day of my life because it's the day I had you."

Now he imagined her saying this again, putting her arms around him, pulling him close, so close he could feel her breath in his hair, so close he could smell her. His eyes were heavy and his breathing slowed. He was stuck in that place between waking and sleeping, and the last thought he had was of dust and wind. Finally he felt himself being blown away.

The next morning the nurse on duty in the infirmary, which was housed in a flimsy trailer next to Bunce Hall, assured him the ambulance was already on its way. In the next cubicle was a freshman girl, just a kid, poor thing. She did something stupid and lost a lot of blood last night and was nearly comatose. They could ride to the hospital together.

The nurse took his blood pressure and temperature and asked what happened. Al said he fell in a ditch and landed on his ankle. The nurse rolled her eyes, but when he winced in real pain, she cupped the side of his handsome face in her warm hand and told him everything would be alright.

He was in Cooper Medical Center, Room 423, by noon. His anklebone had, indeed, been shattered, and the place where he cut his hand on the barbed wire was already infected. They packed his ankle and foot, swollen beyond recognition, in ice. His toes were the size of thick sausages. A young nurse giggled at the grotesque foot that looked more like inflated rubber than living flesh. His confidence waned. How had he come up with such a hair-brained idea? What in the hell was he thinking? There was no way his birthday would be called, even in the top half. Wouldn't his mother, wherever she was, be looking out for him? Now he worried if he'd ever be able to walk again.

They gave him antibiotics and pain meds. They were beginning to kick in, and he started to relax. He asked if the radio could be left on, even though he felt as though he'd drift off to sleep any minute. What was about to happen didn't involve him anymore. He had seen to that.

There were three hundred and sixty-six wooden balls in the metal cage, each bearing a birth date, including February 29. Even the leap-year boys would not be left out of this lottery. Representative Pirnie, R-NY, reached in and pulled out a blue ball.

"The first draftees to be called to duty would be those young men born on…" Al tilted his head toward the radio. "September 14."

He couldn't believe it. He felt such…relief, followed by such… justification. He, Alexander Murphy, had been clever enough and yes, damn it, lucky enough to save himself. Yet, in this almost exuberant moment, he was careful to keep his poker face on. Since he'd been smart enough to figure a way out for himself, then he was also smart enough to know that he didn't want anyone to think even for a moment that he might have done something devious. He wasn't dumb. He knew how lame his story sounded and that saving himself had cost him something.

The drugs were beginning to make the haunting specters of shame ethereal. What he did truly was the best thing. He'd tell Janet he couldn't see her anymore because he wouldn't be going back to Glassboro State College after his ankle healed. He was already figuring out how many of his credits he could transfer to Trenton State so he could graduate from there. After all, that's where he probably should've gone in the first place. It was closer to home, a more prestigious school, and all that. And no one would know him. No one would know exactly when or how he broke his ankle or even give a rat's ass about it. He'd be 1-H, not 1-A, and everyone would figure he just had a serious problem—a physical one, that is.

He leaned back into the soft pillows—the nurse who had giggled brought him two extra ones—and let himself drift off to sleep. He forgot to listen for Steve's birthday. None of it mattered to him now.

When Al finished his confession, he downed the rest of his beer. "Now put that in your pipe and smoke it," he added and looked in the direction of Chet's kitchen window. "The old news-bag was probably listening to the whole thing."

Hester watched her husband get up and wobble into the trailer, where she knew he'd plopped into his La-Z-Boy, the bedroom too far away for him in his present state of inebriation. What Al told her was the last straw. His confession rocked Hester to her core. She wasted decades feeling sorry for Al because he had a bad ankle, because he was in pain, because he was mortified that he didn't get to go to Vietnam and fight for the United States of America, all because of a football injury!

She gathered up the empties and quietly put them in the recycling can. She picked up the remains of the chicken and took it inside. The television was on, and Al was snoring. She dumped the skin and bones in the trash, rinsed the plate, and went into the bathroom. She closed the door so she wouldn't have to hear the racket Al was making.

Coward, liar, hypocrite! Hester could barely contain her fury. *He slammed a hammer into his own ankle because he was afraid to go to war. He lied to everyone about it. He pretended he hated Glassboro, said the college sucked and was full of the sons and daughters of hicks and trailer trash. He bragged about graduating from Trenton State College, and he was there for what? One semester!*

Hester stood at the sink and looked in the mirror. She was having a hard time focusing on her image. She turned and looked at the toilet. The seat was down. All she had to do was lift it and do it. Do it. Make herself gag and get it over with.

I was that girl in the ambulance. I couldn't stop the bleeding. I tried. I shoved a washcloth up my vagina. It didn't help. She was on a stretcher in the ambulance and was too weak to turn her head to see who was on the other stretcher.

Al was disgusted with me. I got not an ounce of sympathy from my own husband when he learned what I had done. I had to bend over backward to keep our marriage going, to make Al happy; it became my life's work. He had no right to throw stones when he lived in a glass house.

She came out of the bathroom and walked past her pathetic husband. She went out and laid on the lounge and thought about all that happened since the hurricane swept through the park, wreaked havoc, and passed into oblivion, and she thought about Nina.

Our interest's on the edge, the dangerous edge, the edge of dangerous... that line from Browning, she still couldn't get it right.

Hester fell asleep. When she opened her eyes, bright shafts of sun cut through the leaves of the bo. It was a beautiful, hopeful sight, but Hester felt none of that. A realization came to her. She'd been clinging to a slender branch over a precipice. It was going to snap and she was going to plummet into the chasm of failure. More was at stake than her wounded heart and her misspent life with Al. She retired too early. She listened to Al. "We don't need your pension, Hester, because mine is going to be plenty for the both of us," and, "You don't need benefits, Hester, if I have them."

She should've waited until she could collect her own pension and her own benefits. Should've, could've, would've.

She felt like slapping herself in the face.

Forty-Five

"The master bath—why is it called the "master" bath?" Hester asked Al that question, and he said, "Because it is the bigger and better bathroom, just like men are the bigger and better sex." He was joking, naturally, but Hester wasn't laughing. She had, mistakenly, thought there was an historical or etymological explanation she was unaware of.

When she arrived home from Kintersville, Hester took the rustic wooden Madonna, which she'd recognized at once as Peruvian, not Mexican, and put it on the vanity between the sinks in the master bath. It did wonders to warm up the sterile space.

Al didn't think so, and he made a point about the sacrilegious placement of the religious artifact. After all, he pointed out, they did take a dump in there, whereupon, Hester countered that they didn't, because they had a separate water closet. Al claimed that was a stupid technicality, but he was too busy watching *The Price Is Right* with Nina, and since Hester reluctantly agreed to leave with him for Florida on the first of November, he stopped arguing.

Nina, sitting on the low-backed sofa with her feet curled up under her, was an arm's reach away from Al in the Eames chair. Both of them had their eyes glued to the television screen. The late-afternoon sun cast its last steely light through the floor-to-ceiling windows.

"Nope, no classes today, Mrs. M," Nina answered between bites of her apple when Hester asked.

"How's the whole college thing going?" Hester kicked off her flats and went over to the fireplace to turn it up.

"Can't you wait for a commercial before you start your inter-rogation of the poor girl?" Al picked up the remote and increased the volume. Nina looked at Hester and shrugged as if to say, sorry. Hester shook her head and smiled. She was happy to see Nina. It made her think she hadn't wasted all those years being a teacher. Look how her former student made such an effort to visit her. Nina didn't have a car and had to take a southbound bus from Moretown to Trenton, to catch a northbound bus to Lambertville. The trip probably took over two hours. After Hester made a nice dinner for them, she'd drive Nina back to her aunt's, and all it would take is about fifteen minutes.

From the kitchen Hester could see the back of Nina's head and Al's profile, and through the windows the darkening sky, the blotches of heavy clouds. By the time the show was over, Hester had set the table, made a salad, broiled the flounder, nuked the potatoes, and opened a bottle of Rioja. She poured a glass for Al and herself, and milk for Nina.

Al clicked off the TV, extended a hand to Nina, and pulled her up off the sofa. "Come on, little girl, time for dinner."

She giggled just like a little girl, but said, "Mr. M, come on now. You of all people know I'm no little girl anymore."

"Me of all people? What do you mean by that? Little girl?" Al winked.

"What I mean is, I'm almost eighteen and grown-up, so don't tease me about it anymore, all right?" Nina was taking her seat at the table. She flipped the long wispy curls of her hair off her shoulders. Al sat down next to her and across from Hester. He took the napkin off Nina's plate and handed it to her. She shook it out and dutifully placed it on her lap.

The meal was delicious, and the wine warmed Hester from the inside out. Nina told them all about community college. She loved her professors, especially her biology teacher. She was thinking now she might want to go into medicine.

"Imagine me a doctor! Could you imagine that?"

"Of course we can, Nina," encouraged Hester. "We've always believed in you, haven't we, Al?"

"Yes we have," Al agreed and poured another glass of wine. He sat back and looked at the young woman next to him. Hester watched her husband's eyes soften when they rested on Nina. Al would've been a good father. Hester hadn't been able to give Al his own daughter, but at least she nurtured their connection with Nina.

Yes, thought Hester, *Nina was a gift to us. Maybe the only good thing that came out of 9/11.*

Hester, Al, and Nina worked together to clear the table and do the dishes. Nina chattered about the job she got as a waitress at

Wildflowers and how she couldn't go to the shore with her new friends because she need to work as many hours as she could to pay for college

"Al, don't you think we could help Nina out?" Hester said knowing fair well that with Nina right there it put Al on the spot. When Al shot her a look, Hester knew she misjudged the degree to which Al felt responsible for Nina.

"Well, Nina, we did just retire. Maybe Mr. Murphy hasn't figured out our own bills yet?" Hester back-pedaled.

"Don't worry, Mrs. M, I'm fine. I don't expect you or Mr. M to give me anything. You've already done too much, helping me get into college, helping me with the student loan applications, helping me pay for my books. Why, I couldn't ask anything more from either of you." She stood in the center of the kitchen. The overhead light lit up her face. Her skin glowed, her cheeks were flushed, her lips pink. She folded her arms in front of her. Three feet away, Al stood in the same position.

"Look, little girl, it's not that I don't want to help you. It's just that if you don't work for something, you'll never appreciate it. I was never handed anything on a silver platter. I had to make my own way and solve my own problems. To get where I am today took sacrifices, big sacrifices." Al words, ping, ping, pinged through the air at Nina. His eyes boring right through her.

Nina stared back and locked eyes with the man who was probably the closest thing she ever had to a father, her face rigid with defiance. She pursed her lips as if to stop herself from saying something. Hester saw the tears welling up in Nina's eyes. She wanted to go to her, hug her, comb her fingers through her curls.

Before Hester could move, Nina said, "Didn't I say I was fine, that I don't want anything from you? Didn't I just say that?" Her lips quivered, tears ran down her face. Hester went to her and wrapped her arms around the small shaking body.

"Hester, cut it out. She's alright. I'll handle this." Al stepped forward and took one of Nina's hands and led her away from Hester into the living area. "Calm down. We'll work something out so you have enough to do some fun things once in a while with your friends." He put his hand on her back and patted her. Nina had her head down and picked it up to turn and look up at Al. She blinked a couple of times, and her tears were gone.

"I'll drive you home, and on the way, we'll figure the whole thing out." Al gave Nina a quick hug and went into the bedroom to get his coat and keys.

"Do you want me to go with you, honey?" Hester hollered after him.

He reappeared. "No, we'll be okay. Won't we, Nina?"

"I know you'll be okay," interrupted Hester, "but this might be the last time I'll see Nina for a while since we're leaving for Florida next week. Hester turned to Nina and took her hand, "I am going to miss you. You have to come down to visit. You just have to."

"I will, Mrs. M, if I can save up enough money." Nina squeezed Hester's hand and dropped it.

"Maybe I should go with you, Al. You might want some company for the ride back."

"Oh, he likes to listen to the radio, Mrs. M. You know that." Nina grabbed her heavy sweater from the back of one of the dining room chairs, put it on, and pulled the hood up. The tawny curls spilled forward around her face and made her look even prettier. She hurried over to Hester, hugged her quickly, and kissed her cheek. She and Al were halfway out the door before she turned slightly and said, "Thanks for everything."

"Be careful!" Hester warned, but the door had already slammed shut as though caught by the wind.

Forty-Six

It was April 1, the day after the closing. The night before, reluctant to leave, Eve, Marvin, Dee, and Hester sat in the rockers on the clubhouse porch, opened several bottles of expensive wine, and drank them. No one was worried about counting pennies. They were rich now, even though the million dollars had dwindled to half that by the time everyone stuck their fingers in the cookie jar.

Al, who couldn't wait to get the money into an interest-bearing account, had Hester sign the back of the check and drop him off at the airport. She'd drive the Odyssey home when she was ready.

The only thing Hester and Al talked about since his drunken confession was money. They went around with a realtor and discovered the only thing they could afford on their "windfall" would be an inland condo—talk about a step down. Even though he loved Florida, Al decided it would be best for them to stay in New Jersey and put the money into this fund handled by some guy named Maddork, or something like that, where they would get almost 30 percent interest.

In a few years they'd have enough to come back to the Sunshine State and live in style.

Hester went through the motions with Al, but the truth was she couldn't think straight anymore. She cared about the money. If she left Al, her half might end up being all she'd ever have, but she wasn't up to making any kind of sense out of what to do with it, so she would trust Al this one last time.

After finishing the wine and making one last toast to Pleasant Palms, Eve and Marvin drove to the Marriott in Delray, and Dee caught a limo for a flight to Connecticut. Hester went back to her trailer. So what if Clayton slapped her with the $10,000 fine? Too bad. She had unfinished business.

The next morning at the sound of the first trucks, Hester, who hadn't slept, dressed and walked up to where the first trailers were to be demolished. The abandoned units were left mostly intact by their owners, who wouldn't need any of their old stuff once they cashed those big fat checks from the developer. Patios still had furniture on them. An array of schlocky lawn ornaments like plastic flamingoes, concrete pelicans, and "To the Beach" signs still lined the narrow lanes.

Hester sat on the concrete wall by the shuffleboard courts and watched an army of workers toss everything that wasn't nailed down into a giant pile. Another platoon began disconnecting the electrical boxes and turning off water valves to the ill-fated trailers. An excavator pulled off A1A, stopped in front of the first unit, and ripped into it with its giant claws.

By noon the park looked like somebody dropped a bomb on part of it. Everything, including Hester, was covered with dust. She walked past the detritus to the deli, and got a hoagie and a coffee. She was killing time.

On the way back, she turned onto Fish Tail Lane and headed toward her place. Their custom sign, "Our Castle by the Sea, Unit 23, Al and Hester Murphy," was askew. She didn't bother to straighten it before she went inside.

It was stuffy and humid. Hester flipped on the air-conditioner. Luckily they hadn't shut everything off. She noticed how dirty, how forlorn the little place looked. Had it always been like this? Or was she just seeing it for what it really was? A dump. The room and every-thing in it was about to fall even further from glory. Hester wanted to have a yard sale or donate their belongings to Goodwill. Now all of it was destined for a landfill where, eventually, it would rot away.

"It's junk we don't need, Hester," Al said in a stern voice. "Just leave it behind."

You're not the boss of me, Hester thought. Her students used to say that. "You're not the boss of me, Mrs. Murphy."

Hester picked up one of her favorite things, a saltshaker in the shape of an orange with a face on it and "Florida" written around the base. "I don't need you, but I want you." Hester said to the small orange face. *Landfill, my foot. This whole place might be going down, but not Mr. Orange.* She went to the closet and got some tissue paper and wrapped Mr. Orange up, then his pepper twin. She dumped Al's old paperwork out of the box in the bedroom and spent the next half hour filling it with her things.

The crunching, booming demolition team was getting closer. Hester didn't have much time left. She began trembling at the pros-pect of what she still had to do.

She looked out. Dust rose up and met the clouds. *Ashes to ashes. Dust to dust.*

When the air cleared, when Pleasant Palms was gone, condos, like phoenixes, would rise from the park's ashes on the wings of big money. The towering buildings would block the sun from the beach. Concrete and asphalt would replace the lush tamarind, necklace pod, and wax myrtle. The towhee would search futilely for the bloodberry. The birdsongs would be gone, replaced by the droning of the gas trimmers. At night instead of the rustle of sea oats and satinleaf, the clink of champagne flutes would fill the air. The bright lights of the new condos would outshine the constellations. The first moon would wane in comparison, and the pregnant leatherbacks, bewildered, would swim away from, instead of toward their ancient destination. The trails of perpetuation in the sand, the fertile mounds, and the hatchlings would be gone. And since the female instinct cannot be thwarted, since she must lay her eggs or die trying, the great turtles would become extinct. And the silver gray fox. And the copper snakes. All the frightened creatures would slink away, never to return.

As the noise grew into a deafening buzz, Hester thought of flies buzzing around dead meat, the rotting pig's head, the lord of the flies, the beastie, the flies landing on it, eating it, laying their eggs on it. Oh, yes, she believed in the beast within.

Her eyes itched from the dust, and her head ached from trying to make a decision. She was scared, but this was not the time for her to weaken, it was the time for her to move forward, face the music, put the cards on the table. She felt the blood pulsing in her temples and the flutter of anxiety in her chest.

If only she had knocked Al off that pedestal she'd put him on sooner, she might not have let so much of what he did, as James Joyce put it in *The Dead*, "fall faintly through the universe." The Irishman was writing literally about snow, but figuratively it was exactly how she reacted to all of Al's shenanigans—she just let them drift down in the endless darkness inside her and let the heat of her anger melt them away.

Hester went into the living room and packed a beach towel on top of her things in the box and taped it shut.

Someone banged on the window. "You have to get out. Your place is next. You know you shouldn't be here. If you get sick from all this dust, you're at your own risk." It was Clayton in his good clothes, his mouth covered in a white mask, screaming through the closed window.

"Okay, I'm going," Hester shouted over the grinding noise, but Clayton was already walking away. She surveyed the small interior. Everything that happened here that was good was over. And everything that happened here that was bad would never be over. Reluctantly, she went down the hallway and into the guest room.

The whole trailer began to vibrate. Nearby a jackhammer rumbled. Hester pulled Nina's suitcase and carry-on from under the bed. *Funny how Al never knew they were there, never snooped around his own place.* His utter and dependable laziness kept Hester's secret safe and allowed their sham of a marriage to bungle along for a few more months.

Hester blew the dust off the suitcase and opened it. She wanted to take one of those pictures of Nina, the one of her smiling with the two pearls of her baby teeth showing. Hester couldn't stay mad at Nina.

She was the victim. Whatever happened between Al and Nina—Hester was no longer in denial that something did—was all on Al.

And Hester couldn't take Nina's foolish teenage bravado seriously either. Nina wrote those nasty things in her book probably because Hester had given her a D on her *Gatsby* essay. Nina defended Tom. Her argument was a rant about Daisy. If Nina was a man and had to live with a person like Daisy, she'd cheat on her too. There wasn't much else, no textual references, no insight into any of the other characters.

Hester unzipped the pocket of the suitcase and took the photos out. The one she wanted was on top. She put it aside and beneath it was the photo she hadn't seen. It was a picture of baby Nina and her mother. Hester stared at the photograph, at the mother holding her smiling daughter, at the smiling mother…Jennifer Masterson.

That cold day in the dugout, Al with Jennifer. Al lying—she knew the minute he opened his mouth, he was lying—about checking for smokers, class-cutters. Al blocking Hester's view of Jennifer. Jennifer leaving school without graduating.

Hester's mouth went dry. The truth dropped down on her like a hammer.

Al is Nina's father?

The excavator was chewing away at Chet's place. Something scraped the side of Hester's unit. She heard men hollering to each other in Spanish.

Hester rummaged quickly through the carry on, found Nina's hairbrush, and pulled a handful of hair from its bristles. She took the photographs and the hair into the kitchen and shoved the hair into a baggie. She went back into the bathroom and got Al's used razor and put it in another baggie. She shoved everything in her pocketbook, picked up the box of her things, and headed out into the heat.

Before she could close the slider, the sky opened up, and it was pouring rain. It was the way it was in Florida, dry one minute, a deluge the next. Hester backed up into the trailer, put the box down, grabbed Al's yellow slicker, and threw it on. As she was about to leave, though, she remembered something she'd been trying to re-member, and ran into her bedroom. In her underwear drawer, balled up in the back, was the soiled pink thong. She stuck it in the pocket of the slicker and left.

Forty-Seven

Everything was quiet except for the screeching parrots in the top of the bo tree. The workers were in their trucks waiting out the rain. Let Clayton slap her with a fine. Hester didn't care. She walked to the tree, pressed her hand against the scar, and looked down. Drops of water clung to the blossoms of the flowers she'd planted. She kissed her hand, knelt, and touched the wet earth where Nina was buried. If only she could turn back time.

Hester walked away past a row of refrigerators, rotting food spilling out of their open orifices, toward mounds of debris. Like refuges from better times, sofas, mattresses, chairs, draperies, jagged chunks of Formica countertops, light fixtures, lamps, and rugs were jumbled up together waiting to be loaded onto some truck and hauled away. As Hester circumnavigated the rubble, she was nearly run down by a Bobcat, whose driver seemed blinded by his goggles.

Once she got beyond the construction site, the rain stopped as suddenly as it had begun, and the noise resumed with a vengeance.

Hester knew it wouldn't last long. *The truth will change everything*, she thought.

Yes, she hid Nina's body. Yes, she lied to Al about what happened. Yes, she told him the girl had gone back to the community college. And, yes, Hester knew how hard Al tried to get in touch with Nina. Hester checked his cell phone, saw all the fruitless, unanswered calls to what must have been a cell phone he'd given Nina. Hester knew, despite his silence, he was desperate to find his secret lover. He was probably walking around the campus at this very moment searching for her. Hester could almost pity him if she weren't so disgusted by him.

She didn't really need a DNA test—even though she was hell-bent on getting one done—to be certain.

In the end Al was a stranger to her. She was married to him, cooked for him, cleaned up after him, worried about him, fought for him and with him, soothed him, flattered him, and had sex, lots of sex, with him, without really knowing him. So how had she loved him all these years? By turning a blind eye to what was right in front of her? By acting clueless when she already connected the dots?

She had invented the Alexander Bruno Murphy she loved. That man was a figment of her imagination and not the real person with whom she'd spent most of her life. Why she should've spent the past three decades writing an epic novel instead of putting up with the real Al. Oh, she'd done a spectacular job of fictionalizing their existence. From afar, as a couple, they glowed romantically like the moon; but as the astronauts found out when they touched down on it, that shining magical sphere was, in reality, cold, cratered, and barren.

All Hester desired now was to salvage some shred of dignity from the wasteland of her life. She had plenty of regrets concerning Al, but none as immutable as the sin she'd committed before Al came into her life. Her abortion distorted everything forever after. That single loss was a stake in the center of her being upon which any chance for happiness was quickly impaled.

And then there was what she did with Nina.

The day of the hurricane.

Nina's dead! Dead! She had to do something. She was washing the young women's body. She was... She lost track...

She knelt on the floor whispering the Hail Mary. *Forgive Nina. Help me.*

She looked up, tucked a strand of Nina's wild hair behind the girl's delicate ear, caressed Nina's face, touched her lips. Nina's lips were warm. Inside her flesh was still warm. *This part of Nina is alive.*

Quickly, Hester sat on the bed and cradled Nina in her arms. *The Grapes of Wrath.* It flashed through her mind. Hester thought of Rose of Sharon, her baby dead, her breasts agonizingly full of milk. The old man would starve to death. Rose could see it in Ma's eyes. If Rose didn't help him, if she didn't cradle him and feed him from her own breast, he would die. Rose wasn't always a good girl, but now she could do something exceedingly good—she could save someone's life.

Gently, Hester leaned forward, pressed her breast into Nina's open mouth, and felt the warmth. *Maybe, just maybe.* Nina's head was in the crook of Hester's arm. Her eyes were open and vacant. Still Hester stared into them lovingly. *Is this how it feels to have a child of your own?* Hester's flesh throbbed with contentment. She felt at peace imagining Nina to be her own, longed-for child. Hester half-believed she could perform the miracle. She could bring Nina back to life.

Hester lost track of time. Soon Nina's mouth grew cold. It made goose bumps rise on Hester's skin. She laid the dead girl on the bed, kissed her on the forehead, and went to get the trash bags. She came back, and as she stuffed Nina into the black plastic, remorse, and horror, descended on her.

She hadn't broken Nina's neck. Al, or the hurricane, did, but she had been the one who cast the net that captured Nina and gathered her to them. If she hadn't loved Nina, if she hadn't been so desperate to make her part of their family...

By the time Hester reached her car, which she'd parked on A1A the night before, she was drenched in sweat beneath the slicker. She put the box on the ground and removed the heavy garment. She wiped her damp hands on her pants, took out her cell phone, and flipped it open.

Nine-one-one.

When Hester heard the ringing, she hesitated for a fraction of a second. *If I don't tell them, they'll probably never find her. They'll just plow everything under, grind everything up. If they do see it, they'll just think, oh, it's only a big dog. Lots of Pleasant Palmers had dogs. Dogs barking night and day. Plenty of dogs are buried in plastic bags all over the park.*

But if she did tell them, what she said could never be taken back.

A dispatcher answered, "What is your emergency?"

"The body of a young woman..." Hester's voice faltered, "...is buried in Pleasant Palms Trailer Park on A1A. It's buried under the tree at 23 Fish Tail Lane."

"Please, stay on the line while I determine your exact location."

The dispatcher put Hester on hold. She kept her cell phone to her ear, turned, and walked back toward the demolition site. Dust hung in the air, the palms lolled, the marina flags drooped. It took several minutes before the noise stopped, and all she heard was the sound of her own uneasy breathing. Everything had come to a halt, just as she knew it would.

The drivers of the steam shovels and cranes shut off the engines, descended from their cabs, removed their goggles. By the time she reached Fish Tail Lane, Clayton was hurrying down the street with several workers with shovels. He was on his cell phone too. Hester ducked behind the Buchanans' unit, which they hadn't gotten to yet. She didn't want Clayton to see her.

"What the hell is wrong?" hollered Clayton into his phone. "What the hell do you mean stop everything?" A pause. "Yes, I'm at 23 now. Yes, they're digging under the tree right now."

It didn't take long for the strong men to dig down a few feet before they struck something. Ginger leaves, impatiens petals, gardenia blossoms dotted the dark soil they piled to the side of the hole. Two men reached into it and pulled out something in plastic bags that were duct-taped together.

"Officer, I can't hear what you're saying. You're breaking up," shouted Clayton.

"Open it up," he ordered one of the workers. "I don't know what the hell's going on. The police said something about somebody called about a dead body. They're on their way, but I'm not waiting. It's probably only a dog. Lots of these old people had dogs."

The man ripped at the duct tape, then hesitated. The smell was disgusting. He backed away and said, "Man, I can't do this."

Two other workers grabbed the ends of the bags and pulled them apart.

Nina's decomposing body, the mushroom-colored skin rotting off the bones, slipped out in front of them. Despite its condition, the body was clearly that of a woman.

"Oh my God," whispered Clayton. "It is a dead body. Now what in the hell are we going to do? This is going to screw everything up." He punched some numbers into his phone and turned away.

Hester tried not to look at Nina, but she couldn't help it. Nina's face was pulsing with squirming maggots. A sudden breeze caught the long curly hair and unfurled it into sort of a halo above Nina's head. Hester couldn't look away from the writhing countenance, from the black holes of Nina's empty eye sockets.

A voice on the cell phone. "I'm patching you through to a supervisor. Stay on your phone."

Hester was numb. She stepped back, turned away, and leaned against the trailer to wait for whatever came next. In this in-between moment, Hester envisioned herself, in the not too distant future, sitting in a Florida courtroom with Al, who would be on trial for the murder of Nina Tattoni. Exactly how it happened, the coroner would be unable to determine conclusively. However, the DNA test done on the sperm found on the pink thong was irrefutable—Nina Tattoni, immediately prior to her death, had engaged in sexual intercourse with the defendant, Alexander Bruno Murphy.

The prosecution built their case around that fact, and one other scandalous piece of information—the results also revealed that Mr. Murphy was not only the young woman's lover, but he was also her father.

Forty-Eight

Hester would, of course, have uncovered this horrifying piece of information long before the trial. She had a plan. After she told the police everything she knew, she'd hand over the pink thong. When they released her on her own recognizance, she'd find a lab and pay to have a DNA test on both the strands of hair she'd taken from Nina's brush and skin cells from Al's dirty razor.

When she had the results, she'd drive as fast as she could, north to the Lambertville condo where she'd most likely find Al sitting in his Eames chair channel-surfing, trying—Hester was sure—to distract himself from fuming about what she'd done. How Hester could have done such a dumb thing, would be going through his mind. It was a stupid accident, was what he told the Lambertville cops when they questioned him. He didn't even know Nina Tattoni was dead. And look at the mess his stupid wife had stirred up, now. She was the criminal, putting the poor girl's dead body in a hole and lying about it to everyone. Saying she buried Nina to save him? And their marriage?

Why he hadn't done one thing to Nina Tattoni, except to try to protect her from the hurricane. She'd jumped into bed with him because she was scared half out of her wits.

Oh, Hester knew now how Al's mind really worked. She knew how he would be so pissed about the whole thing. The development of Pleasant Palms Trailer Park would stop, maybe the developer would pull out all together. Dead bodies weren't part of the deal. They'd have to give all that money back.

But the worst thing for Al would be if, damn it to hell, anyone found out about what he'd gotten away with for all those years at Sourland High. All those teenage girls. Well, that couldn't happen to somebody like him, it just couldn't.

All of this would race through his mind in the time it took for Hester to hand him a manila envelope.

He'd frown at it. "What the hell is this?"

Not wanting to tip her hand, Hester would say as sweetly as she could, "Al, just open it. Please."

"Look I'm so furious with you right now…"

"Please, Al."

"Shit, it better be good news. I am not in the mood…" He wouldn't be able to finish his sentence because as soon as he saw the photograph, he'd recognize Jennifer Masterson. But he'd be clever enough to say, "Where the hell did you get this, Hester? And why the hell are you showing it to me?"

"Just read that paper, Al." Hester would calmly point to the DNA report. Inside she'd be roiling with anticipation. What will Al do when the light goes on?

His eyes dart over the words as he scans the document, his expression hardens. Feverishly he tries to strategize. How can I worm my way out of this? His panic so tangible, Hester would smell it.

He's shocked alright to learn Nina was his daughter and sickened to think he fucked his own flesh and blood, his own longed-for child. Despite this initial pang of guilt, though, Hester knows his knee-jerk reaction will be cowardly. He will rue the public humiliation. He will fear the punishment he so richly deserves and will surely be forced to suffer.

Al Murphy will plead, project, berate, and maybe even try to choke the life out of Hester. Hell hath no fury like a pervert exposed. No, she won't give Al a chance to defend himself or put the blame on her, or on Nina. She'll turn and leave and never go back.

The wail of a siren distracted Hester. She still had her cell phone to her ear. "The officers are approaching Fish Tail Lane. Please stay on your phone."

Hester's mind raced. She foresaw impending doom, bleak days ahead. There was no way around it, she would be punished too, and she welcomed it. It was time she made reparation for her sins.

Despite the fact that her past life was swirling fast in the drain it was about to go down, Hester was oddly at peace. It was difficult for her to put into words— she was rising above what was and drifting toward what would be. She felt light and transparent, like a little less than a god, or, at long last, a part of God. Yes, Hester's retreat from the edge of all that was wrong, had begun.

The End

26968043R00192

Made in the USA
Charleston, SC
21 February 2014